Praise for *When Troubles Rain*

In *When Troubles Rain*, the author deftly draws his characters so they are fully relatable. He builds informative back stories that illuminate the heritage, culture, and beliefs of the Norwegian-American Berg family.

Through love, strong familial ties, war, tragic loss, threats to their way of life, and strong community, the Berg family faces every challenge with grace, faith, and a good dose of stoicism.

The most touching aspect of this historical novel is its absence of bravado. We follow the family in its daily life for a period of time, and therein lies the magic. It is unassuming, yet powerful; serious, yet with humor; The story recognizes the horrors of war, yet stresses the family's dedication to God and country.

This is a book to renew the values of patriotism, hard work, family, sacrifice, and gratitude.

Military Writers Society of America
March 2023

When Troubles Rain

Two boys of a fifth generation Wisconsin dairy farm family grow to manhood during a time of war. Johnny loves the farm, Clark, well, not so much. Will they both be drafted? And, where will they be sent? To Vietnam? Or to Korea's Demilitarized Zone?

While their boys are facing the challenge of possible service to the country, bewildering events begin to happen at the Berg Farm. Who is Gerald Hicks? And why did he send a mysterious letter claiming ownership of part of the farm the family has worked for nearly one hundred years?

Just as with farming when it rains sometimes it pours, so also sometimes in life. The Berg family has a strong Christian faith, except for young Clark who ever manages to doubt and stray. As ever more troubles befall the Berg family, will their faith see them through? Will each member's faith be strengthened, or will some lose heart *When Troubles Rain*?

*This special tenth anniversary edition contains
two new notes by the author.*

The first explains why Jim Hodge wrote the book ten years ago and why he dedicated it to the seven soldiers appearing on the dedication page, all but one of whom North Korean soldiers brutally massacred that night so long ago.

The second note by the author is about "God's Providence and Getting History Right." In this special note, Jim Hodge explains the unlikely but timely finding of old newspaper clippings about that fateful day of the Korean War. He realized the name of one soldier killed in action might have been incorrect. He then details his own perseverance in locating the truth, which, as it turned out, was found in a nearby town. And all of this occurred just before republication of the novel, so that it came to be released by its new publisher on its Tenth Anniversary. This special note, is in itself a lovely story, though a true one. And it illustrates the profound effect we have on the lives of others.

When Troubles Rain

A Novel

**Tenth Anniversary Edition of
Berg Farm**

Works by Jim Hodge

Fiction

When Troubles Rain

Nonfiction

My Father and My Uncles:
One Family's Call to Service in World War II

Short Stories

Every Man a Rifleman

Beer Contraband at 10,000 Feet

A Special Picture Rediscovered

When Troubles Rain

A Novel

by

Jim Hodge

***Tenth Anniversary Edition of*
Berg Farm**

Red Recliner Books
an imprint of
DMS Onge Publishing, LLC
Hartland, Michigan
2022

For information about bulk quantities, please email your request to:
info@DMSOngePublishing.com
or, send a letter to:
DMS Onge Publishing, LLC
ATTN: Red Recliner Books
9552 East Highland Road #30, Howell MI 48843

When Troubles Rain: A Novel
Tenth Anniversary Edition of **Berg Farm**
(previously published under the title *Berg Farm* by Deep River Books)
By Jim Hodge, Revised 2022
ISBN: 978-1-944976-06-4 (First Hardcover Edition May 2022)
ISBN: 978-1-944976-15-6 (First Trade Edition May 2023)

First Trade Printing
Printed in the United States of America

To Sue, Kirstin, Doug,
Kelli, Addie, Devin and Ryann

and

In memoriam

Sergeant James Hensley/Horn
Private First Class John Benton
Private First Class Robert Burrell
Private Morris Fisher
Private Leslie Hasty
Private Ernest Reynolds

and

to the survivor
Private First Class David Bibee

Prologue

"My friends, you have just entered an amazing new country. There is nothing standing in your way to accomplish whatever it is you want to accomplish here. It is all up to you. I myself, and the Immigration Department, wish you the best. Seven years ago America came out of a bitter and deadly civil war. Many people died to preserve the right for each man and each woman, no matter who they are or where they come from, to enjoy freedom. As I am sure you know, we have no king in this country. We have no nobility. When our founding fathers wrote our Constitution they broke the chains of European royalty. Where you go and what you accomplish is all up to you. Make the most of it and God bless you all."

Elmer Berg felt a surge of excitement. The man's words were just what he wanted to hear. Even though he had put his faith in his Lord regarding the success of this enterprise his human frailties gave him cause for concern. Now, hearing this man's words, his heart and soul swelled as full as a fjord at high tide!

* * *

The belief that people will seek familiar surroundings, even after crossing an ocean, seemed to be true. Cold winters followed by damp springs and green, growing summers had brought the people of Norway and Sweden into much of America's heartland. During the last half of the 19th century America's Great Lakes and upper Midwest region drew these robust people by the thousands. Very often these immigrants made their way to Chicago. Those that did not stay in the city spread themselves up both the Michigan and Wisconsin shorelines of Lake

Michigan and into the hinterlands of Illinois, Wisconsin, Minnesota, Iowa, and the Dakotas.

For Elmer Berg, two issues led to his decision to come to America: economic opportunity and religious freedom. The first would come from being unable to have land of his own. The second would come from escaping the increasingly tyrannical and dominant State Lutheran Church in Norway.

As tenant farmers, the Bergs labored on thirty-two acres outside the hamlet of Storen, in central Norway. The icy waters of the narrow and swift-flowing Gaula River flowed close to their small, thatch-roofed home as it made its descent to the huge Trondheim Fjord. During the long winter Elmer worked for the lumber company that harvested the birch, aspen, white pine and hemlock trees that grew in abundance on the lower slopes of the mountains that rose to the east of the farm.

The beauty of rugged Norway belied the heavy yoke under which the Bergs toiled. Elmer did not own the land he worked. Mountainous Norway did not have much arable farmland. The land that was tillable had been owned for many years by certain families. Indeed, Norwegian law held that family property was automatically passed on to the eldest son in the family. Though Elmer had only sisters, his father had accrued no property to pass onto him, in large part, because of this arcane law. So Elmer and Muriel Berg, parents of three small children, were tenant farmers, renting only moderately sustainable land. It was a treadmill life of heavy toil without the satisfaction of owning the land.

Berg's second reason for coming to America was religious. In the 16th century, the Protestant Reformation was brought on because, in the opinion of many, the Roman Catholic Church had become more of a political institution than a messenger of the Gospel. In both Sweden and Norway the Reformation resulted in formation of the Lutheran State Church. In the three centuries since the Reformation many, Elmer Berg among them, felt that the

State Church had itself strayed from its mission of proclaiming the Gospel.

As youngsters Elmer Berg and Muriel Ernst's families worshipped at the more conservative Bible Lutheran Church. After their marriage the discrimination by the conventional Lutherans toward the Bible Lutherans that they had known as youngsters became a bread and butter reality. The opportunity to buy one's own land, remote at best, became impossible. It was well known that the tenant property tax that was assessed to the Bible Lutherans was discriminatory. And as a voice in local politics the township's narrow minded policy making board traditionally ignored these folks who dared to stray from the State Church.

And so it went.

* * *

In 1862 Abraham Lincoln and the American Congress instituted the Homestead Act. This was designed to expedite Manifest Destiny. The glorious land west of the Mississippi River that William Clark and Meriwether Louis had first explored at the beginning of the century was vast and untapped. This legislation encouraged citizens and immigrants seeking a new life to come and help settle America west of the Appalachian Mountains. And that news had travelled all the way to the rugged mountains of Norway to Elmer and his wife.

It was for these reasons that Muriel Berg and three small children made the wagon trip to the harbor at Trondheim in the cold April chill of 1872, seeing off the family's husband and father.

Others, like a young married couple, Carl and Sonia Skaleen, were there; heading to a place in America's mid-west to find work where a Norwegian entrepreneur had begun a successful wagon building business. Elmer Berg and the Skaleens befriended each other on their journey.

Elmer told them, "I am pleased that we can begin this venture together."

As was the case with so many who left the homeland, Elmer would arrive in America alone, leaving his wife and children to come later. Limited finances and a fear of the unknown made this a common practice.

The family had carefully planned so that they could survive the coming growing season and the following winter without their breadwinner. Their wellbeing in Norway was now far from certain and there was no assurance that Muriel would ever see her husband again. As she embraced him one last time on the waterfront's ancient wooden docks, she felt, at one and the same time, anxiety and hope. As she watched her husband board the ship to America her thoughts turned to the night before. The couple had prayed together at their bedside that God's will be done in their lives. They had prayed that they would watch and listen for His leading.

As they finished praying Elmer had opened his Bible to Proverbs, and read aloud, *"Trust in the Lord with all thine heart; and lean not unto thine own understanding. In all thy ways acknowledge Him, and He shall direct thy paths."*

She remembered how he had looked determinedly into her eyes, saying, "These will be our verses, Muriel. These verses must sustain our hearts when all else around us sends doubt to our mind."

* * *

When Elmer Berg arrived in America he carried with him the homestead document assuring him that he would be awarded 160 acres of land. In return the document required that he would "build a dwelling and cultivate the soil." If, after five years, Berg had established himself on the acreage to the government's satisfaction, he could apply for title to the land at a modest fee.

For immigrants of meager financial means and only basic education the move to America was a move into the unknown. Elmer knew only that Chicago was a large city far from the Atlantic shore. It was from this city that he hoped to have the promise of homestead land awarded to him. It was not confidence and a sense of adventure that sparked Elmer Berg's journey to America, but desperation and hope for a new and better life.

1

Heritage

*Rejoice with your family
in the beautiful land of life.*

Albert Einstein

From a distance the tractor appeared and disappeared in the contours of the gentle hills. The black earth, turned over by the tractor's field cultivator attachment, stood in sharp contrast to the brown corn stubble that had endured the bitterness of the previous Wisconsin winter.

Thirty-six-year-old John Berg sat high and gratefully proud in the 1953 Persian-orange Allis-Chalmers WD45 tractor, carefully turning the rich, pungent soil so as not to miss even an inch of the precious ground. The drone of the diesel engine and the thump of the tires as they angled across the previous year's furrows did not deter him from humming one tune after another. His large hands, weathered and calloused from years of outdoor work, slapped against the steering wheel in an amateurish attempt at keeping time with his humming. The unmarked blue baseball cap—faded, sweat stained and somewhat rumpled—that crowned his tousled brown hair was as self-effacing as the man himself.

This was his land. This had been his father's, his grandfather's and his great-grandfather's land and he had long ago acknowledged that he was a steward of all that his Lord had entrusted to him. He well appreciated the courageous homesteading legacy of a man he never knew;

his great-grandfather Elmer. On this spring morning in 1957 John Berg felt, as he almost always did, like the most blessed man in the world.

Indeed, life had been good to Berg, but no more so that it had been to most people. It is just that he seemed to know it and appreciate it. He had grown up in the Great Depression and had served his country as a soldier in World War II. He now basked in the relative tranquility of the late 1950s. Though he was not an expressive man—often his quietness left a glum impression on others—he was a contented man. As a husband, the father of three, and the business partner of his father, John Berg was a man fulfilled. Yes, there was concern over the ways of his and Gertie's second born son, but he was realistic enough to know that his family was not exempt from worries. The weight of responsibility for a family and a two-hundred-eighty acre dairy farm did not seem to daunt him.

Back at the two-storied, white farm house John Berg's wife was rolling out the dough for the bread she would bake that afternoon. No one ever called her Gertrude. Very often the people of northern European ancestry gave their children traditional, sometimes cumbersome, given names that were not at all trendy. Gertie, however, was a most acceptable shortening of Gertrude. So Gertie she had always been.

At age thirty-three she was in the prime of her womanhood. Her sandy blond hair was always pulled back in a short, no nonsense ponytail. Her eyes were an open, friendly blue. When she smiled she showed just the beginning of crow's feet wrinkles at the corners of her eyes. Her strong, supple, and striking figure, which she in no way tried to advertise, was very much up to the demands of home and family.

The rigors of farm life were nothing new to Gertie. She was a Mehlborg, born and raised with three brothers and three sisters only six miles away on the farm of her parents, Steven and Karen Mehlborg. Like most of the members of her large family, her conversations were always direct and to the point, unadorned with either unwarranted praise or the scorn of superiority. These qualities endeared her to all who knew her.

"Boys? Johnny! Clark!" Gertie's voice could be heard upstairs. "You need to get on that job that your father gave you. You'll not dawdle away this whole Saturday. You get down here." Her voice was bright and friendly but each of Gertie Berg's three children knew that she always meant what she said.

The thumpety-thump of feet coming down the stairs could be heard by Gertie back in the kitchen. A quick smile crossed her face as she thought of the eleven- and twelve-year-old sons and eight-year-old daughter with whom God had graced her and John's life.

It was their oldest, Johnny, who bounded into the kitchen first. A mop of straight, but still unruly, blonde hair crowned his youthful frame. The junior-sized bib overalls that he was wearing were a testament to the great pride he took at being part of Berg Dairy Farm. He was fully aware of his obligation in the tractor barn but, nonetheless, he was prepared to raise an objection.

"Mom, can't I chore this afternoon?"

Johnny could have reinforced his request by reminding his mother that during the school week he was up each morning servicing the cows; attaching the milk machines and shoveling out the manure troughs. He could have said that Saturday morning was his morning to have a break; however it was just not in his nature to promote himself.

His eyebrows rose above his wondering eyes in hopes of a softened response.

Gertie did not look up from the bread dough she was kneading.

"John Berg, Jr., your father said he wanted that seeder cleaned up and lubricated this morning, not some time this afternoon. Your father also said the job shouldn't take more than a couple of hours. A strapping twelve-year-old youngster like you should have a lot more responsibility on a Saturday than one job out in the barn."

She paused for a moment, still kneading, then asked, "And where is your brother?"

"Upstairs still." Johnny responded, without concern for his brother's usual apathy.

Gertie looked up. She wiped her flour-covered hands on the apron she wore over her checkered house dress.

"Now, out you go. I don't want to see you back in here until dinner at noon time."

The youngster, knowing full well this would be his mother's response, gave a shoulder shrug and a resigned, yet cheerful, "Okay" and headed out the back door.

Gertie wasted no time in summoning her other son. "Clark! Get a move on!"

It was another two minutes before she heard the slow footsteps of her eleven-year-old coming down the stairs. With hands in pockets, Clark sauntered unenthusiastically into the kitchen. His hapless attitude was as large a contrast to Johnny as his brown eyes and dark, curly hair.

Gertie had little patience for Clark's general lack of interest in seemingly everything, but as she looked right at him she was calmly resolute.

"You need to get out there and help your brother with that seeder."

Expressionless, and without a word, the boy shuffled out the kitchen door.

As she returned to her bread dough Gertie could but shake her head.

***

First Lutheran Church stood at the corner of Washington and Fourth Street, just a block off State Highway 51, the road that served as Stoughton, Wisconsin's main street.

9

As on all Sunday mornings the church parking lot had as many pickups in it as it had sedans, for the farmer was a major presence in this community.

In the same pew as always, John and Gertie Berg, their three children, and John's parents sat together as a family. Their presence each Sunday was a reflection of the anchor of support that family had been to the congregation for many years. In 1909, John's grandfather Gus had been instrumental in building an addition on the original church, which had been located across the street.

In 1942, the church suffered a devastating fire. For the next four years the congregation met in the Dunkirk Town Elementary School at the other end of town. World War II had left few resources and even fewer men to rebuild the church. In 1946, after the war, John Berg and his father Mack helped build a new church on property across the street from the original building. The new church was much larger, but retained the same traditional design. The wood frame, however, gave way to a traditional gray block stone, complete with leaded stained glass windows.

The church was certainly much grander than the humble Evangelical Lutheran Church that Elmer and Muriel Berg had been a part of for so many years when they homesteaded their property. When the survey officer showed Elmer his land that day in 1872, he was delighted to find the church perched on a prominent hill within sight of his land, just off the wagon trail that served as a Dane County road. He had come so far and hoped to find a fundamental Bible-based church like their own in Norway, and here it was! The church was often called the Bovre Congregation because it was built on property donated by Lars Bovre. For the next fifteen years the Bergs did their best to be good stewards of their church until that day in 1887 when the tiny congregation felt it could no longer support itself and closed its doors. The Bergs then began to attend First Lutheran and were delighted to find that it too was very much a Bible believing, Bible preaching church.

Johnny and Clark Berg, true to the restlessness of youth, each silently rejoiced when Pastor Keil announced the closing hymn. An hour for Sunday School and another hour for church were a test of the boys' energy restraint.

***

Back at the Berg house, after church, the two chickens that Gertie had slow-roasting during church service were almost done.

"Woman, I thought I saw you putting an apple pie together yesterday afternoon."

Mack Berg peeked under the clean dish towel that covered the two pies that Gertie had baked on Saturday, knowing full well that if Gertie were any closer to him he'd get a light smack on his hand for peeking.

The senior Berg, at age sixty, was still a full-time dairy farmer. His once blond hair had turned a gleaming silver in just the last couple of years. His blue eyes showed a man of earnest, hard-working character and jovial spirit with their ever-present hint of a smile. He retained a rugged, heavily muscled frame. He had the full face and strong jaw typical of men of Scandinavian descent.

In 1917, Mack, at age twenty, had been thrust into the family's leadership when his father, Gus, died from a wicked strain of influenza which had ravaged much of the upper Midwest in that that year. The next year Mack married. He and his wife Ann had spent a lifetime building the farm, fulfilling the vision that had led his grandfather, Elmer Berg, to this land.

"You just stay away from those pies, Mack Berg," ordered Gertie. "I just might have some for you after your dinner."

Mack gave his characteristic, "Ha! I guess I'll just have to live with it. A man getting bossed around by his wife *and* daughter-in-law! What's a man to do?"

Gertie gave him a mock scolding as she mashed potatoes on the stove top. "Mack Berg, as far as I know

11

you've never missed a meal around here—or a pie—whether it's my cooking or Ann's. Unless you want me to change that, you had best leave the kitchen to us."

With the hint of an amused smile Ann supported her daughter-in-law. "Gertie, he is incorrigible."

"As for you," Ann turned to her husband, "out you go!"

Mack rumbled his subdued, throaty laugh as he backed away from the women's kitchen domain. Gertie had certainly been a favorite of his ever since she became their daughter-in-law in 1945. Her willingness to keep Mack in his place was a trait he loved about her. The two jousted in good-natured fun all the time.

Mack and Ann, with the help of neighbors, built the house over parts of three years, beginning in 1922. That summer the basement was dug. The footings, the basement floor, and the walls were poured that autumn.

During that winter Mack and his neighbors, most notably his friend since boyhood, Harold (Skorpie) Johnson, did the back breaking work of cutting virgin white pine from the twelve acres of high, heavily wooded ground on the southeast corner of the property.

Using block and tackle the men mounted the logs on Mack's horse drawn wagon. In three separate loads he took the logs to the Tornquist sawmill in Stoughton. There they were they were cut and milled into lumber to satisfy the specifications of the Sears and Roebuck "Gabled Farmhouse No.6" plans he had bought three years prior.

Roughing in the house began early in the coming spring. In wet falling snow, icy rain or the blessing of a cool springtime sun, the men worked in a race against the warming of the land. Soon field work would take priority over house building.

Soon the house was enclosed and shingled. With its three stately dormers the place took on the look of a classic American farmhouse, as promised by the Sears plans. Sunlight flooded the interior through the many windows.

Before the coming winter Mack and Ann painted the place white with navy blue trim. During that second winter Mack and Skorpie Johnson plumbed and wired the place. With the help of others they had the place plastered by the middle of May.

When he came home from World War II John built a modest home for Gertie and himself on the northwest corner of the farm. In 1952, with a young, growing family, they sold it and bought the family homestead from Mack and Ann. Three generations now shared the home. Where the long driveway leading to the home met Spring Road Mack had, many years before, hung a small wooden sign. It was painted white with navy blue lettering spelling out BERG DAIRY FARM. The sign was a visible indication of the pride this family took in their home, their family, their farm, and their five generations that had worked this land.

Elmer and Muriel Berg would have been pleased to see the progress made by their descendants. Gus and Ruth Berg also would have been pleased to see all the progress after they had invested years of toil and converted it from strictly a grain farm to a dairy business; the Holstein cow being their preferred species. As the Berg legacy entered the 1930's, Mack and Ann had created a place of refuge for themselves and now, in the 1950's, it was also home to John and Gertie and their children. Mack and Ann could not have been more delighted than to sell the home to their son and his family.

The family gathered around the long, farmhouse table, all seven of them, and John said grace for the Sunday dinner.

"Our Lord, we give thanks to you for the great gifts you have given us and for the everyday gifts that you have given us. Though we try to be honest and dependable in our work we need to understand that all we have is from your grace to us. We thank you for providing this family with the necessities of life. Thank you for the greatest gift of all, the gift of eternal life through the sacrifice of your Son, Jesus. Amen."

Being typically Norwegian, the conversation at meal time was subdued. This is not to say that things were not discussed. In fact, the conversations that occurred could be quite effective in resolving issues, supporting one another, or discussing events of the times. It was just that it was done with a lack of emotion that might be seen at other dinner tables.

"Ike said that if the Russians want to keep threatening with the nuclear stuff we are going to match them," Mack said, referring to President Eisenhower. Mack would sometimes throw out a broad statement just to create some conversation.

"I don't know about that but I do know that since the Russians launched that Sputnik up around the world the amount of homework the kids are getting has greatly increased," Gertie said.

"I have lots of homework now, mama. Our principle said that it is shameful that we should fall behind the Soviets. I think she said that the Soviets are the same as the Russians."

Elsie had chimed in. She was eight years old, John and Gertie's youngest. She had freckles, straight blond hair, and was quite tall for her age. She had the same blue eyes and the same no-nonsense way about her as her mother had.

"I expect you can handle any work they send your way, Elsie." Ann Berg was certainly not a big talker but when she spoke it was usually something sincere and supportive. She was grandmother to ten children. Beside John and Gertie's three she and Mack's two daughters, one living in Madison and the other in Milwaukee, gave her the other seven.

"Did you get the seeder cleaned up and lubed for me yesterday?" John looked straight at Johnny while asking him.

"Yep. We got all the grease fittings. Had to use a hammer and a piece of pipe to knock out a lot of the dirt that was jammed up in there." Johnny met his father's gaze, eye to eye.

John had not questioned his sons about the chore until now, even though he could have mentioned it anytime from Saturday afternoon on. He felt that questioning the boys too soon would be hovering over them, showing a lack of confidence in them. With a degree of uncertainty he accepted Johnny's use of "we" to mean that his brother had helped with the work.

"Good. I'll spring-tooth the two west sections starting tomorrow and we should be ready to plant later in the week. That's if it doesn't rain."

A look of uneasiness crossed John's face.

"It's not right. The government pays cash crop farmers to leave some acreage fallow. It doesn't affect us because we use our own stuff for feed, but it just always seems strange to me."

It was Elsie who chimed in again. "Dad, Mr. Long says that the American farmer should accept subsidy payments proudly because he succeeds so well in producing. The American farmer feeds the world!"

John Berg mulled over her words for a few seconds. "Who's Mr. Long?"

"He's my social studies teacher."

The farmer stared blankly at his daughter while he let her statement sink in.

2

Concerns

So do not fear, for I am with you;
do not be dismayed . . .

Isaiah 41:10 (NIV)

As she did each morning, rain or shine, in the heat of July or the frigid temperatures of January, Gertie walked the 200 yards to the mailbox that stood where the Berg driveway met Spring Road. It was now 1965 and on this day, a damp, blustery morning in early May, the mailbox contained a letter addressed to Johnny, now a strapping twenty year old, almost two years a graduate from Stoughton Area High School. The letter's return address said The Pentagon, Wash. D.C.

Gertie thought of how she and John had talked about the possibility of their two sons being drafted someday and how they would respond should such happen. Now it appeared the time had come and the Bergs were ready to stand behind their son and behind their country. The war in Vietnam had its critics and there were questions about our nation's commitment to such a war. But Johnny was being called and both John and Gertie felt it was a responsibility he should respond to positively.

As she began to walk back to the house Gertie's heart sank for a brief moment. She thought of the families across the nation who lived day to day concerned over the safe return of their sons. She realized how her family was no more immune to the tide of world events than any other family. How they could soon be one of those families. She then stopped and stared at nothing in particular as she righted herself with a brief, audible prayer.

"Lord, in your Word it says that you will not give us anything more than we can bear if we will just put our faith in you. I don't know what you have in store for us but I pray you will give me the strength and the wisdom to hold on to that truth."

* * *

At this time in the spring the Berg men worked their fields relentlessly. Once the soil became firm enough it had to be prepped for planting. The chisel plow, spring tooth, cultivator-seeder, these tractor implements were their allies. Any delay meant planting was moved back. John, Johnny and Mack each had their roles in this process. They were in the fields at dawn, went at it hard all day, came in for supper and then worked with headlights burning until roughly ten o'clock. Clark was finishing high school but he was expected to work a few hours immediately upon getting home.

Despite this schedule the men did not lack for nutrition. Gertie and Ann brought breakfast and dinner out to their men, meeting them individually or as a group on whatever ridge line the women were able to maneuver the family's trusty Ford pickup.

Supper was different. Gertie and Ann insisted the family sit down together and have a full meal. For the men to stuff down a breakfast and dinner at their tractors was enough. The women would not let the demands of work overshadow the stability a family supper offered.

During this time of spring field work it was Johnny's custom, when he came in for supper, to relax for a few minutes on the parlor's davenport before supper. After a hard day in the fields he loved to wash up and then, even if only for a few minutes, lean back into the deep cushions of this piece of furniture, his lanky 6'2" frame recovering from the vibration inflicted by the tractor work.

Gertie called from the kitchen. "Johnny, can you come here?"

Though he heard his mother's call the young man did not immediately respond. In a few moments, and only half awake, he walked down the hallway into the big kitchen. With his eyes half shut a contented smile crossed his face as the scent of his mother's cooking filled his senses.

"Oh yeah! Meat loaf. And is that homemade bread I see?"

"It is," Gertie responded weakly. She picked up the letter off the counter. Looking directly in the eyes of her son she handed it to him.

When he saw the return address Johnny's reaction was typically low key. He gave a grunt of recognition. "Ugh. Well . . . I think I know what this is all about." He gave his mother a quick snippet of a smile and returned to the parlor.

Ten minutes later John and Gertie, their three children, and Mack and Ann were at the supper table. Gertie wondered if and when Johnny would mention his letter. He didn't wait long.

"I'm being drafted. Got the letter in the mail today. Have to report to Camp McCoy for a physical and induction on May 16th."

Not a word was said for a number of seconds until Elsie, now sixteen-years-old, spoke up quizzically. "You have to work the farm. Aren't you exempt, or excluded, or whatever they call it because you have to take care of the farm?"

"Nice try Els but this is grandpa's and dad's farm, not mine." After a pause he continued. "Besides . . . I wouldn't try to get out of this. I've been having a funny feeling seeing other guys go. I'm sort of glad I got drafted. I want to get on with it. It's only two years."

John Sr. did not immediately respond to his son's announcement but the joy that he always experienced at eating the meals prepared by both his wife and his mother seemed to leave him.

The Bergs were not a people to speak quickly. It could be said that they were slow to move off center with their thoughts. Really though, they were just reflective people, more than willing to give consideration to something before speaking.

After a few moments it was the grandparents who spoke up.

"Uncle Sam will be getting the best." Mack spoke with assurance. He looked around the table at everyone when he said this. "I know you will make us all proud."

Ann had a request for her grandson. "Your grandma has but one thing to ask of you, Johnny. Please hear me and take heed. Do not go out of your way to seek danger. Ask the Lord to use you as He will and ask Him to give you the courage to handle that task, but I urge you, don't go out of your way to seek danger."

John Sr. supported his mother. He stared at his oldest son.

"Your grandmother is right. I saw it for myself. Men who volunteered to come to our unit so that they could see action. They were the first to crack. Probably because they realized that they had brought on the whole thing themselves." He paused for a moment, then continued, "Or maybe they just didn't realize how bad it could get."

"I think our son is level headed enough to know all this, and besides, you've all got him in Vietnam already." Gertie spoke with annoyance in her voice. She put an end to the subject. "Goodness sakes. There is many a place the Army could send him."

But it was eighteen-year-old Clark who broke the sullen atmosphere. "Besides, he probably won't even make it through basic training. Pass the c-rations buster."

The mood around the table lightened except for John Sr. Memories of North Africa's Kasserine Pass flashed across his mind.

* * *

Johnny Berg's draft notice should have been enough for the Bergs to digest, but the next morning the strangest bit of news arrived, once again, in the mailbox. The letter was addressed to Mr. Mack Berg. When Gertie retrieved the letter she would have thought little of it except that the return address was from the Pleasant Springs Town Property and Zoning Board. Pleasant Springs Town was the small, very rural township just north of Stoughton where Berg Dairy Farm lay.

That morning Mack came in from the fields to make a repair on his tractor. He spent about forty-five minutes in the barn closest to the house—the service barn, where the Bergs did their maintenance and repair work—replacing a leaking hydraulic hose. The repair finished by eleven o'clock he decided to eat his dinner in the kitchen, before the women took food out to the fields. Like many farm folk the Bergs referred to the noontime meal as dinner, not lunch. The evening meal was always supper.

"Grilled cheese, tomato soup, and coffee. That should keep you going 'til supper."

It was Gertie's habit to announce what was to eat for dinner, whether it was around the kitchen table or out in the fields. She would, however, never let on what she was going to be cooking for supper. It was just a little game she played. Her way of saying, 'this is Ann's kitchen and my kitchen; you just bring your appetite and we'll make sure you get plenty to eat'.

Mack kicked off his muddy boots at the back door. "That sounds good to me, I'm hungry. I'll bet you made that grilled cheese on homemade bread. Where's that wife of mine?"

"Mack Berg, I've never known you when you weren't hungry and, yes, your grilled cheese is on homemade bread. Ann wanted to lay down awhile. She was feeling a little tired."

The farmer had washed his oily hands at the repair barn's wash basin so he sat right down. Gertie handed her father-in-law the letter. "Here. I know you're in the habit of opening your mail just before suppertime but this letter is from the property and zoning board. Thought you might want to see what it's about. Have you been up to some no good that we don't know about?"

"Ha! Haven't done anything wrong lately." He fumbled to open the letter. "That husband of yours keeps me too busy to have time to get into trouble and, besides, I'm too scared of that wife of mine to be out gambling, drinking or chasing wild women."

After a slurp of coffee and a bite from his grilled cheese Mack began to read. By this time Gertie was at work over the kitchen sink, her back to her father-in-law, when she responded.

"Goodness knows, you and John have never given Ann or I concern over such things. We've enough frustration just picking up after you."

When she received no response she looked over her shoulder to see the strangest look on Mack's face. It was a look of puzzlement, astonishment and annoyance, all at the same time. She turned, leaning where the small of her back met the sink counter, as she folded her arms. "What in the world has got you looking like that? You look like you were the one who just got the draft notice."

"It wouldn't surprise me anymore than this. Have a seat."

Mack's strange look was replaced by his deep, throaty laugh and a shake of his head. He handed the letter to Gertie. She started to read aloud. The farther she got the softer her voice became until she was reading silently.

From:
Pleasant Springs Town
Property and Zoning Board

May 3, 1965

When Troubles Rain: A Novel

Dear Mr. Berg:

This letter is to inform you that a "Right to Purchase Land Claim" has been filed in the office of Pleasant Springs Town. The land in question belongs to you.

By law the claimant has the right to a hearing before the town supervisor to present the claimant's case. Be advised that you are requested to attend this hearing. The purpose of the hearing is to expedite the resolution of said claim, thus preventing the need for a legal confrontation in the courts. Barring an amicable settlement upon the conclusion of this hearing the claimant has the option of filing a law suit against you. Be advised that you may wish to have legal counsel present at the time of the hearing. Filing information for the above stated claim follows:

Claim No. 24-5:
Right to Purchase Land Claim

Wisconsin State Real Estate Code reference:
section 12, paragraph 7

Date of Claim Declaration:
April 30, 1965

Claimant:
Mr. Gerald Hicks

Description of claim at issue:
Concerning deed of property sale and pursuant addendum between Oscar Knudson (seller) and Mack Berg (purchaser) dated December 5th, 1936.

Property in question are two sections (eighty acres) from coordinate plat line longitude 34 to coordinate plat line latitude U, Town of Pleasant Springs, County of Dane, State of Wisconsin. Common language border recognition is at north acreage of Berg property along the north side of Koshkonong Rd. to intersection at Kinney Rd. to where it meets Knudson Lane.

Time of claim hearing:
Tuesday, May 24, 1965; 9:00 A.M.

Location:
Pleasant Springs Town Hall, room 3.
1325 County Highway B,
Pleasant Springs Town, Wisconsin.

Any request on your part to change the time of this
hearing may be addressed by calling the following
number:
Su 8-4407.

Thomas Evans
Supervisor
Pleasant Springs Town

Gertie felt a great sense of irritation upon finishing the letter. The idea that someone, somebody named Gerald Hicks, whom none of them had ever heard of, was claiming the right to buy some of their land was so preposterous that she felt not a sense of concern, but just a sense of irritation.

Mack could see the irritation in his daughter-in-law and he knew that it would soon turn to anger.

"Gertie, let's keep this our little secret until supper. We'll let everyone know about this at the same time."

* * *

"Mother, I have no doubt that you make the best pineapple upside down cake in the entire state of Wisconsin." This was Clark's favorite dessert and in one way or another he always let his mother, and his grandmother, know that he appreciated their efforts. Despite his sometimes irreverent behavior he could be a real charmer.

Upon the conclusion of dessert it was normal for Clark and Johnny, and sometimes Elsie, to leave the table to their mother, father and grandparents, who would relax over their coffee for another ten minutes. On this evening Gertie asked her kids to stay put, grandpa had something to

23

say. Clark's expression showed his impatience with staying at the table, but then he received that glare from his mother that told him it would be wise to stay put.

Mack put on his reading glasses. "Got a letter today. Want to read it to you."

When he finished there were a few seconds of stunned silence.

"Who in the world is Gerald Hicks?" John Berg leaned back in his chair. "Is this really addressed to us? There has to be some kind of mistake. My great grandparents settled here in 1872. I haven't got time to go to court on May whatever it is for a hearing about being forced to sell some of the land we've been farming for the last ninety three years."

He took the letter from his father and read it himself. He looked up quizzically, at no one in particular. "Gerald Hicks?" He shifted his gaze to his father with an expression of amazement and concern. "You or I need to call Tom Evans tomorrow and see what this is all about. In the meantime you've got the homestead land grant deed somewhere, don't you? In your safety deposit box at the bank?"

"Yep. Got it somewhere," replied Mack. "I don't know where, but we've got it somewhere. I think it's in our dresser, in the bottom drawer with a lot of other papers. I don't believe I ever got around to putting that stuff in the safety deposit box."

"And the receipts or the deeds from when you bought the acreage from the Knudson place?"

"Oh yeah, got those too. And I know I've got the deed from when dad bought the north forty acres from the state shortly before he died." He rubbed the back of his neck and continued.

"You know, the two sections this letter is talking about. That's the land Oscar Knudson sold me when he retired. He said he had had enough. He was only in his sixties. Said he and Margaret were going to retire down south somewhere.

Mack stared into his coffee cup for a second or two and then repeated the thoughts that his son had just expressed. "What kind of a crackpot is going to come along and claim the right to buy a person's land away from him?"

Clark was now glad he stayed at the table. "Grandpa, maybe this is a practical joke. Maybe this is another one of Skorpie's practical jokes. I wouldn't put it past him."

"Ha! That old bird isn't smart enough to come up with something this good. Harold Johnson has been sticking it to me since I was five years old but that dumb Swede isn't smart enough to come up with something like this. Besides, look at the letterhead. This looks pretty official."

John did his best to put an end to the nonsense of such a letter. "I'd be happy to know that this was some of Skorpie Johnson's mischief . . . but I don't think so. I'll call Tom Evans tomorrow and see what this is all about."

He sat at the table motionless for a few moments before thinking out loud. "Who in the world is Gerald Hicks?"

3

Setback

Spring field work notwithstanding, it was Johnny Berg's practice to stop at two o'clock each Saturday. He spent the rest of the day with the girl who had been his sweetheart since his sophomore year in high school.

Jenny Watson had moved to Stoughton with her family when she was eleven years old. Her father had bought the hardware store in town in 1956 when his career as an engineer at the American Motors plant in Kenosha seemed to have no real future.

Jenny was the oldest of three girls and one boy. She was bright, sincere and had a mind of her own. If the latter quality indicated stubbornness it was of a positive nature. She was a person, even at the young age of twenty, who thought independently. She could not be easily swayed from what she believed to be right and she was more than willing to speak up for those beliefs. Young John Berg was not the same. Though just as principled as Jenny he was so laid back that he often let the comments of others go unchallenged.

Johnny received his draft notice on Thursday and had only talked to Jenny on the phone Friday night for the briefest of moments. The intense field work left little time for talk and besides, the telephone at the Berg home was considered a tool to be used as needed, not as an instrument for extended conversation. He did not mention the induction notice over the phone, preferring to wait until he saw Jenny in person.

As they often did, the couple drove the Berg's Ford pickup twenty five miles into Madison to eat. They liked a place on Highway 12 called Tom's Grill. The place offered a great club sandwich that Johnny enjoyed.

While waiting for their food Jenny challenged him.

"I know you are one of the most soft-spoken guys on this earth, Johnny Berg, but you hardly said two words on the way over here. Sometimes I wonder how you ever put the words together to say that you want to marry me."

Jenny tilted her head as she met John's gaze. "In case you forgot you did say that you want to marry me. You do remember saying that to me, don't you Mr. Berg?"

She gave her boyfriend that smile that always brought him around to her way of thinking.

Johnny cracked a smile. "Of course I want to marry you." He gave a long hesitation that made Jenny take pause for concern. Her tone was upbeat, but demanding.

"What is the matter, John? It's like you are about to tell me something that I don't want to hear. What is it?"

He leaned back in his chair and rubbed his left hand on the back of his neck. It was a mannerism—not uncommon to his grandfather—that he unconsciously used when concerned about something. He took a deep breath and looked directly into Jenny's eyes.

"I've received my draft notice. I have to report to Camp McCoy for a physical and induction in twelve days."

Jenny was caught totally by surprise. For a brief moment they just stared at each other.

"Camp McCoy. It's over near LaCrosse. Dad says it's an old Army camp they closed a few years ago and they probably reopened some of it to process new guys since Vietnam started."

He knew that his girlfriend was not really interested in the history of Camp McCoy, but it was an awkward moment and he did not know what else to say.

Jenny's eyes went down to her coke. She took a sip, gathered her thoughts, squared her shoulders and returned her gaze to the young man she loved.

"I don't know if this war is right or wrong or what. The one time we talked about it you said that if they called you then you would do your best."

Though she was not finished with her thought she stopped for a moment. She was fighting her disappointment while trying to face this news head on.

"Well, now the draft board has called you, Johnny Berg. I won't be the first girl to have her fiancée, well, almost fiancée, called into the Army."

"Is that what it is; the Army? Or is it the Navy or the Air Force or the Marines or the paratroopers? I would prefer that you not be jumping out of airplanes."

Johnny smiled. At that moment he felt a wave of love for this girl that went beyond anything he had yet known. Here she was getting the news that her future with the guy she wanted to marry was going to be put on hold for the next two years and yet she took the news bravely. He reached across the table and squeezed her hands.

"I want to go and get this over with, Jen. Then I want to come back and marry you and share your bed and make babies with you and all that goes with it."

Jenny was speechless for a moment before responding. "Wow! I've been waiting for the day when you would sound so authoritative about our future. Looks like it took a draft notice to get it out of you."

Johnny took on a self-conscious smile. He raised his eyebrows and shrugged his shoulders in an 'I hadn't thought about it that way' gesture.

"Anyway, I don't know much about the military Jen, but I do know that they don't draft guys into the paratroopers. They are a part of the Army. I think paratroop training is something you volunteer for."

Jenny loosened her hands from his and squeezed one of his forearms. "Well, I hope you have the good sense not to be volunteering to jump out of airplanes."

John laughed softly. "Jen, I don't know what I'll be doing. I could spend the next two years cleaning out toilets."

"Besides," he spoke with light hearted conviction, "I've already been told by grandma not to volunteer for anything."

Jenny took a long drag on her coke and controlled a smile that was trying to break out. "Does that include cleaning out toilets?"

"It certainly does!"

It was well past dark when the couple returned to the Watson house. At the front door Jenny gave her boyfriend a kiss with a passion she had never previously offered. She immediately turned and went into the house.

As he drove home a number of things raced through Johnny's mind. One second it was Jenny and how special it would be when he returned from the Army so they could begin their lives together. Then he realized how much he was going to miss his family and how amazing his life, this simple, unglamorous, but amazing life, had been. He then thought of the uncertainty of these next two years. Would he be up to whatever experiences were ahead of him? Would he be the kind of soldier, the kind of man, that he should be? Would he be the kind of person that, as his grandfather said, 'would make them all proud'?

He knew before he pulled into the farm that he needed for he and Jenny to become engaged before he went away. Before the next week was out he would take her to the Christianson Jewelry store in town, buy her a ring, and do that very thing.

Johnny quietly entered the back door of the house. It was 10 o'clock and everyone was asleep. He knew that at 10 o'clock on a Saturday night much of the world was out trying to make life fun and exciting. He stood there in the dark kitchen. A feeling of gratitude came over him as he realized that all the fun and excitement, and all the contentment and peace that he needed had already been his for the twenty years of his life.

4

Uncle Frank

Sail away from the safe harbor.
Catch the trade winds in your sails.

Mark Twain

Brothers can be so much alike and yet so different. Clark Berg was different than his brother. Unlike Johnny, Clark was not one to hide his light under a barrel.

He was a handsome young man. He was of solid build, almost six feet tall; dark hair and brown eyes. Some said he reminded them of a popular actor of the day, Montgomery Clift.

His choice of friends had never pleased his parents, even in elementary school. And now, a senior in high school, he was part of a crowd that could charitably be called fast. Clark never drank or smoked anywhere near the farm but John and Gertie had not just fallen off the turnip truck. Elsie and Johnny had never been any trouble but Clark was another matter. He could be very much a rebel. He possessed a charm that could endear him to people one minute, and insincerity that left people feeling betrayed the next.

Where Johnny always knew his life's work would be to carry on the farm Clark seemed less interested in his future and more interested in the delights of the next weekend. He had always managed to pass from grade to grade in elementary school, not because of a strong work ethic, but rather because he possessed a natural aptitude for memorization and deduction. Then, in the ninth grade, part way through the fall term, his behavior got him expelled for the reminder of the term; playing poker in the boys' bathroom. When he came back his attitude was so poor that he flunked that same first half of the ninth grade. He had lost an entire year.

Clark graduated from Stoughton Area High School on May 18, two days after Johnny left for the Army. He faced graduation with no plans other than to spend that summer working on the farm. Tending to the needs of the Holstein cow was something he did not want to do; but then a stroke of good fortune gave young Berg the direction he needed: occupational direction, anyway.

Clark's Uncle Frank, husband to John Berg's sister Catherine, was sales manager for WWMR, a 50,000 watt, major radio station in Milwaukee. It competed staunchly with the likes of WGN and WLS out of Chicago for a share of the Wisconsin, and beyond, audience. Like many stations of the day the morning and afternoon drive time programs featured music with an adult appeal. Conversation was light hearted, covering subjects from human interest stories to occasional interviews with local athletes and politicians. Though the station did not cover the game play-by-play of the Green Bay Packers, it thoroughly followed every aspect of the beloved team. They did cover the play-by-play of the Milwaukee Braves and had done so since the team came from Boston in 1953. The mid-morning slot included a popular, Peabody Award-winning documentary program. The farm report came on after the noon news and Arthur Godfrey's syndicated radio show followed. The station was a CBS affiliate.

WWMR attracted blue ribbon businesses with large advertising budgets.

Frank Smith had been sales manager at the station for eleven years. Selling radio advertising was a difficult, high pressure business. It required perseverance and discipline. Smith was aware that Clark had little of these qualities. But over the years he had come to see likeability in his nephew that—if channeled correctly—could go a long way in sales. Could Clark learn the discipline he needed? Frank Smith felt it was worth a try. After all, Clark was family. He was the son of his wife's brother. Smith felt that somewhere inside of the young man must reside the character so abundant in the rest of the Berg family.

And so on the Tuesday after the Memorial Day weekend, just five days after his high school graduation, Clark borrowed the family station wagon to keep an appointment with Frank Smith at his office, one floor above the WWMR studios in the Kramer Building in downtown Milwaukee.

Frank Smith was an imposing figure from behind his desk. With the sleeves of his white dress shirt rolled up, the shirt unbuttoned at the top and a conservative blue tie dangling loosely, he appeared all business. He was a rangy, athletic looking six foot two inches tall. His black hair, graying at the temples and receding just a bit, was conservatively cut. From all of his outdoor activities he was already well tanned, despite the cool spring weather.

Smith came around the desk, welcomed his nephew with a handshake, and asked him to take a seat. Smith sat on the edge of his desk. He skipped over the family small talk and got right to the point.

"Clark, I told you over the phone that I had a job offer for you. I didn't tell you anything about it over the phone and I did that purposefully. I believe the most important thing I do as advertising sales manager here is to hire the right people to sell time on this radio station."

Frank Smith paused.

"I want to make sure you understand that you sink or swim here based on your own performance, just like everyone else."

A formal, "Yes sir," was all Clark could manage. Smith had succeeded in getting and holding his nephew's attention. This, Clark could tell, would be no family favor hiring.

"If you're interested you are going to have to look at the big picture. Our advertising account execs all have university degrees. What I see in you is some raw talent. Over time, with some long range planning and commitment on your part, I believe you have the opportunity for a lucrative career in radio ad sales."

"Before I go any further . . . do you think that this holds any interest for you?"

For one of the few times in his young life someone had Clark's complete attention.

"Yes sir, I'm interested. I'm very interested."

Smith moved right along. "What I am proposing is this. I know you are a senior. Have you finished school?"

"We graduated last week." Clark was sitting ram rod straight on the edge of his seat.

"Fine then. If your answer is yes to this be ready to start here next Monday morning. Your position will be assistant ad exec. What that means is you'll be doing everything from assisting the ad execs with their paper work; taking phone calls when the execs aren't available; going out on presentations when the execs need a hand; organizing files and whatever else might be required. When we bring a client in you may be setting up the coffee and donuts! You get the idea. We have six ad execs here and we have one assistant. It's too much. We need a second assistant. Your starting pay will be $150.00 a week. If all goes well, and by that I mean you become a valuable employee, there will be incremental increases as soon as I deem appropriate."

Smith held up his hand to stop an immediate response from his nephew. He wasn't finished yet.

"Now, before you give me a final answer as to whether or not you want this I need to know something. I want to see you make every effort to get yourself enrolled in college for the fall semester. I know that it's a little late to get started in this effort and maybe your grades are not the most impressive but I am of the belief that a person can accomplish most anything if he puts his mind to it. We will deal later about how you go to school and work here at the same time. They do have a thing called night school. Are you still interested?"

Clark knew full well that this was an opportunity that he must take. Here he was, one minute drifting along with no plans after high school but the dismal prospect of the farm, and the next minute having a chance to get started in a business with a future that appealed to him.

"Yes sir. I'm very interested. I do want this opportunity."

Smith continued to stare directly into his nephew's eyes. "And the discipline? Are you going to be disciplined enough to work and go to school? I don't need you to be an assistant sales exec forever. You'll have to be energetic enough and disciplined enough to work toward a future."

Clark stood to meet his uncle. He exhaled the air of tension that had accumulated in his lungs. His uncle had been upfront with him and he owed the same to him.

"I want this opportunity very much. I, ugh. Well, I may be telling you something that you already know when I tell you that I don't have the best work reputation. I've sometimes been one to . . ."

Smith held up his hand again. "I know something of your work ethic. And I know something of your good time Charlie reputation. What I am interested in is what lies ahead of you. There's no reason why you can't be an achiever. You work hard, be willing to learn, and to be sincere with your employer and with our clients, and I believe you can make it."

Smith held out his hand and the two shook.

"So I'll expect you Monday morning at 8:30." He spoke matter-of-factly to his nephew.

Clark responded with a, "Yes sir. Thank you." It came upon him that this was no moment for a 'thanks Uncle Frank' good bye.

5

Uncertainty

And I will make them
and the places round about my hill a blessing;
and I will cause the shower to come down in his season;
there shall be showers of blessing.

Ezekiel 34:26 (KJV)

John brought the Ford F-150 to a stop when it reached the crest of the rise. He occasionally took this bumpy, two-track trail along the edge of the Berg's land, the very high ground from which Mack had harvested the pine to build the family's home in the 1920's, to take in all the farm's 280 acres.

Having been born and raised in the dairy business John accepted without need for acknowledgement the demands on the American farmer. It is unlikely that in any other work are the qualities of self-discipline, physical endurance, optimism, patience, pragmatism, business savvy, and the acceptance of disappointment so well required. And then, beyond all else, the need for humility is essential. A humility that says a higher power than man has control of the weather that is needed for success.

On this morning, looking beyond the farm to the southwest, he saw the reflection of the sun off of Lake Kegonsa. Farther on, he could make out the top of the Romanesque style bell tower of Stoughton's town hall.

He smiled as he thought of the town's Norwegian heritage. So much was owed to Targe Mandt, the Norwegian immigrant who began a wagon building business in Stoughton after the Civil War. Mandt solicited for those in his birth country to come to America and work in his factory. The town's annual Syttende Mai Festival—the seventeenth of May—was celebrated each spring during the week culminating on the weekend closest to that date; the date that Norway declared its independence from five hundred years of rule by Denmark.

John thought of how his father proudly flew the family's Norwegian flag during that week. Mack always broke out his elaborately embroidered Norse sweater—sent to him years before by distant relatives near Trondiem—for the Sunday parade. It had been an especially warm May afternoon this year, but Mack proudly perspired through the festivities.

On this morning John had called for a nine o'clock meeting with Mack and his two hired hands at this location. He thought that from here the young man he had hired through the University of Wisconsin placement service could get the best view of the entire farm on this, his first day of employment. As he heard the station wagon strain, making its way to the top of the hill, John's gaze settled on the eighty acres that was now, thanks to a man names Gerald Hicks, in doubt. The contented feeling that he was experiencing began to slip. He was of a belief that the Lord was in charge, but he was also mindful of the expression that God helps those who help themselves.

"Georgie, welcome to Berg Dairy Farm, home of the Vikings. If Mack here or John get on your case just remember that Gertie and Ann's cooking will make it all worthwhile."

It was Rollie Leach, the farm's regular summer help, who offered an official welcome to young George Wistoff once all four men were gathered around John's pickup. Though Rollie and George had first met while working in the milking parlor earlier in the morning, Rollie now had an audience.

"Where's home, Georgie?"

The soft spoken, broad shouldered twenty-year-old was put at ease by Rollie's outgoing style.

"Minot, North Dakota. It's about nine hundred miles west and a little north of here. My folks have a farm there. It's a grain operation."

He was quick to explain why he would spend the summer on a Wisconsin dairy farm instead of working his family's business.

"I just finished my first year at North Dakota State. I'm lookin' to get an Ag degree. I need work on a dairy farm to satisfy my animal husbandry requirement."

Rollie jumped all over it.

"North Dakota? North Dakota! Do they have electricity out there yet? This place must seem like the Las Vegas strip to you!"

They all chuckled; then Mack put in his two cents worth. "Don't mind Rollie here, George. I thought that Canadians were a soft-spoken bunch. But I think Rollie here's been hit too many times in the head by hockey pucks."

Rollie gave a quick retort. "Oh mighty Thor, like I've said before, it's the stick that does the damage. A hockey player will get clobbered twenty times in the head by a stick for every time he gets drilled by a puck."

Leach had come to the University of Wisconsin on a hockey scholarship in 1958. In his sophomore year he suffered a severe knee injury that ended his playing days. Being unable to play, and with his scholarship money partially revoked, the starch had been taken out of him regarding school. When the opportunity to take work as the team's equipment manager presented itself he quit school and took the job. During the slow summer months he had endeared himself to the Bergs as their loyal, irreverently humorous hired hand.

There is no doubt that Rollie had taken on the appearance of many an ex-hockey player. He had the thick calf and thigh muscles and the high, rumpy glutes of a man who had been skating almost from the time he could walk.

He had a barrel chest and the beginnings of a pot belly. The barrel chest was the result of the aerobics of his sport. The pot belly was from the favorite form of hydration of many an ex-player—full bodied Canadian beer. He always wore one of two baseball caps over his reddish brown brush cut. One was red and white with the word Badgers spelled out, the name of his university's teams. The other was blue with white letters spelling Hespeler. With unabashed pride Rollie Leach loved to tell anyone he could about his beloved hometown of Hespeler, Ontario.

John brought everyone's attention to the work at hand.

"I brought you all up here so George could get the lay of the land. Dad is going to continue with his tractor work for the rest of the week. Rollie, between morning and afternoon milking today I want George and you to spend your time cleaning out those three culverts in the field near Koshgonong Road. We've neglected them for a number of years and they can't take much more erosion before they start backing up. I'll be in the service barn for the rest of the week with repairs. Kaiser's called yesterday and said the yoke was in for the little Massey."

Rollie couldn't help but make young George feel more at home.

"John, I think old Georgie here might be cleaning out culverts for the first time. Up in Minot it stays so cold the damn, I mean darn, drains never get a chance to thaw out, eh!"

By this time George Wistoff could sense an unfamiliar lilt to Rollie Leach's speech pattern.

"Where are you from, Rollie?"

George could sense that both Mack and John stiffened; as though he shouldn't have asked the question.

"Georgie, I'm from the greatest little town in North America: Hespeler, Ontario. It's a great main street community. Not so many Vikings to put up with. Mostly Scotch and English up our way. Hespeler is the hockey stick capital of the world. Most all your major brands are cut and milled there. Bauer, Sherwood, our own Hespeler brand. A lot of the Northland Pro brand is done in Hespeler for teams in the National Hockey League. And some of the minor league teams."

"You can't beat it; right John!"

Berg shook his head in resignation to Rollie's enthusiasm. "Right Rollie. Scotch, English, and hockey sticks."

He redirected his conversation toward his new help.

"You're replacing a good man, George. You shouldn't have any trouble adjusting to the dairy business. We're glad to have you."

The kid was already aware that Johnny was away in the army. "I've got two older brothers. Twins. They got drafted about a year ago. One's in Vietnam."

It was quiet for a few moments as the uncertainty of America's commitment to this war gripped these men, along with the shared concern for those now in harm's way.

Mack broke the silence, speaking with Berg pragmatism.

"We're just gonna have to see how it all works out."

Before the summer was gone both Mack and John were to find out that Johnny's army time and the land dispute with Gerald Hicks would become secondary to yet another concern.

6

Rasmussen's Diner

and we have fellowship one with another . . .

1 John 1:7 (KJV)

When Mack Berg turned the financial responsibility and day-to-day operation of the farm over to his son he continued to work a schedule that would exhaust most folks. He routinely put in an hour or so of work before breakfast. Good work habits are not soon abandoned.

On Saturday mornings he allowed himself a little down time. He made the six mile trip into town, where he met for coffee at Rasmussen's Diner with three of his peers, farmers in semi-retirement.

Bud Rasmussen had maintained the business on his own since his wife had passed away two years previous. The place opened at 6:00 a.m. for breakfast and closed after the lunch hour. Save for one enlarged and framed photograph that hung above the doorway leading back into the kitchen the place had no atmosphere at all. The picture was a black and white print of Bud and three other locals showing off an impressive stringer of walleyes. In the bottom right corner of the picture was scribbled "Lake Kegonsa, spring, 1948".

The place was always kept clean and it had a decent following. It was well supplied with old world baked goods from Kronberg's, the outstanding Danish bakery on the other side of Main Street. It was all Mack Berg and his buddies needed.

On this morning Mack walked in with a pointed question for Harold (Skorpie) Johnson.

"Are you up to no good with me again, Johnson?" Mack had the words out of his mouth before he plopped into his chair.

"I'm up to no good every chance I get when it comes to you, Mr. Berg," replied Mack's life-long friend. "Trouble is, you're just too easy a mark. What did I do this time?"

Mack shook his head and grunted. "I wish it were one of your shenanigans." He rubbed the back of his neck. "Got a letter yesterday from the town office. Some guy has claimed that he has the right to buy some of our land. Those eighty acres that Oscar Knudson sold me in the thirties. I've got to go for a meeting to see if it can be resolved to avoid a legal action. Can you believe it!"

Skorpie Johnson stared over his reading glasses at his friend for a good five seconds. Over the years he had kept himself almost in as good a physical condition as Mack, although he now carried a few extra pounds on his six foot, two inch frame. His blue eyes looked gleeful as he saw the humor of it. "Ah! That's a classic. I'd a loved to have thought of that one."

"Thought of what?" Tom Edgerton asked the question as he and Edgar Friske found their seats.

Mack began to explain what little he knew; that someone was claiming the right to purchase part of the Bergs' land based on an obscure state law; that he had to go to the Pleasant Springs Town office to try and settle things.

"What's the guy's name?" It was Friske who asked, hoping the name would ring a bell with one of them.

"Ugh? I donno. Forgot. Got it here." Mack fumbled for the letter and put on his reading glasses. "Ugh. Name's Gerald Hicks."

They all reflected for a moment.

Friske shook his head.

"My family's been here almost as long as yours, Mack. I don't recall anybody named Hicks from around here."

"Yeah. Well, whoever he is he's got a lot of explaining to do come the twenty-fourth," grumbled Mack.

The mood at the table was always jovial with a great deal of kidding and exaggeration. But now the mood turned somber. A man's land was being questioned. In this part of the country, where the business of farming was passed on from one generation to the next, where pride and tradition were as important as making a dollar, a man's land ranked only behind his God and his family.

Betty Smith, Rasmussen's longtime waitress, filled coffee cups and put a plate with a generous number of slices of Kronberg's cardamom coffee bread on the foursome's table.

"Eat up boys; it's not getting any fresher." It's the same line she gave this group every Saturday.

Skorpie looked up. "Betty, you get better looking every day. If I wasn't so afraid of that wife of mine I'd be sweet talking you every chance I get."

Indeed, Betty Smith was a good looking woman. Now forty-five years old she had been widowed seven years previous when her husband, Tom Smith, Stoughton's postmaster, passed away after a long struggle with colon cancer. Betty had a million dollar smile, had been able to keep an attractive figure and, possibly with a little help from the right hair color, had been able to retain her shiny, naturally curly chestnut brown hair. Better than all that Betty Smith had a great sense of humor and a no nonsense way of keeping her customers in line.

"Harold Johnson, you mind yourself. If I were to tell Ruth how you carry on here I believe they'd try to cancel your life insurance."

The men chortled and Eddie Friske asked Betty if she knew anyone named Hicks from around Stoughton.

"Beats me," she replied, as she took off for another table.

Five minutes later she was back. "You know, I think I do know that name Hicks. When I was a young girl my mother's best friend was Maggie Knudson. You guys knew the Knudsen's, Oscar and Margaret."

"Yeah, sure." replied Mack. "They had the farm right next to us. Oscar Knudsen sold out to Bobby Pierson and me during the Depression." He did not attempt to explain the issue at hand.

Betty continued. "Anyway, they had two daughters. Maggie was the oldest and she had a younger sister. Name was Gretchen. No. No, it was Greta."

"It was Greta." Eddie Friske seemed to have the sharpest recall of the four of them. "As I recall, a good looking girl."

"Oh yeah. I remember now," chimed in Edgerton. "A very attractive young woman."

Skorpie grunted. "It's good to know that a couple of geezers like you can still remember such things."

"Do you people want to hear what I have to say, or not?" With hands on hips and a look of mock impatience on her face Betty continued. "Greta married somebody from Chicago named Hicks. I remember they lived in Chicago and I don't believe they ever came back here much. Come on! I'll bet you guys were at the wedding."

After a second of reflection none of them could remember being at such a wedding.

"Had to have been thirty some years ago," said Mack. "That wedding isn't ringing a bell to me."

"Ah!" Betty shook her head. "That's because you're men. It's beyond your powers to remember any-thing as significant as a wedding. I remember and I was just a kid."

She folded her arms and softened her voice. "Anyway, there it is. I'm pretty sure you all remember hearing about the car accident. Fifteen years ago, or so. Maggie was killed. Somewhere down south where she had moved. She never had married."

Betty left for another table.

Eddie Friske spoke to no one in particular. "Yes, I think we all remember hearing about that one. When you think about it the Knudson name is gone. That is if Margaret is gone, which most likely she is. She'd have to be somewhere in her nineties."

"She's gone alright," said Mack. "I remember reading it in the obituaries a number of years ago. Knuddy died first. Funny, they brought him back up here, had a memorial service and all, but they must'da planted Margaret down south somewhere."

"Gone but not forgotten," said Edgerton. "Old Knuddy was a hard, hard worker." He looked to Mack. "You think this might be the Hicks guy that married Greta?"

"Must be. Still doesn't make any sense to me." Mack reached for another slab of coffee bread. "How in the world could this Hicks character have any claim on our land? I'm going to forget about it for now and just be at that meeting."

7

Lawyers

In the house of the righteous is much treasure:
but in the revenues of the wicked is trouble.

Proverbs 15:6 (KJV)

John Berg's phone call regarding Gerald Hicks and the so called Right to Buy Property Claim had been fruitless. The law prohibited the town supervisor from discussing the subject prior to the scheduled meeting.

On May 24 Mack and John appeared at the Pleasant Springs Town Hall. Quite understandably they arrived with chips on their shoulders, a great deal of curiosity, and a keen desire to confront Mr. Gerald Hicks. The Bergs never had need for a lawyer, save the time papers were drawn up to create a partnership of the farm, bringing John into ownership with Mack. They brought no lawyer with them on this day either. They were, however, armed with the property deeds and bills of sale for the transactions that had occurred at the farm going back to the homestead award to Elmer.

The Pleasant Springs Town Hall was a modest, one-story office building. It had a reception area and three rooms. It was in the conference room where the meeting was to take place. When Mack and John walked in the town supervisor, Tom Evans, was already seated at the head of the conference table. Along one side were three men, all of them dressed in three piece suits and each sporting a leather valise filled, no doubt, with pertinent papers. If some people felt intimidated by such a legal looking battery it was not the Bergs. Besides, Mack had known Tom Evans for almost forty years. He was a man of unquestioned integrity. He wasn't going to let any intimidation take place. The job of Pleasant Springs Town supervisor was a part time position. Evans was a life-long resident of the area. Now retired from running his own insurance business in Stoughton he did light farming on his forty acre Pleasant Springs Town property. He had accepted the supervisor's position when the members of the town board had asked him to take it thirty-one years before. The compensation he received was nominal. It was out of a sense of duty to the community that he had kept the position all these years.

Evans made the introductions.

"Mack and John Berg this is Gerald Hicks, the petitioner, and his two lawyers, John Patterson and Charles Diehl."

Hicks sat between his two lawyers, as though insulating himself from the very process that he himself had set in motion. At the introduction he said nothing, giving only an expressionless nod of recognition. He appeared to be in his late fifties, possibly early sixties. His well-greased hair was parted in the middle and combed straight back. If he had any gray it was hidden by jet black hair coloring. The wire rim glasses that he wore did little to soften the hawkish look of his eyes.

The Bergs were not judgmental people but they later agreed that the man left an untrustworthy impression. Considering the situation they now found themselves in it was easy enough to feel that this man made his living manipulating other people.

Evans continued. "Mr. Hicks, would you get this started with your statement."

One of Hick's lawyers read the contention. As far as the core content was concerned the message was the same as the letter received at Berg Dairy Farm. However the legal wording: party of the first part, party of the second part, etc., brought a look of uneasiness from both Mack and John. They glanced at Tom Evans for reassurance.

"A very legal way of saying the same thing your letter says. Gerald Hicks is claiming the right to purchase those two sections of your farm."

Mack turned his gaze toward Hicks. The twinkle that normally was present in his eyes had turned steely.

"We are aware of what you are claiming. What I want to know is how in blue blazes you can make such a claim."

Mack displayed an air of calmness but John knew his father was working up a head of steam inside.

Evans interjected. "That comes in a second statement. Shall we hear it, gentlemen?"

Before reading, the lawyer, Charles Diehl, held up a copy of a handwritten note for all to see. He then read.

> *If one of our daughters or a member of her immediate family should want to buy the eighty acres of property sold by Oscar Knudson to Mack Berg on December 5, 1936, Mack Berg is obligated to sell the property to that person. The price of the sale would be based on market conditions at that time.*

Diehl continued his reading, noting "This is signed by Oscar Knudson and Margaret Knudson," he paused, looking up at the elder Berg, "and you, Mack Berg, on December 19, 1936, and notarized with his seal on the same date, by Thomas L. Evans, Supervisor, Pleasant Springs Town, County of Dane, State of Wisconsin, followed by his signature."

Diehl hesitated for a moment before continuing

"On February 18, 1940, Greta Knudson, daughter of Oscar and Margaret Knudson, married Gerald Hicks. We have here in our possession a copy of that marriage certificate. Last year, on October 13, 1964, Greta Hicks passed away. We have in our possession a copy of that death certificate."

Diehl held up both of those certificates for everyone to see. He then offered all three documents to Mack and John for viewing before he continued. "Gentlemen, based on this documentation just presented and on the Wisconsin State Real Estate Code, section 12, paragraph 7, Mr. Hicks has a perfect legal right to purchase the property in question."

In an attorney's voice, trained to be separated from the emotion that he knew resided in the Bergs, he continued.

"Gentlemen, Mr. Knudson's note is straight forward. We do not know if you have in your possession a similar handwritten note, Mr. Berg, but the significant thing is that you put your signature to this one. State law indicates that this note stands as a legal document when placed as an addendum to the notarized deed as registered in the Pleasant Springs Registrar of Deeds. We have researched the deed relating to this sale and found, in fact, that this information is legally attached to the deed in question. Oscar Knudson, Margaret Knudson and Mack Berg signed that deed and this addendum. This hand-written note is legal and binding."

There was silence for a few moments, then Tom Evans spoke.

"Mack, do you agree that this is your signature?"

Mack took a deep breath and reluctantly looked at the note. "Yeah, that's my signature all right."

Before he could say anymore John grabbed his father's forearm. He knew that an emotional response to this claim would be of no value. He also knew that an emotional response would be just what a man like Gerald Hicks would like to see. Here was a man, sitting between two lawyers, saying not a word himself, but apparently knowing how to let the law work for him.

Staying as composed as he could, John spoke. "I don't know what kind of game you are trying to play here, Mr. Hicks, but our family has been on this land for ninety-three years. My father bought those two sections from the

Knudson's twenty-nine years ago. Those eighty acres have been good to us, and as a boy I remember the sale of that land during the Depression was a lifesaver for your late wife's mom and dad. Go ahead and have your lawyer here say whatever else he needs to say. We want you to know that we have no intention of selling any of our land to anyone."

Mack could be contained no longer. His normally husky voice took on an even more raspy quality. "Who the hell do you think you are? Are you a dairy farmer, Hicks? I don't think so. I don't think you know a Holstein from a hole in the ground. You're an opportunist. You're somebody who's trying to pad his own pockets at the expense of others. My grandfather came here with nothing and built a shack . . ."

John again grabbed his dad's arm. "These people aren't interested in what we have to say, pop." He looked at Tom Evans. "What else do we need to do here?"

Evans gestured toward the lawyers and Diehl continued. "We just need you to know that this will be turned over to Mr. Hicks' real estate representatives and they will be contacting you about the purchase of the two sections in question. I believe that is all we have, gentlemen. Thank you."

The threesome stood in unison and began to exit the conference room.

Mack repeated himself. "What would you do with this land if you had it, Hicks? You don't look like much of a dairy farmer to me."

In the doorway Gerald Hicks came to a stop and spoke without expression. "Good day, gentlemen." It was the only words he said during the meeting.

John said nothing for a few moments, trying to digest what had just taken place. He knew he had to approach this situation logically and pragmatically. "Tom, where do we go from here on this? This guy is not going to go away."

"You're right. He, *and* his lawyers, are not going to go away. I think you both know that as supervisor I'm supposed to be a neutral facilitator, but I will offer you one piece of advice. You need to get a lawyer and you need to get the right kind of lawyer. You need to get the services of a lawyer who knows something about farm real estate. That note you signed, Mack, will carry a large amount of weight. It was a long time ago and I certainly had forgotten about it, even though I notarized it. But what matters is that it stands as a legal document."

Staring blankly across the table Mack spoke like a man whose zest for life had just been shaken. "I had forgotten about that note. I had completely forgotten about it."

In an apologetic voice, a tone of voice that John had rarely heard from his father, Mack continued. "Oscar and I agreed on the sale as a way to help his family. It was during the Depression. After he had no takers on the sale after about, I don't know, maybe a year, he came to me. I had all I could handle at the time but he was not well. And he had no sons. Knuddy was a happy Norseman when I agreed to buy those eighty acres. I agreed to the price he wanted. Never tried to talk down his price. And then, a little later, he wrote that note. I never thought much of it. I never thought in a million years that one of the girls would want to come back to the farm."

Mack's thoughts drifted off.

"Knuddy sold his equipment off at auction but before he did he sold me his tractor as part of our deal. A good machine. A 1925 Case A 25-45. Still got it; stashed back in the corner of our repair barn. Gave me a real good price. It helped me a lot to offset equipment expenses."

He looked over at his son. "I'm sorry John. Now we've got a big mess on our hands."

John Berg was frustrated but he made sure his father knew that he was not at fault. "You did nothing wrong, dad. Everything you did was honorable." He looked to Evans. "I want to get that right lawyer you mentioned. Who do I go see?"

"I know some people at the Law School in Madison," replied Evans. "I'll make some phone calls and get back to you."

As the Bergs began to leave Mack turned to the supervisor. "Tom, what about the other property; the two sections that Bobby Pierson bought? I don't know if Bobby signed that same kind of note or not."

"He did. I notarized that one, too. But that doesn't apply here. Such a note applies only to the original purchaser. When Pierson sold his farm to his nephew, what, about fifteen years ago, that note became null and void.

"Ugh. State law." Mack spoke distantly, to neither Evans nor his son. "Seems to me this Hicks guy is breaking a greater law. He wants something that isn't his."

8

Stroud

God is our refuge and strength,
a very present help in trouble.

Psalm 46:1 (KJV)

There is an old, but untrue, saying that if you ignore bad news it will go away.

Gertie went to the mail box one morning in the second week of July to find two letters. One was from Johnny, now in his sixth week of basic training at Fort Knox, Kentucky. The other was from Devries Real Estate Brokerage in Milwaukee.

Johnny had been writing to Jenny Watson almost every day and to his family once a week since he had left home in the middle of May. In his letters to the family he always spoke of how he missed everyone and how he missed working the land. When he mentioned how much he missed his mother's and his grandmother's cooking he always referred to particular items—homemade bread, cakes and pies, meatloaf and Swiss steak suppers, and grandma's homemade grape juice.

He wrote of how there were so many guys from so many places in his training company.

Even though we are all so different we seem
to get along and I think that is for one reason, we all
want to get through basic. I've really had my eyes
opened to some of the crummy circumstances that
some of them come from. Makes me know more than
ever just how blessed we are back home.

He always liked to sign off his letters with a light hearted P.S. after his signature. Johnny Berg wasn't much on sarcasm but he couldn't help this one.

P.S. How's Rollie? I sure miss hearing about Hespeler.

The other letter was the bad news that wasn't going to go away. The real estate firm said it specialized in the buying and selling of farm land. It had been hired by the law firm representing Gerald Hicks to make an offer on the acreage in question. Mr. DeVries would soon call, requesting permission to look at the acreage. "A fair and equitable offer would then be forthcoming."

That night John, Gertie and Mack sat on the porch of their beloved farmhouse as the last rays of the summer sun still shone off to the west. Ann had been tired and already gone to bed.

Mack and Skorpie Johnson had added the covered porch, as well as a hardwood floor in the parlor, in 1924. The porch was as much a gathering spot for the family during the summer and fall as their kitchen table was at any time of year. Hanging flower baskets, made of cedar years ago by Mack, adorned the length of the porch. Ann took great delight in growing a variety of flowers in them.

Ann and Gertie were diligent in keeping the area tidy, but in the summer months this spot was so central to the Berg family life that it always had a very lived in feeling. Two swings were hung from the porch ceiling, one on each side of the front door. Six rocking chairs held their places, in no particular arrangement other than to allow family and friends to visit easily. A table that could accommodate eight people was at the west end of the porch. Over the years it had been the sight of many a summer evening meal.

"It's unlike Ann not to be out here, especially on a Saturday night," said Gertie.

Mack was in his familiar pose; his hands behind his head, fingers interlocked, as he gently rocked in his chair.

"Oh, I think she knew we would wind up talking about the Hicks thing and she's had enough of it. But there's nothing more to talk about right now."

He rocked in silence for a few more seconds and then spoke with a tone of disgust in his voice. "A fair and equitable offer. Ha!"

John leaned forward in his rocker.

"Dad, you've made me partner in the farm and you've given me free range to make decisions. I don't ever want to take that flexibility for granted, but I'll say this. Tom Evans sent us that list of lawyers to choose from and I don't want to let any more time go by before we speak to one. You're going to be sent an offer on those sections and we need to know what to do to fight it."

For a few moments Mack stared straight ahead with a sour look on his face. "Yeah. The time has come. I never thought a simple dairy farmer would have to seek out a lawyer. But then, some people would say I'm behind the times."

Gertie spoke in her usual plain spoken way. "You have worked hard your entire life to build this place. You men have to make the decisions here but I will tell you this. You can be sure that Oscar Knudson would not have wanted you to lose that land to someone like Gerald Hicks. You need to settle on a lawyer. He'll know where to go from here."

Mack gently smacked the arms of his chair with his weathered hands. "What a time of year to have to take time out to go explain what this is all about to some lawyer and then hope that he's the right one to help us."

"No." John was resolute. "We are not going to go chasing after a lawyer. I'm going to make a phone call or two on Monday. If one of these outfits is interested they can come out and talk to us."

* * *

Monday morning at about ten o'clock John roared up behind the house on his tractor. Gertie was hanging out laundry to dry when she saw her husband walk very purposely toward the back door. She knew he was about to make a call to find a lawyer. With a clothes pin clamped between her teeth she mumbled audibly to herself, "Lord, help us out here."

It wasn't but ten minutes later when John came out the back door and walked over to his wife. She could tell immediately that the call went well. Without much expression but still with a tone of relief in his voice he told her that the lawyer he contacted would be out to see them on Wednesday at seven o'clock.

Gertie gave her husband a long hug then looked him in the eye. "Did he give you any idea of what he thought? Did he think he could help us?"

"He said from what I told him the law looked to be on Hicks' side, but there are always a few skeletons in the closet. I asked him what he meant and he said he'll have a better idea once he sees the letter from Hicks and the note that Oscar Knudson wrote."

Gertie's voice was uplifting, as usual. "I'm glad your father found his copy of that note. You've done the right thing, John Berg. We'll look forward to Wednesday evening."

They gave each other a quick hug and John turned to go back to the Massey. He stopped, turned back and looked at Gertie. With his spirits buoyed by the phone call he made a suggestion. "I think you and I should take a break . . . Right now, I mean."

Gertie didn't say anything for about ten seconds as she returned to hanging her laundry.

"John Berg, along with you I have three other men looking forward to dinner in the field in another hour and fifteen minutes. I haven't got time for the kind of break that you've got in mind."

John smiled and returned to the tractor. As he was climbing into the cab he heard Gertie shout over the noise of the idling diesel engine. "We'll take that break tonight."

* * *

Wednesday evening at five minutes to seven the lawyer that John spoke to was at the Berg's door. His name was Charlie Stroud. He appeared to be in his mid-fifties. He sported a brush cut of once black hair that had gone mostly gray. He was not a distinguished looking man, as some folks would expect a lawyer might be. He had a modest middle-aged spread. He appeared work worn, with pronounced bags under his tired, but earnest looking eyes. The suit he wore hung on him in a bit of a haphazard fashion. No three piece suit here. No doubt he had already put in a full day.

As was customary for the Bergs when anything of family concern was discussed everyone sat around the kitchen table. During coffee and some of Ann's wonderful Danish sweet rolls Charlie Stroud explained himself.

"I have my own firm in West Allis. I'm not a partnership. I just feel that I can do a better job representing people when I can work with them one on one. It's a matter of wanting to know each client directly. You could call me a no frills country lawyer, I suppose. Anyway, John, you told me Tom Evans said you needed a lawyer with some farm real estate experience and that he recommended me."

Stroud continued. "After you called me I spoke with Tom. He told me your story, but I'd like to hear it directly from you folks."

It was John who explained. The lawyer gave a half smile and gently shook his head affirmatively. "Could I be forward enough to ask you ladies for another cup of that great coffee?"

"Oh! Where are my manners?" Gertie bounced to her feet, came back with the coffee pot and filled everyone's cup. "Mr. Stroud, you have another Danish."

"They are most delicious." As Stroud reached for another of the sweet, buttery, tender and flaky raspberry Danish he said, "My dad used to call this his boarding house reach." His attempt at a little down home humor drew courtesy smiles. The lawyer knew it was time to get down to business.

He looked around, making eye contact with each of the four Bergs. "I want to tell you that I do believe I can help you."

"After I spoke with Tom I did a little research on Gerald Hicks. I knew I had heard the name before. He's in the real estate business. In fact, he's president and owner of Midwest Properties, a large commercial outfit in Chicago."

"Real estate!" Mack set his jaw hard as he looked at John. "We knew he didn't know one end of a Holstein from the other. But real estate! He's got to be up to no good."

As was his habit while he was thinking John had his chair tipped back on its two back legs, allowing a gentle rocking motion back and forth. "It makes sense, I guess, but the outfit that contacted us was Devries Real Estate in Milwaukee."

"Sure. A guy like Hicks wants to keep a low profile. He wouldn't want to advertise to you that he is in the real estate business. He just wants to be the beneficiary of his father-in-law's note. Anyway, I stopped over at your town hall this afternoon and took a look at the plot of the area around you. I see that Midwest Agra Group owns and operates two hundred and forty acres that butts up to the north side of your property. If I'm not mistaken that north side of yours is the acreage that Hicks is after."

"Yes, that's the acreage, all right. Midwest butts up against us there. They bought the Buhl farm a few years ago. That's it then," said John. "He'll just turn around and sell to Midwest and make a little profit."

"Maybe make a big profit, if he could get a so-called *fair price* from you folks." Has Midwest Agra ever talked to you about buying some of your land?" asked Stroud.

"'Bout a half dozen times," Mack said emphatically. "And not just some of our land. They offered to buy it all."

"Sure," said the lawyer. "The two hundred and forty acres Midwest has is not near enough for a commercial enterprise like they run. It has just allowed them to get their foot in the door."

Stroud continued. "I talked to a friend of mine in real estate. Residential, actually. I asked him if he knew anything about Gerald Hicks. He knew about him, all right. He said Hicks was very successful and he also said he had a reputation of being ruthless. He was aware of two deals where attempts to sue him had been made. Anyway, that note you signed, Mr. Berg, is, under Wisconsin law, a legal document. It is binding."

There was silence. The lawyer could sense an air of inevitability at the table.

He gently clasped his hands together and continued. "That is the bad news. However, state law most certainly has some qualifiers that could make Hicks' claim invalid. Those skeletons in the closet that I mentioned to you on the phone, John, could trip up Mr. Hicks."

John righted his chair on all four legs. "How so? What kind of skeletons are you talking about and how could that help us anyway?"

"May I see the note?" Stroud grabbed his reading glasses, then carefully handled the twenty nine year old piece of handwritten paper. He read to himself and then aloud.

If one of our daughters or a member of her
immediate family should want to buy the 80 acres of

property sold by Oscar Knudson to Mack Berg on December 5, 1936, Mack Berg is obligated to sell that property to that person. The price of the sale would be based on market conditions at that time.

Duly signed on this 19th day of December 1936

Oscar Knudson
Margaret Knudson

Mack Berg

Notarized on this day, December 19, 1936

Thomas L. Evans
Supervisor, Pleasant
Springs Town
County of Dane
State of Wisconsin
Thomas L. Evans

"And, I see it has the notary seal affixed," he said as he concluded his reading of the letter.

The lawyer then stated the obvious. "Of course the biggest obstacle in Mr. Hicks plan has been removed with the death of his wife. It's very likely she objected to buying back the eighty acres or else he would have pulled this stunt years ago."

"Now that phrase, *reestablish themselves on the Knudson farm*. That, arguably, will be interpreted as requiring that the purchaser reside on the property."

Mack's eyes darted hopefully from the lawyer to John and back to the lawyer. "If that's the case we should be able to beat this. I can't picture this guy leaving his business in Chicago to move out here. Believe me, he's no farmer.

Stroud held up his hand to slow Mack down. "Unfortunately, state law interprets the concept of residence very liberally. There are some legal alternatives here. Hicks can beat this rather simply by taking up legal residence on the farm. That doesn't mean he has to actually live there. Then again, he may need to physically live on the property for a certain period of time, or even be required to farm the land for a certain period of time. Whatever the stipulation might be Hicks would just wait for a prescribed period of time before selling to Midwest."

As Stroud said this it reminded him of another question.

Who lives in the Knudson's old house now? Is the house still there?"

Once again Mack stretched his mind back almost thirty years. "Knuddy sold the house with about five acres when they moved south. Been a couple of folks in there."

As Mack said this he could see a puzzled look on the lawyer's face.

"Knuddy, that's how we all knew Oscar back then. Anyway, it was the Depression, Mr. Stroud. I wasn't looking to buy any land."

Mack told his story about the purchase.

"Anyway, I never put a plow to it 'til five years' time. Now we've got an operation big enough that without those eighty acres we couldn't support our herd."

Stroud kept the conversation moving right along. "I think I know the answer to this but I'll ask anyway. Is there any chance Mrs. Knudson is still alive?"

Mack was gulping down a mouthful of coffee so he shook his head before speaking.

"No sir. They both passed away down south. Knuddy first, then later Margaret. She had to be well into her seventies somewhere. They brought Oscar back up here. Had a memorial service before they put him in the ground. I remember seeing in our newspaper's obituary about Margaret's passing. I was a little surprised that they didn't bring her back up here for burial. It said she would be buried down there somewhere."

Ann spoke up. "Why did you say you think you know the answer to your question, Mr. Stroud?"

"Because Gerald Hicks is much too knowledgeable to make a move for this land before both his father-in-law *and* his mother-in-law had passed away. If Mrs. Knudson were to object to him buying the land it would stop him cold. But now, with no one to stand in his way, and Midwest Agra Group an eager buyer, well, he decided to make his move."

"Dad and I are partners in the farm. We formed the partnership about twelve years ago." John thought perhaps the partnership might negate the Knudson agreement.

"Does the partnership stipulate you as senior partner? If so, then you may be on solid legal ground." Stroud was quite sure he knew the answer before he continued.

"Oh no. Not at all. Dad is senior."

Mack let out a deep breath of frustration. "Yeah, I'm senior partner. But why would it matter who is senior?"

"The state won't allow it. Too great an opportunity for people to hide themselves from responsibility. A person takes on a junior partner; maybe just a small percentage partner, to deflect all kinds of litigation against himself. The state still considers the senior partner the one subject to all kinds of litigation. In this situation I'm sure, Mr. Berg, that your partnership with your son would not void your written agreement with Knudson." Stroud spread his hands in a gesture of sympathetic frustration.

In her quiet and gracious way Ann Berg spoke. "It appears that there are some variables here that cannot be answered around this kitchen table." She looked at both her husband and her son. "We *are* going to need help."

When neither John nor Mack responded the lawyer spoke. "You're correct, Mrs. Berg." He clenched his fist and tapped the table resolutely. "This is an unusual case, but not a complex one. Whether you choose me to represent you or not you are going to need counsel on this. As I said I am not in a partnership with anyone so I do not have the resources that some firms do. But I do have a small staff that will work hard for you. And I have two private investigators that do work for me."

John was quite sure that Stroud was right, but he wanted his father to say something first. After a few moments Mack questioned the lawyer. "Mr. Stroud, how much would all this cost us?"

"It works like this. I have a one-time retainer fee of three hundred dollars. Beyond that you pay me by the hour. My fee is thirty dollars per hour. This can add up to a lot of money, I know. But I don't foresee a lot of hours in a case like this. And you should know that a larger firm would charge as much as forty five dollars per hour."

Stroud knew well enough to let the Bergs digest this news before continuing, even if it meant getting no answer until later.

John questioned. "By the hour? How does that work?"

"If this were a situation where you were seeking punitive damages I would be paid by receiving a percentage of your award, if you won. In this situation the time spent by myself and my staff is compiled."

Silence.

Finally, Mack spoke. "I want to ring his neck. I just want to ring his neck!"

Stroud looked a little startled. "I guess you're talking about Hicks."

"Uh? Ya, Hicks." Mack cracked a smile. "Hicks, not you."

The lawyer offered a ray of sunshine. "That was the bad news, but here's the good news. If Hicks brings this to court, and is deemed to have brought you into court under a fraudulent claim, he can be held liable for your legal expenses. For example, let's say I was to find that Greta and he had divorced before her death. The judge could determine that Hicks is responsible for dragging you into court fraudulently, since he no longer is a family member. Now, Hicks and his lawyers know this and if they know you can present him as making a fraudulent claim they most certainly will back down."

Gertie shook her head. "He would have some nerve trying to pass himself off as a rightful family member if he and Greta had divorced."

"Yes," said Stroud. "I'm sure he's much too smart to try something like that, but you would be amazed at what some people will try and do. His deviousness, if any, is probably of a much more subtle nature. The one thing we do know for sure is that you can expect that call from Devries Real Estate soon."

Some people would have wanted time to discuss in private whether this lawyer was the right choice to help them. Check references on the man. Are his fees really as reasonable as he says? Does he have the resources needed to handle the case? But the Bergs were a family that made their decisions on such things as truth, character, and overall integrity. If they saw sincerity they were inclined to follow that path. They put their faith in the Lord, trusting that He had sent this man to them.

In Charlie Stroud Mack saw an honest man.

"I've known and trusted Tom Evans for almost forty years. There's no one finer. He recommended you. You seem like the kind of man who will help us out here. And I want to tell you this. We try to be a God fearing bunch here. It's my feeling that the Lord's sent you to us." Mack looked over to his son.

"I think we should have Mr. Stroud help us."

John looked at Stroud. "Your honesty with us is what matters more than anything. We'd like to pay you that retainer and you can get started."

Stroud gave a gentle smile. Not a smile like a man who had just closed the deal on selling a commodity to a buyer, but a smile that said I'm glad you're putting you're trust in me.

As they all stood the lawyer put his hands to his stomach. "In closing I have but two things to say. If a man is going to go off his diet he might as well do it in style.

Ladies, those Danish of yours were just wonderful. And, secondly, I hope you'll all call me Charlie from here on."

Mack reached out to shake Stroud's hand. "Only if you call me Mack. I'm getting old enough without this Mr. Berg stuff!"

9

Adjustment

> *but when I became a man,*
> *I put away childish things.*
>
> *I Corinthians 13:11 (KJV)*

Over and over again in his mind it kept repeating to Clark Berg, Frank Smith's words.

"What I see in you is some raw talent that could, over time, with some long-range planning and commitment on your part, make available the opportunity for a lucrative career in radio ad sales."

What I see in you is some raw talent? What raw talent?

Wasn't he the one that no one could really count on? The one shirking responsibility in a family of responsible people? He thought about how, as youngsters, his father had started Johnny and himself working in the service barn: changing oil and lubricating, keeping tractors and equipment fueled, seeing to it that the tools were properly maintained and stored, twice-a-year scrubbing the oily cement pad. He looked down his nose at the work and felt that if he could only be in the milking parlor or out in the fields he would feel some satisfaction. Of course as the years moved along working with the cows or helping in the fields became as meaningless as the service barn work. Unlike his brother, he now realized his restless, dissatisfied spirit could find no meaning in any of the work of the farm.

Wasn't he the jerk that just a few months ago, when confronted by his mother for letting his father down on some work, said "Dairy farming! Milk! Who needs milk when there's beer to drink!"

He apologized to her later, but it was probably because he wanted something. That's how he had always been, manipulative. That's the word that one of the girls at school used. She said he was a manipulative person. He shrugged off the comment, just as he always shrugged off the comments of anyone he let down. After all, he was the Berg who didn't have his head buried in the manure pile. He was the one who could deal with more sophisticated people. He was the good looking one. He was the one that always had two or three girls interested in him at the same time. Not like Johnny. Sure, he was going to marry Jenny Watson, but that's the point. He'd been so slow socially, such a hayseed, that Jenny was the only girl he was ever interested in. Not him. He'd had experience that his brother did not have. A couple of sexual experiences, two different girls, during his senior year. This despite all he had been taught and all he had seen in his own family and their friends.

Now his uncle was saying that he had some raw talent? He was going to start work at the most conservative, most profitable radio station in Milwaukee. He didn't know a thing about the radio business, but even that wasn't the point. He was beginning to realize that he really didn't know anything about anything. Not just about radio advertising, but about how to really treat people. How to be, as he had heard it said, a genuine person.

On the Friday of his second week of work Clark went on his first sales presentation with one of the execs, Andy Quince. The potential client was available late in the day. It was six o'clock in the evening before a successful meeting ended.

"Clark, I'm in a bit of a jam. My wife and I have to be somewhere tonight. Could you get this paperwork filed back at the office?"

"Sure," said Clark, though to himself he instinctively reacted, "What about me? I've got places to go, too."

After they parted Clark decided he would arrive early Monday morning to file the papers.

On Monday, just before noon, Andy Quince asked Clark to stop by his desk. He spoke in subdued tones.

"What gives, my friend? I came in on Saturday to, among other things, get a head start on this new account. I find no papers, yet I get here this morning and, wa-la, here it all is. What the hell is going on? If you say you're going to do something, my man, then do it."

"Andy, I'm sorry. I . . ." Quince held up his hand, indicating that he had said his piece and wasn't interested in Clark's response.

His face red with embarrassment Clark realized he had slipped into some of his "me first" behavior. He realized, more than ever, that he needed to grow up. His brother might be quiet and unassertive but he was fair, sincere, honest, and reliable. These were the qualities that mattered to people. So it took a job offer from his uncle for him to realize these things?

Now he told himself, "You've got to be a whole new person or you're not going to make it."

He paused, "I don't know if I can do it."

The whole thing made him feel weak in the stomach. How was he going to change completely, like a car going from high gear to reverse without first coming to a stop.

"One day at a time," he told himself. "One day at a time." He felt like the lumberjack balancing on the floating log during the Syttende Mai Festival. One more slip and the real Clark Berg would come crashing down.

10

Soldier

*Put on the whole armour of God
that ye may be able to stand against the wiles of the devil.*

Ephesians 6:11 (KJV)

Though the course of the nation's events had taken young Johnny Berg away from his home and had potentially placed him in harm's way he held none of his brother's apprehensions. He was a soldier now. That is, he was being made into a soldier.

Fort Knox, Kentucky, was a world, and a way of life, quite different than he had known. He boarded the Greyhound bus, a military charter full of recruits that had all been given a physical and been sworn in at Camp McCoy. It dawned on him as they crossed the state line into Illinois that he had only been in one other state besides his own Wisconsin, that state being Illinois, twice to see Chicago with his family. Indeed, those two trips had been in winter. Harold Johnson had done the milking for them. To leave Berg Dairy Farm in the spring, summer or fall was not even a consideration; too much work to be done. The influence of the sun on the ever rotating earth was the clock by which the Bergs lived.

Now young Berg would be living by another clock, one set by the military machine known as the U.S. Army. Generations of young men before him had done the same. Now it was his turn. Basic training: every minute accounted for; everything being done by the numbers; strict adherence to military rules and regulations; commands to be followed, whether one agreed with them or not; one's own opinion never solicited; don't think—react. The objective of basic training was as old as the military itself: break the individual down and make him responsive to a higher authority. It was the only way to take a mass of individuals from different backgrounds, most who did not want to be there, and turn them into an effective fighting unit. The alternative would be chaos and disaster. His father's words when he left home were ringing true. John Sr. had told his son, "You'll be giving up your own freedom to help secure the freedom of our country."

Though he was already looking forward to the day two years hence when he would resume his civilian life, when he would go home and marry Jenny Watson, Johnny Berg was also looking forward to fulfilling his military obligation. As he had told his family, others were being taken from their lives to serve and he felt that he should do the same.

In a world full of people trying to impress others young John Berg was an unassuming person that was not one to be anyone but himself. Many a young man of like solid character had entered the service this way, only to be swept up in the cynicism, bravado and worldliness of the barracks atmosphere. It was an atmosphere where young men bragged about their sexual conquests, even if the stories were only half true. Where they told of their beer drinking prowess, as though it were a badge of manhood. The cussing. The oaths. Taking the Father or the Son's name in vain. Sometimes just a fountain of four letter profanities. That transformation of the human psyche was as old as any army. All in an attempt to hold one's ground in the masculine environment these young men now found themselves in.

Berg would have his moments of frustration, but he would keep his temper and his damnations to himself. When he did offer an opinion on something it was said without embellishment. He did not attempt to build himself up at someone else's expense. When others talked amongst themselves and belittled the platoon's drill instructor, Staff Sgt. Hence, as a loser, a guy who had flunked out at life and was reduced to barking at forty army recruits, the forty some year old who was rubbing their faces in the dirt for eight weeks, the loser who was living in a room at one end of their barracks on the second floor, Berg would never join in. He would continue to be the decent person he had always been. A certain vulnerability? Yes. But a superficial vulnerability only. Beneath what appeared to be a worldly innocence John Berg Jr. was rock solid, dependable, loyal, true to his word. He had the valuable quality of being unchanged by circumstances beyond his control.

His physical strength was deceptive. He was tall; six foot, two inches. He was what some might call thin, but a better description would be rangy. He didn't possess a showy muscularity, but rather the deceptive physique of long muscles with great elasticity. It was muscle that had developed working the rigors of a Wisconsin dairy farm: tossing hay bales, shoveling manure, cutting and clearing land with a chain saw and even a manual crosscut saw. A hundred different chores from the time he was first able to help his father and grandfather. His hands were particularly powerful, for despite the presence of automated milkers he had done his share of manual milking.

On the first morning of actual training they assembled in formation at 0515 for personal inspection before being marched to the mess hall for breakfast. While eating they were commanded to remain totally silent. Drill instructors prowled the floor; screaming at any of them that did not maintain a rigid, back straight sitting position. They were commanded to eat a square meal, meaning they had to take the spoonful of oatmeal, raise it up to the level of the mouth and take it on a direct line into the mouth.

They were then marched to the training company's armory and each assigned a weapon, an M-14 rifle. John's platoon spent two hours beginning to learn to follow commands with their rifles. It was called dismounted drill: present arms, parade rest, right shoulder arms, left shoulder arms, left face, right face, about face. The purpose of it all was to learn to respond to an order in the exact same way as the other forty-seven people in the platoon.

They then marched some more, drill instructor Hence screaming at their sloppy incompetence, to the physical training field, where they joined the rest of the training company.

Physical training: PT, the daily dozen. These were the time-tested twelve exercises designed to begin toughening these young men that came from all walks of life. The strong, the weak, the athletic, the softies, the lean, the fat. The brash who needed to be cut down, the timid who needed their confidence built up: the four count pushup, the eight count pushup, the turn and bounce, the airborne squat. All twelve exercises, every day.

Sgt. Christian was the fittest of the company's drill instructors: five foot eight inches tall, one hundred and sixty pounds of rock solid muscle. He stood on the wooden platform demonstrating each exercise to the new recruits, teaching them to perform each movement to his cadence count. After each exercise, when he began to demonstrate the next one, he kept them at rigid attention; arms to their sides; fists closed with the thumb over the top of the index finger; knees locked; chin up, eyes straight ahead. Later, in coming days, he would say, "At ease, shake it out", and they were given a few seconds to relax between exercises. But not in these first few days. They were going to have to earn those few moments when they could "shake it out".

Berg survived the PT quite well. Oh, he was sore the next morning, but not like some of them; hardly able to get out of their bunks. Some of them had been unable to complete even a third of the repetitions demanded by Sgt. Christian. Some recruits "fell out" after four, three or even two repetitions. The other drill instructors patrolled the rows of groaning bodies. They screamed in the faces of those that "fell out" early. They belittled, humiliated and threatened them. Berg made it as far into the counts as anyone. He completed at least nine repetitions of all twelve exercises, ten or eleven of some and he was one of only six recruits to complete all twelve repetitions of the eight count pushup. The quiet one who didn't have any exploits to brag about; the one who didn't pepper every sentence with a barrage of four letter expletives. Yes, they came to call him hayseed or pork belly or John Deere, but they did it with respect.

Basic training was just the beginning. It was eight weeks of learning how to think like, and perform like, a soldier. Then it would be AIT, advanced individual training. The word individual was a misnomer. Nothing in the army was tailored for the individual. But it was training in one of a number of specific areas: communications, radar specialists, hospital technicians and many more. These were the types of career opportunities that the Army publicized, but it was infantry, armor or artillery that most of them would train in. Then many of them would be assigned to a combat unit. Who knew? None of them did. When the training was done, then they would each receive orders telling them where they would go. Career officers in the Pentagon, officers who had the grand scheme of personnel movement in front of them, would make that decision. Wherever any of them should be sent they should all be so fortunate to have a young man like Johnny Berg at their side.

11

Revelations

*Casting all your cares upon him;
for he careth for you.*

I Peter 5:7 (KJV)

Ann Berg was sixty seven years old when her two grandsons left home. She was proud of them both. Sure, Clark was a handful; but it was her job, her privilege, to love them both, unconditionally, just as she loved Elsie and her other grandchildren.

It had been a long and bumpy road for Ann to become the person she was. She knew more than any of them about the value of a strong family. She had been the product of a broken home. Her father had been a professor at the University of Illinois. George Hopkins was also a closet alcoholic; carrying himself well enough in academia, but progressively hurting the ones closest to him as the years went along.

As a very young girl Ann Hopkins had a sweet nature. However, by the time she was ten years old, when her father's vice began to manifest itself in his relationship with his wife and two children, Ann began the long slide to insecurity, cynicism and bitterness. She finished high school with only an arm's length friendship with a couple of girls and a total rejection of boys. How could she trust any boy when her own father had let them down so wretchedly? The stream of broken promises made to her and her younger brother Cal. The evening meals when her mother would try to explain their father's absence with pathetically weak excuses about where he was: after school faculty meetings, helping his mother out, doing after school research for his chosen field of political science. And worst of all, the fights. Her mother and father yelling at each other as once again he failed to admit his shortcomings; instead, accusing his wife of being the source of their problems. Why couldn't he see what he was doing to them? How could anyone so smart, a PhD, a professor of political science at one of the best universities in the country, not realize how selfish his behavior was? How could all he care about be in a bottle of crystal clear liquid? Gin. Distilled grain spirits flavored with juniper berries. Ann could see that nothing else was as important as his gin.

At times he could be contrite with his children. He would sit on the edge of one of their beds, bring them to his sides, put his arms around them and come to tears asking for their forgiveness. But Ann knew that he never asked mother for her forgiveness. And what did it matter anyway? He would come home, sometimes as soon as the next day, and be in a gin-foul mood. His act of asking for forgiveness simply making the hurt of disappointment even worse.

When Ann was a senior in high school her mother and father separated. George Hopkins took accommodation in faculty housing at the university. Ruth and her two children stayed at the modest house in Champaign. She had seen the inevitable handwriting on the wall. Although it was a time when women rarely strayed from the job of homemaker she had gotten a decent job two years previous as a receptionist in the City of Champaign offices.

The couple never reunited, but they never divorced. To his credit, George sent money every month to help support his family until his passing; no doubt an act to ease his conscience as much as anything else.

Ann was an intelligent girl, but she graduated from high school confused and drained of the energy she would have needed to continue her education. Besides, in those years, going on to college was a rare step for any woman. Most often, the mindset for a young woman graduating from high school was to find a husband and start a family.

She took work with the Stratton Leather Works Company. This was a small organization that bought cured cowhide from two different tanneries in Chicago. Stratton's dyed the material and fashioned a number of small leather goods. They sold wholesale, mostly to the two mail order giants, Sears-Roebuck and Montgomery Ward. Ann would come home, hands swollen and sore from hours of cutting and stitching leather for gloves, belts, men's wallets and women's purses. But it was her spirit that was beaten more than her hands. She continued to be timid in her relationships, rarely venturing beyond the certainty of home with mother and Cal.

* * *

In the summer of 1918 Ruth Hopkins managed to secure two weeks off. This was not a paid vacation. Such was almost unheard of, but the City of Champaign considered itself a progressive organization. Providentially, a drop in orders for leather goods made it convenient for Stratton's to grant Ann the time off. Ruth took Ann and Cal, now finished with his junior year of high school, to the village of Stoughton, Wisconsin, her hometown.

It turned out to be wonderful medicine for all three of them. It had been six years since they had been to Stoughton. On that trip, with her husband with them, it had been a trip with its share of anxiety for Ruth. And for Ann and Cal, insecure and confused by their parents crumbling marriage, it was a guarded time with their grandparents, aunts, uncles and cousins. But now, for all three of them, Stoughton was a revelation of family ties; a confirmation that family laughter and support were still tangible things.

Ruth Hopkins was a Steingird. Her father, Hans, owned the feed store down near the railroad tracks on the east end of Main Street, Steingird Feed and Supply.

There wasn't a farmer within a radius of twenty miles that Hans Steingird did not know. Some of the time the talk between farmer and store owner was in Norwegian, or a more than adequate combination of Norwegian and Swedish. And he wasn't bad at getting along with the Germans and the Danes, although he diplomatically made the effort to get those that wanted to speak in their native tongue to speak English. Hans was an anomaly for a Norseman. He was talkative and outgoing with his customers. He was, however, very aware of the limits of the farmer's psyche toward being disingenuous. He never allowed himself to be anything but sincere with customers and friends that walked in.

Hans and Margaret welcomed Ruth, Ann and Cal with open arms. Three of Ruth's four siblings lived in Stoughton or surroundings so the Steingird home buzzed with family laughter. Even at age twenty Ann, and certainly Cal, reveled in the companionship of their cousins.

On Sunday the family was off to church at First Lutheran.

Ann remembered when they were a church going family; before dad began drinking. At least before the drinking became apparent. And then, gradually, the strain of it all. Dad showing up home so late from a Saturday night drunk that he couldn't get out of bed in time to get to church. They missed sporadically at first, then never to Sunday School and, finally, they just stopped going. It became easier, less painful, for Ruth Hopkins to avoid the strain she felt when she was there at church. She just didn't have the emotional energy to praise the Lord one moment and deal with her husband the next. Although the problems were rooted in his drinking she began to feel too inadequate to be in church.

Somehow that service with her grandparents, the first time Ann had been in church in such a long time, was an experience she would not forget for the rest of her life. The hymns, the fellowship, the wonderful feel of it all. Even though she would soon forget the pastor's message, the joy and overwhelming peace that she felt, remembering what she knew as a young girl—that God loved her enough to sacrifice His Son to wipe away her sin—kept her fighting tears throughout the service.

In that same service that morning was Mack Berg. He was only twenty one years old but owner of a then 200 acre dairy farm six miles north of the village. When his father died from the flu strain the previous year Mack was yoked with a great deal of responsibility; but he was up to the challenge. He always knew it would be his duty, his desire, to carry on Berg Dairy Farm. He had learned everything he could when, at age seven, he first tried squeezing milk from a cow's teats. He never expected that time to come so soon.

From the benediction Mack, Inga, Steven, and their mother exited church where they were greeted by the Steingirds. Mack's mother needed no introduction to Ruth Hopkins for the two had been only one year apart at Stoughton Area High School.

Mack and Ann had, no doubt, been aware of each other when the Hopkins last visited, but they were much younger then. Now, as the families paused outside church, they each felt an attraction toward the other. This was a feeling new not only to Ann, but to Mack also. He, so dedicated to carrying on the farm, gave little pause to consider women. So concerned he was for his mother's, sister's and brother's welfare that he hadn't considered the need to share his life with someone. Even though he was only twenty one years old his sister had taken to calling him the "bachelor farmer." It wasn't that he was not yet married. It was just that he was so focused on the farm that he never gave himself a chance with any of the girls around Stoughton.

Mack's unruly curly hair, pure blond as a youngster, was a shade or two darkened now. He was powerfully built on a six foot frame. He did not possess the classic facial features some would consider necessary to be called handsome, but his rugged masculinity more than compensated.

Ann, if she could only learn to smile again, was an attractive young woman. Her English rose complexion, inherited from her father's family, was a joy to behold when she did smile. She stood there on the church steps, one moment feeling so good about what she felt from the service, and the next realizing that she felt an attraction to this young farmer. It was a new feeling for her not to instinctively put up her defenses. Somehow she felt that this young man was not in any way like her father.

* * *

All through the first part of the next week Mack could not get his mind off the Hopkins girl. His concentration on his work was nothing less than a shambles. It was a good thing that it was the end of July, not the end of May. It was still easily twelve hours of work a day, but late spring, the most critical time of year with the birthing of new calves and planting time in the fields, was past.

He experienced something new, a queasiness in the pit of his stomach. His hardy appetite took a turn downward. He always devoured everything his mother put in front of him, but now his normal breakfast of three eggs, four sausage links, four pieces of toast and two cups of coffee was cut in half. Ruth Berg was puzzled by her son's diminished appetite.

By Wednesday morning he made up his mind that if he were any kind of a man he would call on Ann Hopkins. He felt the need to speak to Ann's grandfather, face to face, about such a visit.

Mack made a trip into Steingird Feed and Supply. He bought something he didn't really need and asked Hans for a moment of his time.

He gathered his nerve and spoke. "I'd like to see your granddaughter, Hans. I'd like to see Ann. I guess I'm asking your permission. I'd like to pay her a visit, Friday evening, if that's possible?"

Hans Steingird handled young Mack's request with the same ease in which he dealt with his customers. "You'll not come over Friday unless you come over for supper. Do you think you can pull yourself off of that farm of yours early enough to get over to our place at 6:30?"

"Sure Hans. Thanks. I'll be there. Thank you." Mack exited the store, climbed back on his wagon, flicked the reins on his two horses, and sped away. As soon as he made the turn to go north on County Road N he stopped. He took a couple of deep breaths to settle himself down. All of a sudden he felt like a new man. It was as though a twenty pound weight had been lifted from around his neck. He had summoned the nerve to do what his heart was telling him to do. Ann Hopkins may reject him, but Mack knew that he could deal with that easier than if he made no overture at all to get to know her. All of a sudden he felt powerfully hungry.

When Mack had pulled away from the store, Hans, who had made his invitation to Mack in matter of fact fashion, gave himself a little smile, knowing he may have helped get something good started.

* * *

Friday evening Margaret Steingird served a wonderful chicken pie dinner and for dessert a fine pie from their own black raspberry patch. She took the awkwardness out of the after dinner proceedings when she ordered Mack and Ann to visit alone. "We'll clean up the kitchen; you two young ones go get acquainted out on the porch."

Mack and Ann did just that. They sat and talked for some time before Mack invited her to walk with him in the remaining minutes of the setting July sun.

The Steingird house was just off Stoughton's unpaved Main Street. They walked on the narrow concrete sidewalk that fronted the businesses before returning to the house. Their conversation was quite guarded, as one might expect. She, with her uncertainty about men; he, with his awkward inexperience with girls. But it was the beginning of a familiarity that would grow in the next few days.

Mack joined the Steingirds and the Hopkinses every evening except one for the remaining days of the Hopkinses visit. Sometimes it would be for dinner, other times later in the evening. On the coming Sunday Mack took Ann on a picnic, just the two of them. By this time they were talking much more openly. Mack and his dreams for the farm. His need to gather the confidence to carry on his father's and his grandfather's work, even stating his desire to share those dreams with someone. Ann, for the first time having a feeling of security around a man. She spoke of her family's difficulties. She told Mack how difficult she thought it would be to ever go out on her own. How she thought there might never be a man she could trust. How all three of them were so enjoying this time in Stoughton.

As the time drew close for the Hopkinses to return to Champaign Mack knew he must ask Ann to marry him. They had known each other only nine days. He realized it was such a short time. A nine day courtship, if you could call it that. But they would soon be separated by 240 miles. Mack knew he would never be the kind of man to court a number of women and choose among them to marry. Besides, it wasn't as though there were girls lining up all over Dane County just to know Mack Berg. And above and beyond it all he had been raised to be a sincere person; limited in his number of relationships with people, but always committed to honesty and forthrightness in those relationships. Mack knew what he felt and he had to know if Ann felt the same. Could she commit to a Wisconsin dairy farmer after less than a two week acquaintance? It had been a wonderful time for Mack and he had told her so. She had said the same. Now he was going to ask her to marry him.

He did that very thing just the day before the Hopkinses left for Champaign. They walked that evening and Ann remarked with a puzzled look that he seemed to be far away. Mack had them sit down on a bench along Main Street, close by the bridge that allowed the Catfish River to cross under the road. It was almost ten o'clock. The street was almost deserted and the sun was gone, leaving only an orange glow on the western horizon. Mack spoke slowly and earnestly, as was his nature.

"Ann, I don't know how to say this except to come right out and say it." He looked down, inhaled deeply, and then looked up to her. It was difficult for him to continue, not because he was unsure of what he wanted to say, but because he was afraid her answer would be no.

"I want to marry you." He now increased the cadence of his speech, concerned that any hesitation on his part would allow her time to decline before he said his piece.

"I know I'm asking you this and we've only known each other for a few days, but I know this, that we were all made to share our lives with someone. It's in our nature. It's in my nature. I know that I love you and I want to marry you. I know it's asking a lot to expect you to come up here and be part of this life with me. But I'm asking . . . Will you marry me?"

She stared at him, motionless for a good ten seconds. She then shut her eyes as tears ran down her cheeks. "Yes, Mack Berg. I will marry you. I will marry you and come to Stoughton and help you with your farm."

Twelve weeks later Mack Berg and Ann Hopkins were married in Stoughton at First Lutheran Church.

* * *

And now it was forty seven years later. She was sixty seven years old; wife, mother, grandmother. None that did not know could suspect the heartache of her childhood. She was beloved by all that knew her.

It began to bother her around the first week of August. A raspy sensation in her throat and a raspy sound to the words she spoke. There was no pain, initially. Gertie was the first to notice it and say something. It was in the morning when the two of them were making sandwiches for the men's dinner in the field. She questioned Ann about the little change in her voice. Ann told her it had started off and on about three days earlier. "I don't know what could be causing it. Here it is summer and I have acquired some kind of cold."

They had arranged for one of the men to come in from the fields to pick up their dinners at eleven o'clock. It was Rollie who showed up. He bounded up the steps of the back porch and spoke through the screen door.

"We've got some hungry farm boys out there, eh. Some of that good Berg chow should set us straight. Old Thor himself says he could stand a gallon of whatever we're drinking today."

Gertie had gone upstairs. Ann had just finished putting all the items in two boxes. "Come in Rollie, come in. How is my favorite hockey player this morning?"

Rollie walked in, the gentle clank of the wooden screen door closing behind him. His face was covered with a combination of sweat and the dust of the fields. His red Badger cap was heavily sweat stained. "Ex hockey player, Mrs. B, and I couldn't be finer. But you said morning? You know how to deflate a chap. We've been going at it for seven hours and it's still morning?"

Ann gave her gentle laugh. "Well, it is only 11:15, but I do suppose it seems later to all of you. There is plenty of ice tea in there to keep my husband and the rest of you happy."

Rollie grabbed the first box, took it out to the tractor and was back for the second box. "I'm hearing a little burr in your voice, Mrs. B. Had a hockey coach in bantams with a gravelly sounding voice. I think it was all of the cigars. He used to smoke 'em right down to the end. Burned his nose a few times. A hell of a, excuse me, a heck of a coach."

Ann stood listening to Rollie with her hands clasped gently together. She looked into his eyes with a smile, as though she were delighted at every word he spoke. Rollie quickly realized he had started carrying on about his life in Hespeler. He was happy to burden the men about such talk but he became faintly apologetic to Ann.

"Enough of my talk, Mrs. B. We'll enjoy all this food, for sure. Hotter than a pistol out there, otherwise it's a lovely day."

Ann laughed gently and shook her head.

Rollie was puzzled. "What is it, Mrs. B?"

"Oh, it's the way you use the word lovely so often. We say things like wonderful, great or outstanding. But you say lovely. I think it's very nice."

"I'm glad you like it. Your husband and your son and your grandsons give me a rough time about it. They say, I thought you were a rough and tumble hockey player. How come you say everything is lovely? Your husband is the worst. Says it sounds girly. It's just the way we say things in Canada. At least my part of Canada—Ontario."

"Yes, of course," smiled Ann. "Hespeler."

* * *

The raspy irritation did not go away. By Labor Day weekend it had become painful. Ann agreed to go see the doctor in Stoughton. She who had not been to see the doctor since she gave birth to her youngest, John's sister Catherine. She, who had milked the cows and worked the fields with her husband throughout the first twenty five years of their marriage. She, who had cooked and cleaned and raised three children. She had never been a physically strong woman, but she had a strong constitution. Never ill in all those years, save for a bad case of the flu one winter. She seemed indestructible to all those around her, although she took no credit, regarding her good health as a gift from God.

The doctor ordered tests for her at the hospital in Madison. This included a throat biopsy. When the results were in Mack and Ann went together and received bad news. A malignant tumor had been found in her larynx.

Ann, Mack and the rest of the family took the news solemnly, of course, but with the usual Berg sense of calm. They would be diligent in fighting this cancer in every way possible, but at the same time they were willing to turn it over to the Lord. They would prepare themselves for whatever He had in store for them. Does the Word not say to cast your cares upon Him?

12

Mantlund

The eternal God be thy refuge,
and underneath are the everlasting arms.

Deuteronomy 33:27 (KJV)

By the last week of September the sights and smells and feelings of autumn were beginning to show themselves everywhere. The first frost was still a few days away, but the cold night air hung persistently through the morning hours. The ground stayed damp until it was dried out by a sun that made its appearance a little later each day. As the thawing ground in the spring had its own special scent so too did the ground in the fall. It was a vaguely musty scent; leaves and vegetation lying down for the coming winter, their juices having left them. Only the pleasant smell of the brown plant remains hanging in the air.

The time of decision for John and Mack, and farmers everywhere, was fast approaching. When to harvest? When to 'beat the weather'? When would the corn be as dry as necessary so that it could be layered with hay, alfalfa and grass without fear of it rotting? A well-proportioned silage would see their stock through the winter months.

It was on a crisp mid-October afternoon when John and Mack had driven out to the two sections planted in corn to check its moisture content. Mack rarely expressed sentiments with his son but his concern over Ann's health and the realization that the years were moving along prompted his comment.

"When you were a kid it was my concern whether you could become a man who would love this land. It's been a prideful thing for me to know that you, and Johnny too, love this place." He paused. "Ha! Funny how it goes. One day I'm ready to drag this son-of-a . . . this snake Hicks across a barbed wire fence. Next thing I know your mother is sick and . . . well, the land thing just doesn't seem so important.

* * *

Ann began a series of treatments that did little to slow down the rapid progression of cancer in her voice box. The growth soon invaded her esophagus.   It became even more difficult for her to swallow.

Difficult though it was Gertie was the first to be pragmatic about it. She gently, but firmly, confronted her husband. When Ann's condition put her in a state of not being able to feed herself, and soon after that she showed early signs of incontinence, Gertie told John he must speak to his father.

"He must be made to see that keeping her here at home is more of a consoling thing for him than it is a comfort for her."

When John spoke to his father Mack would have none of it. He took alliance with Elsie, whose tender young emotions resisted any thought of her grandmother being cared for somewhere other than at home. And so as the days moved along the strain began to show on Mack. His hearty appetite waned, as it had when he first knew he had love for this woman.

At John and Gertie's insistence Mack agreed to a home visit by their pastor. In all their years as members of First Lutheran, stretching back to Elmer and Muriel, the family had never requested pastoral counseling. They were indeed a low maintenance family. But now, as he thought about it, even Mack agreed for the need to speak to someone outside the family.

Pastor Fred Mantlund was fifty four years old; a tall, rangy figure with earnest looking eyes and a personality to match. He had been First Lutheran's pastor for six years, succeeding Edwin Keil. Keil had been much loved by the congregation when he retired in 1959 after thirty years at the church. It was no easy task to follow a man of such revered stature, but Mantlund had been well received. He was born and raised in Minneapolis, the third child of Swedish immigrants.

Though the heavily Norwegian congregation had great affection for their new pastor he was made to suffer the good natured Norse superiority. Mack would often chide him for not being fortunate enough to be Norwegian.

"A thousand Swedes ran through the weeds, chased by one Norwegian!"

Mack had repeated the old Norwegian folk rhyme a number of times when Mantlund first came. He now saved the verse for once a year, having realized that too much of a good thing does lose its punch. But he still delighted in hitting Pastor with one of his Swedish jokes from time to time. However, this meeting with Pastor at the Berg kitchen table was one without levity.

One of the things that the Bergs liked about Fred Mantlund was that he was to the point. Whether it was from the pulpit, or now at a home visitation, he engaged little in small talk. He possessed a sincere Christian spirit but he never exhibited a forced upbeat personality. He was just himself.

As soon as they sat down and Gertie poured the coffee Mantland asked the penetrating question.

"At this point in Ann's illness I suspect there are decisions, tough decisions, that you are facing."

Mack showed no visible response to the comment. He stared at his coffee cup. John was prepared to be the one to have to open up to Mantlund.

"That is true, Pastor. Mom is suffering dearly now. She has trouble talking to us much of the time. We are concerned that soon she may not be able to swallow soft food or even soup. There are times, because of the pain, it's possible she doesn't understand us."

"She hears me. She knows what I am saying." Still staring at his coffee cup Mack spoke in an irritated and defensive tone.

John waited a few seconds before responding. "Yes, she does, some of the time, dad. But a lot of the time I think she is in too much discomfort to understand." He shifted his eyes from his father to his pastor. "Especially when the pain medicine wears thin."

Mantlund said nothing. He waited for John to continue.

"We're having a tough time deciding on what to do." John's voice suggested just the hint of the loss of composure. The pastor leaned forward in his chair and stepped in.

"Decisions like this were a lot easier in years gone by when there were no such things as convalescent homes and rehabilitation centers." He paused as the thought took hold, even in Mack. "As wrenching as the decision is, having the option of full time care is a blessing."

Mantland could have spent the next moments consoling with the anguish of the decision facing this family, but he moved forward.

"I want to read you something."

Like any good minister he had his Bible with him. It was a small Bible that he had tucked in his jacket pocket. Now Gertie knew why he had insisted on just hanging his jacket on the back of the kitchen chair.

"There are two different things. They seem to be opposite each other in one respect. In another respect they seem to work together. The first is stewardship. In Proverbs it says this. *'Be thou diligent to know the state of thy flocks, and look well to thy herds.'"*

He closed his Bible and spoke resolutely.

"I see that verse and I think of stewardship. Of taking care of what we have been blessed with." He was in no rush to finish his thought.

"Well, I don't need to tell the Bergs about that. About the wonderful farm you have here and the great discipline it takes to make it a success."

Again he hesitated.

"Even more importantly is the stewardship of family. I don't believe there is a family anywhere that shows better stewardship of family than you folks. The pride and the love you all take in this family. What is it now, four or five generations, right here together, supporting each other? That doesn't happen without the discipline of good stewardship. A personal responsibility as individuals and as a family."

"I know, Mack, that you, that all three of you, have done your utmost for Ann. There's no greater example of stewardship than taking care of your family. So that's one thing, the stewardship."

Mantlund turned the pages of his Bible. "Then, the second thing. It's in Matthew. We've all heard it before, but let's look at it. Jesus said it. *'Take my yoke upon you, and learn of me, for I am meek and lowly in heart: and ye shall find rest unto your souls.'"*

The pastor again said nothing for a few seconds. It was just not in his nature to rush his speech.

"I know you folks have taken this principle to heart as well. Different concerns, different problems. I know. I've seen it in you, being able to lean on the Lord. And now you've got a really tough one. The thing is, for a person who does not have Christ in his life, and even for those of us who are Christians, we don't always see the help that He affords us."

Mantlund gently closed his Bible. "The thing is . . . you've got to decide if having a place for Ann to go to is a gift from the Lord? Is it a practical kind of yoke that He is providing that will ease the burden on Ann . . . and on yourselves?"

No one spoke a word. John, Gertie and Mack each struggled with emotion. They had just been reminded from the written Word that He wants to help; that He sustains us if we will just give our concerns over to Him. That a care facility could be a gift from Him.

The pastor waited a good twenty seconds. If any of them wanted to discuss how these words applied to them, he was leaving the door open for their thoughts. But he was not going to preach at them. The Bible's words were clear.

Mantlund continued. "I'm going to take us to prayer."

"Our Father, You have promised to never give us a burden that is more than we can bear if we will seek You for our wisdom and our strength. Help these good people in the days ahead. Make it clear to them the decisions that must be made. May they know, more than ever now, that their hope and assurance is centered in You. Amen."

13

Furlough

*A good sense of humor
is an escape valve for the pressures of life.*

Richard G. Scott

It was just a few days later when Johnny completed his eight weeks of advanced individual training in infantry at Fort Leonard Wood, Missouri. John and Gertie prepared themselves for the strong possibility of their son being assigned to a unit in Vietnam. John Sr. knew that it would be the foot soldier that would bear the biggest burden in Vietnam. It was a war without front lines.

Young Johnny Berg had been gone twenty weeks. It had been twenty weeks with almost no personal freedom. Rigid training, rigid discipline. First basic training and then AIT. Now he was going home.

As he rode the Greyhound bus from Fort Leonard Wood to Chicago his mind was spinning with a number of thoughts. Jenny had been in his thoughts every day since he left home. The actual thought that they were engaged to be married now made him realize that much of his future had already been set in motion. From Chicago he transferred to the route going to Milwaukee. From there he took a Trailways bus to Stoughton. He knew Jenny would be at work so he decided to first go home. He sought out one of his friends to take him the six miles to the farm.

Upon his arrival all work stopped. John and Mack had been testing that morning's milk collection for butterfat content. Rollie and George Wistoff had been in the milking parlor clearing the manure trough and power washing the floor. Gertie had been in the middle of preparing Johnny's favorite dinner—rolled pork roast and gravy, with potatoes peeled and halved and roasted with the pork, plenty of homemade apple sauce, homemade bread and the very last of the green beans from the garden, with rhubarb pie for dessert. They didn't know if he would arrive Monday or Tuesday but Gertie wanted to be ready with his favorites.

To Johnny they all seemed to be the same, mostly. Mom, in her bright, industrious, in-charge way. He could see how excited she was to have him home. His father, giving him a hug along with the handshake. He was not a hugger, except to his wife and mother. He looked into his son's eyes with a look that said 'I'm proud of you. I know you've done well'.

Grandpa Mack was the last one to get back to the house. They shook hands as Mack looked at his grandson. "This is a good day. This is a good day."

Johnny held his tongue about his grandma. Both men fought back a little emotion as Johnny put an arm around his grandfather. It was a moment when not a word needed to be said.

And then there was Rollie. His cheery thoughts helped everyone through the moment.

"Bergie, what'ya think you're doing, eh; running off to the Army, leaving me with all the work this summer?"

He slapped Johnny on the shoulder with his beefy right hand. It was good old Rollie all right, but not quite the same. He was, as always, full of life; but at the same time showing just a touch of reserve. Was it that he felt a little out of place, being there with the family at such a special time, greeting their son after twenty weeks away? It's possible, but Rollie Leach felt completely at home with the Bergs. Was it because of the seriousness of Ann's illness? He did care deeply for Mrs. B. Or was there a little respect for the soldier?

Despite her weakened state Ann lit up when Johnny came to her bedside. They visited for more than an hour.

On this special day Gertie wisely served dinner early so that her son could get over to Jenny Watson's.

* * *

The Watson home was just off Main Street on Harrison Avenue, one of the beautifully shaded streets lined with early twentieth century homes where oak, hickory and maple trees predominated. The October temperatures had brought out the reds, golds and oranges of the turning leaves in all their nuances. It made for an awesome display against the backdrop of the cobalt blue October sky.

Some of the homes, including the Watson's, were a modest two story frame. A covered front porch for sitting was a prominent feature of this style home. It was small town mid-west Americana. Just three houses away from the Watson's was the home that once belonged to Hans and Margaret Steingird, both deceased many years now.

Jenny met Johnny on the porch with an embrace that seemed to go on forever. He was hesitant of letting go because he was raging so for this girl. He was afraid he could not control his feelings once he looked into her eyes. They pawed at each other as they made their way to the swing that hung suspended from the porch ceiling.

Howard Watson was working late, taking inventory at his hardware store. Jenny's mother and sister were in the back sitting room watching television. They were not yet aware of Johnny's arrival.

"Oh John. Are you all right? You're out of breath and all the color is drained from your face."

They held each other tightly for the next few moments. Jenny could feel the tension in his body. She too felt a surging emotion as tears flooded her eyes. She pulled back slightly, looking at him with a mixture of amazement, delight and caution.

"You're a freight train of passion, Johnny Berg. I think you missed me."

Slowly he seemed to catch his breath and begin a muffled laugh that went on at length.

Jenny watched in amazement as he finally got control of himself enough to put some words together. "A freight train of passion? I guess so."

She put her head on his chest and joined him in a soft, affectionate giggle.

She had defused her fiancé's urges with the skill of a bomb squad expert removing the firing pin.

Jenny's father soon arrived. He, Jenny's mother and sister all greeted their daughter's fiancé and welcomed him home to Stoughton, before leaving them on the porch. The cold night air soon drove the couple indoors. They talked until well past midnight. As he had told his family at dinner he now told Jenny where he was being sent after his furlough. Beyond that they kept the talk about the two of them; with Jenny, as usual, carrying most of the conversation.

"My orders are to the First Cavalry Division. They're in Korea. That's where I'll be going. Somewhere in South Korea. It's a thirteen month tour."

Jenny gave a puzzled smile as she kidded him.

"That sounds like horses. That is what the cavalry means.   Wouldn't they rather have cowboys from Oklahoma or Texas than a dairy farmer from Wisconsin?"

Johnny shook his head. "You do know how to keep a guy loose."

"Well, what's so funny? I may not know too much about, what are they calling it, the military-industrial complex, but I do think they gave up on horses some time ago?"

"Yes," Johnny replied. He went on to explain.

"The First Cav stopped using horses some time ago. I don't know, sometime after the start of World War II, I believe. From what little I know they travel by APC's now, and by helicopter."

Jenny drew back with an exasperated look. "And I'm supposed to know what an APC is?"

For the first time since he arrived at Jenny's house he was relaxed enough to let his lanky frame sit back. He was chuckling again.

Jenny made a fist and knocked on her fiancé's head.

"So what is an APC? It sounds like an all purpose capsule to me." She gave a muted smile at her own humor.

"It's an Armored Personnel Carrier. I rode in one just one time back at Fort Leonard Wood. It's a track vehicle, like a tank, but it's not a tank. It's used to carry guys from one place to another. It's a way of moving foot soldiers quickly."

He shrugged his shoulders, as though to say, "That's about all I know, let's talk about something else."

Jenny had to have the last word on the subject.

"I'll bet it is terribly noisy. I think you had better take some of those all-purpose capsules with you."

Jenny gave herself but an instant to enjoy her own wit. She almost immediately broke down. She covered her face with her hands as she quietly sobbed.

Johnny was startled. One minute his fiancée is full of humor and then, so suddenly, her emotions overwhelm her.

Jenny heaved with a sigh. "I should be happy. I should be happy. They're not sending you to Vietnam and here I am getting all upset. It's just the finality of it. You'll be gone for over a year and, I don't know, it's just not what I thought would happen."

14

Embarrassed

The secret to getting ahead is getting started.

Mark Twain

Despite the long bus ride from Missouri and only a few hours' sleep after getting home from Jenny's house, Johnny was ready when the work day began the next morning, though not with the enthusiasm that he had anticipated. Jenny's anxiety about their impending long separation had put a damper on his spirits. After hooking up the milkers he came back into the kitchen for some breakfast. After the great roast pork dinner the night before he realized his mother was on a mission to spoil him when she slid a plateful of waffles, eggs and sausage under his nose.

"I don't understand how a woman thinks. Seems like out of a clear blue sky last night Jenny just seemed to fall apart for a few minutes. Emotionally I mean, at the thought of me being gone for the next thirteen months. Sure, neither one of us likes the idea but it was like someone had turned a switch on."

Gertie stopped her work at the sink with the unexpected statement from her stoic son. She joined him at the table.

"I believe you're right; you don't know how a woman thinks. When it comes to relationships women are a lot more inclined to fret. You see yourself as going off for a short while . . . taking in a new experience. Oh, the Army may not be something of your choosing, but you see it as an obligation that's no more than a bump in the road. For Jenny it's a whole different way of seeing things. She's most likely concerned that the two of you will somehow be changed in this next year."

He gave a puzzled look and responded with a, "Changed?"

"See what I mean. You and your father. Like two peas in a pod. I've told him, 'Look around you.' We are seeing the end of some golden years around here. You and Clark off on your own. Elsie, determined as ever to go to college in just another year. I'm realizing change is in the wind and he doesn't see it. Sure, he sees that we may lose his mother and he sees that we might lose eighty acres of valuable farm land but he's not realizing that the golden years of raising a family are about to become a thing of the past for the two of us."

"I realized years ago that there's just a plain and simple difference in the way a man and a woman look at things. Same with you and Jenny. She'll do just fine."

* * *

Clark had been working at WWMR for four months. He surprised even himself. Oh, there were two or three times when, what he called the old Clark, surfaced. But he refocused. He kept his nose to the grindstone.

Frank Smith was an experienced manager. Just as he did with his other employees he let Clark alone as much as possible. Smith did not breathe down a person's neck. If they had a problem they wished to discuss with him his door was always open. Otherwise, he expected his employees to work through to their objectives using their own chain of command. He was especially careful not to be peering over Clark's shoulder.

But Smith didn't miss a thing. Every few months he conducted a performance review with each employee on his sales staff. Back in early September he had called Clark into his office. He was as to the point with his nephew as he was with everyone else.

"You're doing well, Clark. I like what I see and I know the ad execs are satisfied with your performance. Whenever you've stumbled you've corrected your mistakes." He paused for a moment. "But there are two times you showed up late in meeting an exec for a presentation. Mistakes are mistakes. We all make them. Showing up late is not a mistake, it is negligence. It's irresponsibility."

He did not dwell on the subject, nor did he give Clark a chance to respond. He moved right into a question.

"Now, how have you done in getting yourself enrolled in classes this fall?"

Clark could feel himself sinking in his chair. Had there been one available he could have crawled into a hole. He had spent most of his free time having a good time. Other than read a couple of pieces of literature about Carroll College he had not even made the first effort to get himself enrolled for any classes. He'd spent many of his evenings playing cards with friends he had acquired at Kleindeinst Bar and Grill, a restaurant and watering hole across the street from his apartment.

Clark was a work in progress. Yes, he had taken his uncle's challenge to be responsible and unselfish in his work ethic. It was not always easy, for his nature, or at least his habit, was to put himself first. But he was making great strides in the right direction.

But now he was face to face with the man who had given him this opportunity, despite what he knew about him. His uncle had just asked him what he had done about getting enrolled in school. How could he tell him he had done nothing?

Clark straightened himself in his chair. He had been hired in the expectation that he would put his boyish behavior behind him and start acting like a responsible man. Among many other things that meant being truthful.

He swallowed hard. "I haven't done a thing. I've let you down and I've let myself down. I was feeling so good about having this job that I just kept putting things off until, well, before I knew it the summer was gone and I hadn't done a thing."

Smith leaned back in his chair, giving himself a few seconds before responding.

"You said you would make an effort to get enrolled in some classes. The fact that you didn't, well, there's no two ways around it Clark, you were not honest with me."

Smith hesitated again before continuing. He had a knack for using the pause to squeeze the most out of what he wanted to convey.

"But you were forthright enough with me right now, just now, to say what you just said. To lay the responsibility, and the blame, on yourself."

"Yes sir," responded Clark. He felt weak in the stomach and totally defenseless against whatever his uncle might say.

Smith leaned forward with that penetrating eye contact of his. "Clark, do you like this job? Do you like this business?"

"Yes, I do." He waited for the ax to fall. He waited to be preached to or to be told he was finished at WWMR.

"I can use you just where you are, Clark. You can stay as an exec assistant and that will work out fine for me." Again the pause.

"But did you hear what I just said. I said, 'I can use you'. Maybe that's what you want. To be used by me. Maybe you're willing to be used by myself and any number of other people so that they can attain their goals. In the meantime you remain as good old Clark, the guy that other people can rely on to use."

"We both know that you came here with a reputation of being self-serving. A 'me first' outlook. We've been over that ground and I feel you have worked pretty hard at trying to overcome it. But if you fail to improve yourself, to prepare yourself for something better, then you are just sliding off in the opposite direction. Other people will just be using you. Not because they're out there trying to manipulate you, but because you've failed to live up to your own potential and you're just out there."

Smith's words were a revelation to Clark. Here he was, always believing that he was the one too good for the farm; that he had a special talent for getting what he wanted. Now his uncle was telling him that the opposite was the real case. That he was the one who was going to be the sap that others could use. These thoughts raced through his mind in the few seconds he had before responding. He clenched his fists as he often did when he wanted to be emphatic about something.

With his uncle saying he could use him just where he was Clark felt safe in offering this thought. But now he offered his words not to maneuver himself into a satisfactory position, or to say what he thought Frank Smith wanted to hear, but because, in these few seconds he realized how true Smith's words were.

"I'd like to do this. I'm going to apply for school in order to begin next fall, a year from now. That will allow me to save more money in the meantime. Does that sound alright with you?"

Smith stood and walked around his desk. "Up to you." With an expression on his face that was unsympathetic, yet showed a willingness to accept Clark's new plans, he extended a handshake. He brought the discussion to a close by changing the subject.

"How is your grandmother?"

Lost in his own thoughts Clark almost didn't hear the question. "Oh! Yes. I haven't been home in some time. Mom says she is not doing well."

He hesitated a second and began to speak in regard to his work.

Smith held up his hand to stop him. "No need to talk about this anymore. If starting school next fall works for you that would be fine. Up to you."

15

Mrs. Baldwin

Consider it pure joy, my brothers,
whenever you face trials of many kinds,
because you know that the testing of your faith
develops perseverance.
Perseverance must finish its work
so that you may be mature and complete,
not lacking anything.

James 1:2-4 (NIV)

After his two weeks home Johnny's orders sent him to San Francisco, where his training battalion from Fort Leonard Wood was to assemble for the trip to the Korean peninsula. It had been mildly surprising to them all. When so much of the military's resources, both men and equipment, were headed for Vietnam it seemed inevitable to them all that they also would go to the war. But the United States considered its continued commitment to the United Nations presence in Korea as essential.

When he came home on leave and told them that he was being sent to Korea Gertie was so relieved. To her the Korean Conflict, as they had called it, was only a vague memory. It ended in 1953. It had been over twelve years now. She had paid little attention to it because it was not 'their war.' It was World War II that John came home from. She was busy raising two little boys and a baby girl and keeping a home. She was committed to helping her husband and her in-laws keep Berg Dairy Farm a success. The nasty business of Korea was the worry of others.

John Berg Sr. realized that the Korean peninsula was not just any place of American military occupation. The war had no definitive conclusion. It ended in a truce, a cease fire. Twelve years later, the peace was still held together only by that truce. From what he knew the situation was still a fragile one, with both sides, the communist North supported by China, and the democratic South, supported by the United Nations, still armed to the teeth. But still, his son was going to a place of occupation, not the hot war of Vietnam. For this, he too, was grateful.

Throughout the summer months and now into the fall the land dispute with Gerald Hicks continued to remain a gloomy prospect. From Devries Real Estate the Bergs had received Hick's offer for the eighty acres of land back on August 15th. A week later Mack formerly refused the offer. Two more offers followed, both again refused by Mack. In mid-October the inevitable notice of a law suit filed against Mack Berg by Gerald Hicks came to Berg Dairy Farm. It included a court date of November 15th.

Charlie Stroud told the Bergs not to be overly concerned. He would ask for a two month stay to give time to prepare a defense against the suit.

The most urgent concern was Ann. John and Gertie were grateful that Mack had consented to full time care for his wife. The concern for Johnny's well-being and the land issue paled by comparison to the emotional strain of putting Ann into the convalescent home.

"Just coffee for me this morning, Gertie." Mack had no appetite on this, the morning they were taking Ann to Vanstessen's. John and Gertie likewise had no desire to eat.

Mack's husky voice took on a shallow tone.

"Do you think Ann is going to resent this? Taken away from her home; living with a bunch of strangers? Do you think that she is going to feel that I've given up on her and that I'm just dumping her off?"

A few moments passed when Gertie responded.

"When Elsie was an infant her head was so soft that it was forming a flat spot in the back . . . because of the way she slept."

"The doctor recommended that she wear a helmet, even when she was awake, to allow her head to regain its proper shape. It seemed like just an awful thing to do. I remember John and I having such a hard time consenting. But then the doctor said, 'It's going to be harder on you than it is on your baby.' Once I understood that, I was okay with the helmet. The circumstances are different, Mack, but the idea's the same. You need to know that it will be harder on you than it is on Ann."

They dressed her warmly for the ride to the Vanstessen Care Home in Madison. Through the rear view mirror of the family sedan John could see his father with his arm around his wife in a scene that was heartbreaking. When they arrived at Vanstessen's front door an orderly immediately arrived with a wheelchair. He insisted that, as an employee, he was required to wheel Mrs. Berg into admittance. Mack politely brushed him aside and wheeled her into the building.

When the social worker recognized the Bergs as a close family she offered some comforting words.

"I know this is a difficult day for you. I know your hearts are full for Mrs. Berg and it is a heartrending experience, bringing a loved one to us. The fact is we receive some residents from families that have little kinship. Those families may feel less heartache when they entrust us with a loved one, but I think we can agree that a close family such as yours is a blessing.

John and Gertie stayed at Vanstessen's until ten o'clock that evening. Mack spent the night on a visitor's cot in Ann's room. John picked him up the following afternoon.

Both Gertie and John knew that to over empathize with Mack would not be wise. They agreed that he needed to keep his mind and his body busy with his normal work schedule.

* * *

In Milwaukee Clark continued his one man effort to remake himself. Certainly he was making progress. His relationships at WWMR were a testament to this change. He was working with people, considering their needs, helping them reach their goals. Outwardly he seemed to be maturing.

On November 14th, just three weeks after his brother left for San Francisco and the flight to Korea, Clark Berg opened a piece of mail that severely tested his maturation process.

"Greetings from the President of the United States."

He was stunned. How could this be? He was eleven months younger than Johnny, yet he was now receiving his draft notice. Surely he had another six months or so before they would want to draft him; if they were drafting at all by then. He had only been out of high school for six months. He was about to apply to four different schools: Carroll College, Concordia University, Wisconsin Lutheran College, and even Marquette University.

He knew college students were exempt from the draft. Surely there had to be some leeway for a young man who was attempting to enter college?

He paced around his apartment for the next hour. What about his plans? In his mind he took the position all too familiar to him. This was unfair. He didn't deserve this. He was better than being another military draftee.

Finally, he calmed down. It was unusual for him, but he stepped outside of himself long enough to at least realize he was pouting. He wisely realized that a calm approach to this situation was what would help him the most. He would call his draft board officer. Better yet, he would pay a personal visit. The Federal Building was right downtown, only three blocks from WWMR. His draft board officer was there. He would state his case in a calm, rational manner. He planned to start college next September. He already had four applications that he planned to submit. Surely that would make a difference.

And his brother! He had a brother already in the service. Didn't that mean something? He would say he was needed on the farm. He would say he had to get down to the farm on weekends until winter closed in and then he would be helping again in the spring. Surely he could talk his way through this with, who was it, Mrs. Baldwin, his draft board officer.

He had three weeks before he had to report to Camp McCoy. He would get this straightened out.

Two days later Clark found himself in the Milwaukee Federal Building. The place was imposing. Everything about it spoke of the mighty power of the United States of America. He walked up ten steps of elevation to reach one of the four heavy hardwood and glass doors. Once inside those doors he negotiated one of three revolving glass doors, allowing him into a rather austere looking lobby. The lobby extended all the way to the other side of the building where, it appeared, an identical entrance to the one he had just come through existed. A battery of four elevators flanked each side of the lobby. Most impressive of all was the high ceiling that secured six huge, unadorned chandeliers, hung by thick steel chain-link cables.

Clark felt relieved when he saw the information desk in the middle of the place.

The sixth floor, he was told. Room 623.

As he approached one of the elevators he saw a glassed-in directory mounted on the wall. He realized this was a place where the hand of Washington rested heavily: The F.B.I., The Department of the Interior, The Department of Health, Education and Welfare, The Department of the Treasury, Internal Revenue Enforcement, as well as Alcohol, Tobacco and Firearms were here. The field offices for both Wisconsin senators also were here.

On the sixth floor Clark entered the small draft board office of Mrs. Marion Baldwin. There was no receptionist or any other person, only Mrs. Baldwin. She appeared to be in her mid-fifties, with platinum bleached hair and dressed in a very proper manner: gray skirt, medium blue jacket, a white blouse with some sort of pink scarf. Her makeup had a decided pink accent to it and her telephone was pink, as well as a couple of other items on her desk.

Clark introduced himself, mustering all the charm that helped him get his way many times before.

Mrs. Baldwin invited him to sit down. After filing some papers in a folder and placing it aside she gave him a courtesy smile and her full attention.

"Now then, Mr. Berg. Is that spelt with an *e* or a *u*?"

"Yes, mam. That's spelt with an e." Clark's voice displayed an upbeat tone. As she looked up his records he explained his situation.

"I will be attending school next September and I thought I should get down here and try and straighten things out." He immediately thought that the phrase "try and straighten things out" was not the best choice of words.

Without looking up, Baldwin continued to look through her records until she reached Clarence El Berg. Her voice was not unfriendly, yet she spoke in a detached manner, offering no hint of emotional understanding to the young man seated on the other side of her desk.

"Yes, here we are, I think?" She looked to Clark with a questioning expression. "I have a Clarence Berg here."

"Oh. I'm sorry. Yes. It's Clarence. Clark is what I go by."

"Yes." She hesitated as her smile seemed to warm up a bit. "May I ask? Your middle name. El is rather different. Does that have some family significance?"

Clark was always sensitive about his name. He considered Clarence an outdated name that, in his shallow way of thinking, was a bit embarrassing. Now he was being asked about his middle name, El. To most people he would just lie. He would tell them the two letter name had no significance. However, he did not want to appear evasive to this woman. She held the future of his next two years in her hands.

"Yes. My great, great grandfather homesteaded here in Wisconsin—just outside of Stoughton. He came from Norway."

Clark gulped hard for on the rare occasion when he had to admit to the inspiration for his middle name it was uncomfortable for him.

"His name was Elmer and my parents wanted to remember him so, thankfully, they just shortened it to El. That's it." He shrugged his shoulders and gave a sheepish look.

Mrs. Baldwin stared at him. Though she said not a word her look said, "And why should you, in any way, feel embarrassed?"

She then studied the information in front of her, saying nothing for a very long twenty seconds that seemed to him like twenty minutes.

"Your draft notice was sent out six days ago and you say you received it this Monday?" She looked up, offering another cool smile.

Clark leaned forward in his chair. "Yes, I received it on Monday. As I said, I'll be going to school…"

She cut him off with a curt, albeit polite, request. "May I see your paperwork?"

Clark was stunned for just a couple of seconds before returning to charm mode.

"I'm not sure what paperwork you mean?"

Marion Baldwin summoned her patience, for she had been down this road before. She clasped her hands together on the top of her desk and politely continued.

"I will need to see your correspondence from the school you plan to attend stating that you have either been accepted or that they have received your application and are reviewing it. If you have been accepted we can change your classification to II-S. That will rescind your draft notice. If the school, or schools, are reviewing your application at this time I will call them, establish that you are in the process of being considered, and we will put your report date on hold until we see if you are accepted. If you are accepted your draft notice will be rescinded and, again, you will be reclassified II-S. If you are not accepted your current status will remain in effect and you will be assigned a new report date."

By now Clark had an unmistakable lump in his throat. He tried to mask his mounting panic with his continued innocent veneer. "Well, I haven't actually sent out my applications yet. You see, my employer and I discussed my options a short while ago and he encouraged me to work toward a degree. So I really need to get into school. Is there . . ."

Baldwin cut him off again. "Yes, Mr. Berg, it does sound like unfortunate timing. But your situation doesn't warrant a change in your status, or a postponement of your induction report date."

The color was draining from Clark's face. "But it must mean something that I am planning to go to school?"

She tilted her head slightly, the first indication that she at all sympathized with him. Or was it a gesture that said, "Please, I wasn't born yesterday."

"I must tell you that the intention to attend college carries no weight toward a deferment. If it did the government would lose a great deal of those who receive an induction notice."

"I don't understand," returned Clark, trying to deflect the meaning of her statement. "It is an honorable thing to go to college, isn't it?"

"Yes, of course, Mr. Berg." Her expression turned stony. "However, the government won't allow anyone to use the reason of planning to send out an application to a school or schools as adequate reason for a deferment. Too many people, without the least bit of compunction, would, and do, try to use that as a reason to rescind their induction."

Baldwin flipped the cumbersome records book forward one page and saw Johnny's information.

"I thought your information sounded familiar. John Berg is your brother?"

"Yes. Yes, he is." Clark sensed an opportunity. "Johnny was out of high school almost two years before he was drafted. Yet I get the notice just six months after I graduate. That just doesn't seem right."

She seemed puzzled, but just for a moment.

"I see here that you will be twenty years old next March. That does qualify you age wise to be drafted under the current guidelines. It appears you may have fallen behind at some point in school?" She raised her eyes to Clark.

He had hit another brick wall. He nodded affirmatively, but did not bother to explain his ninth grade blunders.

Clark turned his vision from Mrs. Baldwin to the floor in front of his feet. His complexion, which had gone pallid just a few moments before, now turned red. His insincere friendly visage was melting away. He spoke with annoyance in his voice.

"Is there anything I can do about this? Is there anyone I can talk to?"

"You have the option of contacting one of your senators."

She paused for a few seconds, then hesitantly continued. It was now obvious that she was forcing herself to be patient with this young man.

"But I must tell you that you really have no case here. Senators will occasionally—I should say rarely—grant deferments for family hardship reasons, but that's about it."

Clark Berg looked at the floor in front of him for another few seconds. Then, without a word to, or even a glance toward, his draft board officer, he bolted to his feet and left the office.

16

Viking

> *Enter into his gates with thanksgiving*
> *and into his courts with praise;*
> *be thankful unto him, and bless his name.*
>
> *Psalm 100: 4 (KJV)*

Charlie Stroud had familiarized himself all he could about the Bergs, their land, Midwest Agra Group and Gerald Hicks. Despite his efforts there seemed to be no way around Wisconsin law, which was working just fine for Mr. Hicks.

It had been pancreatic cancer that took Greta Hicks' life. As Betty Smith had reminded Mack and his buddies over their coffee at Rasmussen's earlier that year the Knudson's other daughter, Maggie, had been killed in a car accident in Georgia. There seemed to be nothing standing in Hicks' way.

One mid-November morning Gertie made her trip to the mailbox. It was going to be a brilliant fall day. The rays of the sun were making their way across the metal mailbox, melting the frost in a steady procession.

Stroud had told them to expect a letter formally announcing a new court date for the hearing. When she pulled out the box's contents and saw the letter from the court she knew immediately what it was.

Later that morning Gertie drove out to the fields with John and Mack's dinner. They were both chisel plowing under a couple sections of corn stubble. She decided not to mention the letter from the court. Her father-in-law had enough on his mind. He would see the notice that evening when he opened the rest of his mail.

She arrived at the predetermined spot where the vehicle trail led to the meeting of two tree lines. The men were not there yet. As she set up the food on the truck's tailgate her mind drifted back to all the times she and Ann had done this in the last twenty two years. How young they all had been. Mack and Ann, so full of life and good humor. How she and Mack kidded each other incessantly. It came to her mind about the couple of times she made her usual announcement of the mid-day meal when she shouted, "Liverwurst sandwiches."

Mack was a good eater. He never left a scrap on his plate. But he loathed liverwurst. He heard Gertie's announcement as he dismounted his tractor. He quietly made his way to the tailgate and found one of his favorites, not liverwurst. A few years later Gertie announced liverwurst again, but this time there they were: liverwurst sandwiches. Not to be deceived again Mack had expected something else. When he saw the liverwurst he allowed himself only a split second of disappointment before taking a sandwich. Seconds before Mack's arrival Gertie had brought Rollie in on the ruse. As Mack went and found a place to sit Rollie came up to the tailgate, grabbed a hidden sandwich that Mack had not seen and issued a phony self-conscious apology to Gertie.

"Gertie, I love you dearly and you're the best cook I know, but, forgive me, I just have no taste for this type of sandwich."

Rollie walked over toward Mack. "Here you go Thor. How about a trade?" He dropped the sandwich in Mack's lap as all around, Gertie, John, Ann and Rollie, rolled with laughter. The puzzled Mack sheepishly opened the wax paper and found one of his favorites: ham and cheese.

They had been good times: hard work, laughter, love of family, an appreciation that every day was a gift from the Lord. Gertie knew that there would be many more good days ahead; but they would be good times under different circumstances for—except for His promises—nothing stays the same forever. The boys were off on their own. Elsie was getting more independent every day. Ann was seriously ill. Someone was claiming a right to buy eighty acres of their land. And they all were getting a little older.

That evening Mack opened the letter from the court. The hearing was scheduled for January 10th.

* * *

The Thanksgiving holiday was only a few days away. Though Ann and Johnny could not be there Gertie was determined to make Thanksgiving Day, 1965, as traditional as any. It was their turn to host and that meant that the house would be full of Melborgs and Bergs. Clark would be in from Milwaukee and, as she did when she previously hosted, Gertie invited Rollie. There would be twenty nine people in all.

For this large extended family the special Thursday that was Thanksgiving Day was more revered than it was for many folks. This family lived close to the land. Their faith and the farming heritage of both the Berg and Mehlborg families made them well aware of the blessings to which they owed so much gratitude. For these people Thanksgiving was no mere kickoff to the Christmas season.

Thanksgiving morning dawned with heavy, dark cloud cover and high winds. There was a dusting of snow on the ground. To Gertie this prelude to winter weather just meant that the Thanksgiving atmosphere in the house would feel that much better. She had two sixteen pound turkeys stuffed and in her double oven at 6:00 a.m. In the next few hours she would be preparing the traditional side dishes including enough mashed potatoes to, as John would always say, feed an army.

There would be plenty of help from the other women. They would be bringing salads, rolls and pies: everything homemade, of course.

More so than ever Gertie was grateful for the help. It felt strange to be working in the kitchen on this day without her mother-in-law working with her.

A week before the feast Gertie had made it plain to her husband that she wanted everyone eating around one table.

"We gather together once a year for this meal. I'll not have a table here and there for different groups. This is a family and we are going to have fellowship together as a family."

John borrowed a couple of tables from his in-laws. The combination of tables stretched from the dining room into the parlor. With some help from tablecloths and centerpieces the setting looked good.

The only work that John and Mack did on Thanksgiving Day was to get the milking done. This was finished by seven o'clock. Mack had never lost his appreciation for the automated milk hookups. He traditionally spent the rest of the morning and the early afternoon doing something that was uncommon to him. He was glued to the television.

At ten o'clock the traditional Thanksgiving Day Parade from Detroit, sponsored by the Hudson Department Store, came across the network air waves. Mack was delighted by the high school bands, the marching V.F.W. chapters and the many floats with their themes. He especially enjoyed the Detroit Mounted Police Division. The beautiful Arabian horses, all of them either black or a rich chestnut brown, with white at the ankles. The officers and horses were perfectly matched in their unadorned, rugged leather saddles and reigns, with the dark blue saddle blankets with gold trim. What pride, Mack thought, that each officer must take in his work and in the caring of his horse. Each man looked proud and dedicated in his high top black boots, his thick and shiny black leather jacket and his perfectly formed campaign hat. He long felt that if he had grown up in a big city like Chicago or Detroit, he would have wanted to be a mounted police officer.

Shortly after the parade the traditional Thanksgiving Day football game between the Green Bay Packers and the Detroit Lions came on the television. This was no casual event for both Mack and Skorpie Johnson. They had been devoted fans of the Packers since the mid 1930's when Curly Lambeau led the team to its best years in the young National Football League. In the lean years of the forties and the fifties the franchise twice came close to leaving Green Bay for a larger city.

But now it was 1965 and the years of a great Packer dynasty were in progress. Under coach Vince Lombardi Green Bay was "Title Town, U.S.A."

Mack Berg and his friend were men who had spent their lives oblivious to most of the world that went on outside their own responsibilities. One of the exceptions to this was their long suffering allegiance to the Packers. Now they were enjoying the years of sweet success for their team.

But this Thanksgiving morning was not to be a traditional one for Mack. After milking he went to Madison to see Ann. As he left the house Gertie gave him a big hug, looked him in the eyes and said, "Give her our love."

He promised to be back by two o'clock.

Although Vanstessen's offered the option of a noon hour turkey dinner for residents and their guests Mack and Ann visited quietly in her room. She slowly struggled to swallow soup for her nourishment.

As he promised, Mack was back by two o'clock. The place was teeming with family. The laughter, talk and especially the spoken concerns for Ann were all good medicine for him. His spirits were soon lifted.

Clark had arrived at noon. Both John and Gertie thought they noticed a quietness about him that was uncharacteristic. He seemed to be enjoying himself around so many family members, but with a subdued demeanor.

Under Gertie's direction the women brought it all together. Just before three o'clock John was saying grace and then, like millions of other families across the nation, they celebrated the bounty of this land.

All that work to prepare the Thanksgiving meal and it seemed to be over so quickly. At least it seemed that way to Gertie and, no doubt, to every other woman in America who had worked so diligently putting it all together. But now, before dessert, things would slow down for a Berg-Melhborg tradition.

Glen Masterson took front and center, as he did every Thanksgiving at this time.

He was John and Gertie's brother-in-law. He had come up to Milwaukee from rural southwestern Kentucky as a lanky nineteen year old kid shortly after World War II to seek his fortune in the north country. In 1949 he was working on the maintenance crew at the Milwaukee Country Club golf course when a buddy asked him to go on a picnic with him. There would be girls there.

At the picnic he met Alice Mehlborg. For fourteen years now he had been the loveable hillbilly in a family of Germans and Norwegians. He called himself a rose amongst the thorns.

Glen was happy and proud to promote his country boy demeanor; but his down home manner was only a friendly veneer for a more ambitious and successful man. He had applied himself diligently through hard work and night school classes. He was presently supervisor of the Milwaukee Parks and Recreation Department.

All that aside, he was happy to be just good old Glen to his Wisconsin family. It was now time for him to make his annual presentation of the family's bungling Norwegian trophy. He first thought of the idea nine years earlier when Alice had burned, or as Glen would say, destroyed, a corn beef she was planning to have for dinner. She had placed it in a pot of water and initially turned the burner on high. She soon left the house to run an errand, forgetting to turn the burner down. As Glen put it when he made the presentation and every time he had the opportunity to tell the story since, "She went out to spend money we didn't have and came back to a smoke filled house and a dried up piece of meat that looked, and felt, like a tiny bowling ball."

Now, in these ensuing years, Glen presented the award to a family member who had made, as he called it, 'a bungle that would make a hillbilly look smart.'

He held up the award, or as it was sometimes called, the Norseman trophy, for all to see. It was a wooden Viking sailing ship with its flat bottom and dramatic high prow. It was eighteen inches long. Standing in the vessel was a wooden puppet-like figure. It was a Viking warrior in full battle regalia: high top leather boots, leather vest and leather helmet with horns. He sported a scraggily beard and wielded his Viking spear held in his right hand that was thrust high above his head. He showed a toothy smile and the look on his face was one of blissful bewilderment.

In his best Kentucky drawl Glen began.

"As you may remember last year's winner of the bungling Norseman award went to my dear mother–in-law, Karen Mehlborg. She may have married a German but she is all Norwegian, and she proved it when she drove into your nice town of Stoughton here one day to pick up some grocery items. Well, somehow she locked herself out of her car. Now, I don't know why anyone would feel like they had to lock their car in broad daylight in Stoughton, but she did."

"Anyway, I reckon ya'll remember what happened next. She got to the pay phone in the grocery market and called the police for assistance. The officer who came was our own Gracie Mehlborg's brother, Chuck Flat. Well, ole Chuck used his special tool to pop the lock open. Karen then dropped her grocery bag… *and her car keys*… on the car seat and she and Chuck got into an extended conversation about family until Chuck finally went on his way. Karen then remembered another item she wanted from the market so she locked the door again and went on her merry way back into the market. Well . . . when she came out she realized what she had done. So it was back to the pay phone to call the police and within a few minutes here comes ole Chuck, in total amazement."

By this time everyone, even though most of them knew the story well, were engaged in some form of amusement. Most of them howling. Karen Mehlborg herself was doubled over in her chair, rocking back and forth in self-deprecating laughter; tears rolling down her cheeks.

Glen waited a few seconds before continuing. "Well, Karen was gracious enough to bring the bungling Norseman trophy with her so that we could give it out on this Thanksgiving Day to this year's winner."

It suddenly became quiet.

"I and my spies have done our best to keep abreast of things in this past year of any strange incidents that could qualify and we've come up with three or four. I think the best one involves Ralph Myrdal. Ralphie, you want to come on up here. I reckon it's time to face the music."

Ralph Myrdal was John and Gertie's brother-in-law, husband to John's sister Elsie.

With an innocent look suggesting he had done nothing to deserve the trophy Ralph came forward to receive his due.

Masterson launched into his story.

"Most of you don't know about this but last February Ralph and Elsie made a trip to Cleveland—that's in Ohio folks—to attend a wedding. Now, getting from their home in Green Bay to Cleveland should really be no great task. In fact, with proper efficiency and a little discipline I reckon the trip can be made quite easily in less than a day. That is, unless you are Ralph Myrdal."

Ralph was now staring down at the floor, knowing full well that Glen must have done his homework. Those family members who had not heard about this were about to be enlightened. Those who knew about it were already laughing and hooting

Glen continued. "Well, God bless America and the new interstate highway system that allows us to get around so quickly nowadays. Trouble is when you get to Chicago you have to pay close attention to all those signs to make sure you're headed in the right direction. While Elsie was snoozing Ralphie here was supposed to make his way to I-80 east out of Chicago to get to Cleveland. Well, he found his way to I-80 alright. Trouble is he wound up heading westbound."

"Way to go, dad!" It was one of Ralph and Elsie's three teenagers. They were all hooting, enjoying their father's exposure.

Glen was not finished. "Now wait a minute folks. It gets better. Ralph must have really been in another world because he drove all the way to the first rest area. Folks, that's out near Bolingbrook. At this point he pulls off so that Elsie can take a turn behind the wheel. Elsie pulls out from the rest area and almost immediately she sees a west I-80 road sign . . . not to mention she is suspicious because the sun seems to be coming up in the wrong direction!"

By now everyone is in stitches. With perfect timing Glen Masterson waited for the noise to subside. "One can only imagine the conversation that occurred at this point."

Applause now accompanied the laughter as he handed the bungling Norseman trophy to Ralph Myrdal.

Thanksgiving dinner concluded with hot coffee and the sumptuous pies brought by Catherine Smith and the just mentioned Elsie Myrdal: blueberry, mincemeat, apple, pecan and, of course, pumpkin. From their farm's own heavy cream Gertie had made plenty of whipped cream with which to smother the pies. On this day those on a diet threw caution to the wind. This was not a day for the fainthearted.

By eight o'clock things began to break up. There were special hugs and handshakes for Mack; everyone again offering concerns for Ann. Gertie had plenty of help cleaning up so once the last of the family had gone she, John, Mack and Elsie found themselves relaxing at the kitchen table. Both John and Mack were taking advantage of left over pie. Mack was feeling especially buoyed by the day as he enjoyed his favorite—blueberry.

"To the hosting family go the spoils. It was a good day, Gertie. Thanks for everything. Ann said she was going to have a good day just thinking about everything here at the house. I think she meant it."

"I know she did," returned Gertie. "What do they call it? She has an indomitable spirit." She paused. "I'm hoping Johnny had a good day. Are they ahead of us or behind us time wise?"

"They're ahead of us," said John. "They finished their Thanksgiving yesterday. You can bet one way or another they had a turkey dinner."

Clark had the long weekend off from work and he would be staying at the farm until Sunday afternoon. His footsteps could be heard as he came down from upstairs to join the others.

"Mom, it was a good day. Is there any pie left or has grandpa and dad eaten it all?"

He cut himself a piece of pecan and sat with the others. For the briefest of moments he just stared at the wedge of pie and cleared his throat, as though he had something important to say. He did.

"Well . . . I've got something to tell you."

You could have heard a pin drop. It was not like Clark to say, "I've got something to tell you." He had a history of not telling them much. He would just go off and do as he pleased. If John and Gertie were lucky they would find out about it later. Now he was sitting at the table with them, willing to take the time to share with them. Yes, he had their full attention.

With both his elbows on the table Clark put his hands to the sides of his head, closed his eyes and groaned softly. "Ten days ago I received my draft notice. I have to report to Camp McCoy on the fifth of December. Ten days from now."

There was a few seconds of collective silence. Gertie put down her coffee cup, allowing herself just a moment of frustration. Her tone did not express anger or even annoyance, just resignation.

"Goodness knows, it's worry enough having one son gone. Now both of you?"

She squared her shoulders and questioned her son.

"Well. What do you think?"

It was so like Gertie. Many mothers would immediately offer a consoling word: "Oh dear, what a time for this, you've been doing so well at work, we know you have plans to take some college courses, it just doesn't seem fair."

But not Gertie. She offered a listening ear by saying, "What do you think?" If Clark was going to feel sorry for himself she was not going to encourage it.

"What do I think? I think it stinks!"

"Here I've got this job and I was planning to go to school next fall. I've been to see my draft board officer. She was a lot of help! There's no getting around it. I think it sucks."

Gertie dug in.

"And do you think that everything in this life is going to go your way? Goodness knows it does throw a monkey wrench into your plans but you can be sure that before your life is over there will be many a hurdle to overcome; and some of those hurdles are going to be tougher than two years conscription in the United States Army."

It was no surprise to both John and Gertie of how different their two sons' reactions to the draft notices were.

John kept it to himself, but he thought how the son who most needed the discipline and denial that the Army had to offer was the one so distraught about having to go.

"Have you told Frank Smith?" questioned Gertie.

Clark could see he would get no sympathy from his parents. They loved him, he knew. But this he also knew. John and Gertrude Berg were not whiners. He had never seen them feel sorry for themselves and they weren't about to encourage their son to feel sorry for himself.

With annoyance in his voice he answered his mother. "I told him last Friday. I asked him to keep it to himself until after Thanksgiving."

He raised his eyes to look at his mother, father, grandfather and sister.

"I'll probably be going to Fort Knox, like Johnny did, for basic training, but I don't know yet. Anyway, that's it."

17

Frontier

Poverty is no disgrace to a man,
but it is confoundedly inconvenient.

Sydney Smith

The previous month, in San Francisco, Johnny's departure for Korea had been delayed for seven days. So many men were being sent to Vietnam at this time that departures were backed up. This delay was not without design. For six days he and many hundreds of others with orders for Vietnam or Korea stood on a large asphalt parking area of Letterman Veterans Hospital. Every soldier departing San Francisco was required to give blood before departure. The hospital was full of wounded from the war. On the fifth day Johnny and the others with the same travel orders were called inside to give.

Berg and one hundred and sixty two other soldiers arrived in South Korea by commercial air charter on the last day of October, 1965. They landed at Kimpo Airfield in Seoul just as the sun was going down. As they exited the airplane the young men from America were hit with the odor of a large city with an imperfect sanitation system. It was their first indication that they were now in a poor land.

The air was cold. Johnny reckoned that it was easily as cold as his Wisconsin homeland even though, he would later learn, Seoul was two hundred and sixty miles closer to the equator than Stoughton. The Korean peninsula received the frigid weather that swept down from the huge Siberian land mass across Mongolia and northern China.

Two hours later Johnny and the others boarded Army buses. They traveled in the pitch black darkness of the countryside for about an hour; eventually arriving at the gate of a fenced in installation. The bus headlights illuminated a sign:

Camp Burns
22nd Replacement Depot
U.S. Army

All the troops awaiting assignment were assembled twice a day in front of the orderly room, on the camp's modest parade ground. On the third morning Johnny and Tom Bradley, whom he had struck up a friendship with while going through infantry training, and a number of others, were called. They gathered their duffel bags and quickly boarded another bus. On the side of the bus, up near the door, was painted the yellow and black crest of the First Cavalry Division.

The bus traveled north on the narrow dirt road for another hour. Thatched roof, mud wall dwellings in clusters of three or four appeared along the roadside every mile or so. Johnny estimated the size of these homes to be only slightly bigger than his family's kitchen and parlor back at the farm.

They passed six U.S. Army camps along the way. Like the replacement depot these camps were surrounded by two twelve foot high fences spaced three feet apart. A mass of loosely coiled, vicious looking concertina barbed wire filled the space between the fences. The new arrivals were well aware by now that theft of U.S. Army property was a large problem.

Soon enough the bus came upon a river roughly two hundred yards wide. The bus eased to a stop at a cantilever bridge. It was wide enough and substantial enough to accommodate the Army's M4 Sherman tank. On both sides of the checkpoint onto the bridge were M-60 machine guns.

They stood mounted on their tripods, each nestled in a sandbagged bunker. A few feet away from one of the bunkers was a small concrete hut with smoke eking out of a sheet metal chimney. A number of five gallon diesel cans were stacked next to the hut. The building appeared to be a warming, or even, a sleeping location. The two soldiers manning the machine guns and the two soldiers guarding a swinging gate that blocked entrance onto the bridge were American. They each wore the helmet and arm band of the military police. As the bus came to a stop for inspection Johnny could read the small sign next to one of the bunkers:

**Freedom Bridge
Army Corp of Engineers, 1954
Manned by the 43rd Military Police
Always on Alert**

One of the M.P.'s boarded the bus, reviewed the driver's written orders then slowly walked the length of the bus's aisle—his hand on his holstered .45 caliber revolver—while he observed every seating location. When he saw the wondering look of one of the new arrivals he fought back a faint smile and said, "Standard procedure, mack."

On the north end of the bridge the same installations were in place.

The countryside changed abruptly now. There was no sign of people. There were no rice paddies. The land south of the river was denuded of trees and brush. Here many small trees, bushes and field grass were evident.

The road soon ended at a T. The bus turned right and within five minutes it entered into camp headquarters of the 2nd Brigade, 1st Cavalry Division. Unlike the compounds south of the river no barbed wire fencing, no fencing at all, surrounded the camp.

126

The men emptied out from the bus and fell into formation, duffle bags at their sides. Ten minutes later they were called to attention and then to parade rest as a bird colonel, the brigade commander, came out of the headquarters hut and mounted a small reviewing stand.

"Gentlemen, welcome to sector A, home of the 2nd Brigade of the 1st Cavalry Division. Welcome to Freedom's Frontier."

"When you crossed that bridge over the Imjim River you entered into a special place. No civilians live here north of that river. Approximately three hundred yards to the north of us is the southern boundary of the Demilitarized Zone—the DMZ. The zone is three miles wide and runs across the width of the peninsula in a jagged pattern. The first mile and a half belong to Republic of Korea and, by virtue of our occupation, the United States Army, serving under authorization of the United Nations. The other mile and a half belongs to communist North Korea. Only so many personnel and so much military equipment are allowed in the zone at any given time. We perform a number of functions to ensure that the North Koreans don't cross that line and that they don't mount a buildup of any sort in the DMZ. You will learn those details once you arrive at your unit. Just remember this. Hostilities in Korea ended with a cease fire, a truce, twelve years ago. It has been a fragile truce and not one without violence. Not a month goes by without an incident of some sort on the DMZ. Some of those incidents have taken place in the American sector."

"The United States military has 50,000 personnel on the Korean peninsula. It is up to 2,100 of us to keep watch here on the DMZ. Second Brigade has nine camps along our eighteen miles of responsibility. One battalion from the Seventh Infantry Division is attached to us and it is responsible for an additional five miles on our eastern flank. Each of you will be assigned to one of our brigade camps."

"Gentleman, we have an enemy here that would like to see each one of us dead. I expect each one of you to perform your duties responsibly. That is all."

Three hours later Berg and the others had been processed and taken to their assigned camps. Although he kept it to himself Berg was happy that Tom Bradley was among the twelve of them assigned to the same camp: A Troop, 3rd Battalion, 2nd Brigade, 1st Cav.

Upon arriving they were marched to the orderly room where the troop's executive officer, 2nd Lieutenant DePaul spoke with them. Later that night Johnny and Bradley heard DePaul described as a "green behind the ears drama boy." He may have left that impression; however, that did not mean his comments were untrue.

"Gentlemen, Churchill called it an Iron Curtain, somebody else called it a Bamboo Curtain. Whatever you call it we are on the very cusp of the border where the free world meets communism. This is the physical dividing line of the struggle between good and evil, between freedom and oppression and between God fearing and atheism. No doubt since your boyhood you have heard about the Cold War and now you are at one of the places where the two ideologies geographically meet. Between 1950 and 1953 more than 39,000 American troops died on this peninsula fighting with other United Nations forces and the Republic of Korea Army against invading communist North Korea and, eventually, against communist China. Another 92,000 Americans were wounded and more than 8,000 are still listed as missing. The fighting stopped here; near the 38th parallel. In the ensuing twelve years the ROK Army and United Nations forces, most notably the United States, have stood their ground to contain the communists."

* * *

Everything in Korea confirmed to Johnny Berg how good life was back in Wisconsin. As his father had said, a soldier experiences a loss of personal freedom in order to secure a greater freedom for his country. Far beyond that he was seeing the price a people needed to pay to secure their freedom. The people of South Korea, a poor nation where most of the people struggled every day to meet the necessities of life, had drawn a line in the sand at one of the bleakest places he could imagine. Now, for the next thirteen months, he would be part of the force needed to maintain that freedom.

The affable Bradley was from Hattiesburg, Mississippi. He and Johnny were assigned to the same squad in the same platoon. Their sleeping quarters were in the same hut. That first morning at A Troop they were soon marched, with the other new replacements, to the supply shed. Here they shuttled forward in line to receive winter gear: heavy overcoat, two pair of winter gloves, two pair of mittens, insulated rubber boots, two pile caps, two pair of one piece long johns and six pair of heavy woolen socks. For snow camouflage they were each issued two pair of white overalls and loose fitting white hooded sweat shirts.

It was only early November but the temperature that morning was sixteen degrees with a sullen sky. Bradley was in a real culture shock over the cold air. Seeking re-assurance that someday it would warm up he worked up the nerve to speak to the supply sergeant, who was issuing the winter gear along with one of his subordinates.

"Sarge, when do ya'll believe it's going to warm up here?"

The sergeant, a middle aged black man of ample girth, looked up at the young man in front of him with a look of exasperation. "Son . . . where in the *hell* are you from?"

"Hattiesburg, Mississippi, Sarge. The hub city, they call us." Bradley saw that designation meant nothing to the sergeant. He quickly added, "The meeting place for a number of railroad lines."

The sergeant tilted his head slightly with a look of mock irritation.

"Son, I don't care what they claim for your hillbilly town. I'm from Chicago and I'm telling you it gets colder than an unhappy wife in this place. It's not even Thanksgiving yet and you're wanting to know when it's going to warm up? Son, allow me to educate your tender heart and your virgin ears. Today is going to seem like a heat wave compared to what's coming up. Hattiesburg, Mississippi? I do believe you're going to be wishing they sent you to Vietnam. Now keep moving, you're holding up progress here."

As he moved along the line Bradley tried to get in the last word.

"Yes sergeant; but we're not hillbillies. They're up north of us. Up Tennessee, Kentucky and Missouri. Flat country where I'm from, Sarge. We're deep south folk."

The sergeant kept up an irritated tone. He yelled down the line. "Young man, the only deep *ya'll* are going to see around here is a deep *freeze*."

* * *

On just his third day in country Private E-1 John Berg saw for himself how immediate the South Koreans considered the threat from the north. A day patrol from A Troop had run across, and captured, three Korean civilians inside the DMZ. These men were searching for and collecting scrap metal from the war—expended artillery shell casings and other items—that had lain in this ghostly strip of land since the cease fire was declared. These men were undoubtedly South Koreans who had crossed the Imjim River—probably under the cover of darkness— desperate for the money this metal would bring. They were now under arrest for violating South Korean law and, until proven otherwise, for being North Korean infiltrators.

Later that same day Berg was one of four soldiers assigned to deliver these men down to a South Korean Army intelligence unit. Rifles at the ready, John and another soldier sat on the bench seat in the back of a three-quarter ton pickup, the three Koreans chained to the bench seat opposite them. Upon arrival the soldiers herded the handcuffed Koreans into a building whereupon two ROK Army officers escorted everyone into an interrogation room.

Without a word yet spoken one of the ROK officers used his steel toed boot to kick one of the frightened captors in the shin with great force. The helpless victim crumpled to the floor in agony. The process was repeated with the other two men.

The Americans were then thanked and excused. As they left the building Johnny could hear screaming and sounds of violence.

First the colonel's warning; then the Lieutenant's words, and now this. Berg was aware he was in a troubled land.

18

Providence

Trust in the Lord with all thine heart;
and lean not unto thine own understanding.
In all thy ways acknowledge him,
and he shall direct thy paths.

Proverbs 3:5,6 (KJV)

Early on the morning of December 5 John Berg drove his son Clark to Camp McCoy for his physical and initial processing. Twenty four hours later Clark and a Greyhound bus full of just sworn in recruits were on their way to Fort Knox, Kentucky. The increased military presence in Vietnam had led to taking both Berg sons in to the Selective Service Draft. John and Gertie were grateful that their eldest son had not been sent to Vietnam. Now they would wait while Clark went through training to see where he would be sent.

The young man entered the U. S. Army with a chip on his shoulder. It was simply a continuation of the attitude he had carried for most of his young life.

The experience did not begin well. During the first week of basic one of the other rookies, having heard the name "Berg, Clarence" barked out during more processing made light of his first name. They were in the barracks that night when the troublemaker popped off.

"Hey, Clarence. I love it. The only other Clarence I ever heard of was Clarence Birdseye."

Clark did not waste a second as he landed the only serious punch of their scuffle, a right fist to the side of the big mouth's head. They rolled around on the barracks floor before being pulled apart by the other recruits. The drill sergeant who was "charge of quarters" that evening arrived while the two young men were being held back, glaring at each other. Clark and the other guy spent four days in what was called a minor detention cell of the Fort Knox stockade. When he got out Clark restarted basic training. The incident seemed to mellow him out, to a degree. He had no further such incidents for the rest of basic.

* * *

Without the boys, Christmas at Berg Dairy Farm was quite different. Mack brought Ann home on Christmas Eve for a two day stay. She looked forward to it immensely, but it was exhausting for her.

The tenth of January court date about the property sale to Gerald Hicks came and went with dismal results. The district judge shook his head in affinity to the Bergs but he could do nothing but award Hicks the right to buy the acreage in question. It was everyone in Stoughton and environs against Hicks from a populist standpoint but the words written by Oscar Knudson and signed by Mack Berg, all duly attached into the Knudson deed, gave the court no alternative.

Charlie Stroud asked the court for a one year window before the sale took place so that the Bergs could adjust their operation to the loss of eighty acres. The judge gave them nine and one half months. By October 26, 1966, the Bergs would have to sell the eighty acres to Hicks. Although it now seemed hopeless, it did allow for more time to try and find something that could warrant an appeal. Charlie said he would not close the door on the possibility of discovering something but he was forthright enough with the Bergs to say that the time he devoted to such a pursuit would now be limited.

Up to this time the Bergs had been stubborn enough to refuse to talk about what they would do if they were to

133

lose the 80 acres. Now John and Mack began to talk about how they would manage their herd. To Mack the numbers meant inevitable downsizing. "It takes so many acres of good land to run an operation with so many cows," he would repeat. It had been thirty five years since he bought feed for his herd and the thought of having to do so now was a blow to his pride. But John resisted. He wanted to put a paper and pencil to it. He wanted to consult with the Wisconsin Dairy Farmers Association. He thought they might have some advice, some new feed techniques that could help them. The association was in constant contact with the University of Wisconsin's Agricultural Research Department to stay abreast of any new innovations that could help the farmer, especially the dairy farmer.

It was the men who would make the decisions, but it was Gertie who was both the most pragmatic and, at the same time, the most optimistic member of the family. One early February day she took a break from her work around the house when the phone rang. It was her sister Alice. Neither woman had much time for idle chatter. Their conversations were always practical and to the point. But in the last few years they had set aside one time during the depths of the Wisconsin winter when they would just talk about whatever was on their minds.

"Gertie, when are you people going to get your phone system updated out there? I've been getting a busy signal for the last twenty minutes. I'll bet Ruth Connors has been on that party line of yours." Alice laughed. "We went to private lines about three years ago. It is so nice."

"Don't you say a thing against Ruthie, sister. She's one of the sweetest gals around . . . although she *does* do her share of talking. Now, how are all the Mastersons doing?"

For ten minutes Alice talked about her kids, their impending trip down to Kentucky in the spring, and the decision Glen had to make about whether to run for Milwaukee City council next fall.

"The whole idea of politics just does not set well with me, Gertie. These people are like, I don't know, like butterflies floating around Glen, waiting for him to say yes so they can land on him and be part of the whole process. But you know Glen. He's a born showman, so I know he's interested. We'll just wait and see. How's things at the farm?"

"Awfully quiet, that's for sure. I believe 1966 is going to be a different kind of year around here."

It was the kind of statement, the kind of outlook, that was typical of Gertie. Both her boys were gone to the Army, her mother-in-law was seriously ill, and they were being forced to sell eighty acres of prime farmland. She was never one to use hyperbole. She simply called it "a different kind of year."

She went on to share about those concerns with her sister: being matter of fact, pulling no punches. She told her that based on the progress of Ann's cancer she thought they could lose her by spring.

"Alice, the Lord's going to do what He sees best. I'm praying for her comfort and for her recovery, but regardless of what happens He's got a place in heaven waiting for her."

"Amen to that," responded Alice.

"It is different around here without the boys," said Gertie. "One day they're both here, going to school, working with John and Mack. It seems like just the next day one's in the Army and the other one is working in Milwaukee. Now they're both in the Army. Keep 'em in your prayers. We don't know where Clark will wind up! I'm just glad the Lord's in charge of all this. I sure know that I'm not."

19

Orders

On February 15th Clark finished basic training. Both John and Gertie were pleased to know that he had controlled his free spirit enough to stay out of trouble. They were mildly puzzled that it appeared to take nine weeks to complete training when they knew that it should take only eight. Clark never mentioned the altercation.

He wrote to tell his parents that his AIT would be medic training at Fort Sam Houston in San Antonio, Texas. He called it a ten week medical degree. He said he would demand to be called "doc" when he came home on furlough in May. John, Gertie, Mack and Elsie were all glad to see that the tone of his letters indicated he was adjusting to the military. He seemed to be resigned to making the best of the situation. Maybe he was growing up.

When Gertie first read that Clark would go for medic training she was buoyed by the thought that he would be assigned to hospital work. Even if he were sent to Vietnam he could possibly work in a hospital away from the fighting. But she soon realized what John knew immediately: he could wind up being assigned to a ground unit. The majority of medics were assigned to ground units that had potential for combat. She resigned herself not to dwell on the possibilities.

Regardless of where Clark was sent Gertie was forever positive that her second born would find his passage into manhood.

"John, I think the Army is getting that son of ours squared away. I think we'll see some changes for the good when he comes home."

"To borrow one of Skorpie Johnson's expressions," said John with a degree of optimism, "I think they'll put some hair on his chest."

The winter days passed along. For Ann the situation continued to be agonizingly slow and painful. Mack visited her almost every day. John or Gertie went with him on many of these days. As Mack had said months before, the Gerald Hicks problem, as important as it was, had become an issue of lesser concern.

* * *

In Korea Johnny Berg's unassuming brand of leadership manifested itself in no more pointed way than his friendship with Tom Bradley. Bradley had accepted his friend's invitation to visit the farm someday, "but never during winter." He said he never intended to go north of Hattiesburg for the rest of his life, except in the summer.

In 1966 Hattiesburg was a city of marginal prosperity in the economically struggling state of Mississippi. Tom Bradley's father owned one of the town's two wholesale plumbing warehouses.

One would think that young Bradley was accustomed to working with his hands, having grown up around the plumbing business. To the contrary: he enjoyed music, reading, history and politics. In these areas he and Johnny had little in common.

Bradley had a full head of curly red hair that was common to those of his Gaelic ancestry. His physique was less than impressive. He was five foot eleven inches tall but could only be described as a softie. Even the rigors of basic training and AIT had failed to eliminate the baby fat that characterized his soft appearance. It would be unfair to call him heavy for his weight was only moderately out of line. It was just that a lack of muscular development gave him a plump appearance. His jowls sagged and the freckles that accompanied his fair complexion did nothing to project a strong masculine image. Here again the two young men had little in common. Johnny was fit and he had committed himself to the physical discipline of the Army while Bradley found it uncomfortable, fearing the exposure of his physical inadequacies.

Despite these differences the two soldiers felt a kinship. Back at Fort Leonard Wood, during infantry training, something happened that convinced Bradley that he could find no surer a friend than Johnny Berg.

Hollywood had put many of Broadway's hit musicals on the motion picture screen in the '50s and '60s and Bradley had enjoyed the music immensely: *Oklahoma, My Fair Lady, South Pacific, The King and I,* and all the others.

One morning, while on KP duty, he was singing softly and, so he thought, privately, from *My Fair Lady* while peeling potatoes in a corner of the mess hall kitchen.

An Army mess hall is a noisy place. The banging of pots and pans, the hissing of hot water hoses and the shouting and cursing of the others on KP duty gave Bradley a false sense of privacy.

> *I'm very grateful she's a woman*
> *And so easy to forget;*
> *Rather like a habit*
> *One can always break-*
> *And yet,*
> *I've grown accustomed to the trace*
> *Of something in the air;*
> *Accustomed to her face.*

Unbeknownst to Bradley, two of his fellow kitchen workers who were close by waited for those words to end before howling with laughter.

By that evening almost everyone in the platoon, and half the training company, were calling Tom Bradley "my fair lady," or just "fair lady." This went on for two days until just before lights out when one of those leading the charge in the kidding tried to draw John Berg into the fun.

"Hey, Berg. I guess you're pretty impressed, your buddy being such a high class singer and all."

Johnny was sitting on the edge of his lower bunk cot, half undressed. He said nothing for a number of seconds.

"Guess I'm not much of an expert on music. Just glad to know I can count on Tom as a friend"

There was silence after Berg's response. The next day the "fair lady" jabs quickly dissipated.

* * *

Winter's grip on the Korean peninsula began to slowly soften near the end of March. The twenty first day of April brought a day of welcome warmth for Johnny, Tom Bradley and the others in A Troop. The temperature rose to sixty-five degrees. There would be more days of cool, blustery weather before spring took hold; however, this day was one to be enjoyed.

The entire troop was ordered to assemble in formation at 1500 hours. The runner from the orderly room said that the "old man" was calling for the assembly. Everyone would be there except those on guard post surveillance or day patrol, two of the daylight functions inside the DMZ.

As he and Johnny hustled down to the assembly area Bradley could hardly contain his joy.

"Yes! God's great mercy to us! I thought I'd never live to see my bones warm up again, but I think I'm going to make it. Gracious, that sun feels good. I don't care what the "old man" has to say, nothing can ruin this day."

139

The "old man" was A Troop commanding officer 1st Lieutenant Jacob Flint. He was a wiry, rather bookish looking man in his late twenties. A troop or company sized unit normally would be commanded by a captain, but America was at war and promotions sometimes lagged behind the need to fill command positions. In his five month tenure as troop commander he had given his men no reason to doubt his leadership. It had not been his practice to call for a troop assembly, having done so only twice before.

The first sergeant brought the troop to attention and then parade rest. Flint spoke.

"Gentlemen, I wanted to speak to as many of you at one time as possible to relay some important information. At a meeting at battalion headquarters this morning the other troop commanders and I were informed that 2nd Brigade, 1st Cavalry Division will be leaving Korea. We will join the rest of the 1st Cav in South Vietnam. We will begin preparations for this move immediately. For security reasons all outgoing mail will be censored as of today until we arrive in country. We will continue to perform our duties here and at our new location to the high standards we have set for ourselves. That is all."

The first sergeant brought the troop to attention and present arms. Flint returned the salute, did an about face and walked away. The first sergeant brought the men to order arms and then commanded them to fall out.

That was it. In less than a minute it was over.

Everyone was a bit stunned, but none more so than Tom Bradley. He almost sank to the ground, right there in the remains of the formation. "We have finally made it through this unbearable winter and they're going to take us away? My bones have been chattering for the last five months so that they can take us out of here right when spring is finally going to happen?"

Johnny had little reaction to the news. As they left the assembly area his only comment was, "No more cold weather, Tom."

In the next few days the rumor mill was in full cycle. "When would we leave? Where in Vietnam was the division?" Most importantly the men wondered, "Will our time in Korea be applied to Vietnam?"

There was plenty of speculation but these young men knew by now that the Army was not going to give out any more information than necessary.

Berg had been in Korea a little more than four and a half months. The country had made an impression on him, on all of them. He heard someone call it a boil on the buttocks of the world. He understood the sentiment, but he would not express himself that way. He knew he had been blessed to have been born in the greatest nation on earth. He never considered scorning this less fortunate place, or the less fortunate people that lived there.

Now they were being ordered to the hot war. He simply accepted the news as he had accepted his draft notice. While some around him showed enthusiasm for the opportunity to get into action, and a few quietly exclaimed a hatred for "Johnson's war," he carried neither emotion. Others were risking their lives. If he were now chosen to be among them, then so be it. His faith had taught him that God was in control. That belief was one that was now especially reassuring.

20

Letdown

Family gives us two things;
one is roots, the other is wings.

Unknown

Sometimes the sequence of events in the real world can be more amazing than anything the richest of imaginations can create.

Clark finished his medic training on April 22nd. The next day, a Saturday, his training class graduated. That night he was shuttled into San Antonio where he left at midnight for Chicago by Greyhound Bus Lines. Stopping many times at towns along the way to pick up and let off passengers the bus traveled through the night and the next day before arriving at the Greyhound depot in Chicago on Sunday evening. Clark made himself comfortable on one of the benches in the depot waiting area. He used his duffel bag as a pillow, dozing off and on, until he boarded the 6:00 A.M. bus for Madison, via Milwaukee.

On Monday morning John Berg drove the twenty five miles to Madison in a steady spring rain to pick up his son. He quickly took note that it was a different Clark than had left home twenty-one weeks before. He was much more assessable in conversation than John had ever known him to be. Clark asked about Elsie, his mother and his grandparents. He seemed to appreciate every sight along the way as they drove back to the farm. He asked about the land sale.

"It's like we told you in the letter," said John. "It seems to be cut and dried. We were given a nine and a half month grace period to adjust our operation. By October 26 we have to sell the eighty acres to this Hicks guy. Your grandpa and I haven't decided yet what to do about the stock. We don't want to downsize but . . . I just don't know yet."

John paused and glanced over at his son. "I'm proud of you, Clark." There was an awkward silence for a few seconds and then he continued. "I don't just mean because you made it through your training. You had a lot going for you with your job in Milwaukee. You didn't want to go but you did."

Clark gave out with a soft, "Ha! I wouldn't give me too much credit. I didn't have much choice. How do they say it? It's either basic training or Leavenworth straining."

"That's a new one on me," his father responded.

"I guess you didn't need that one in World War II. Nobody was trying to run to Canada then."

It was the first time in his life that Clark ever acknowledged his father's participation in that war. He changed the subject. "What do you hear from Johnny?"

"He seems to be doing alright. It's cold there. Colder than here, plus they're out in it a lot. Says it's worst at night when he has to remain still." John gave himself a quick smile. "Maybe he'll explain that one when he gets home. If we can get it out of him." Maybe we'll hear from him today. We usually get a letter on Mondays."

John hesitated; then asked the question he'd been wanting to ask.

"Where are they sending you?"

"They didn't give us our orders until Thursday night. I figured I'd beat the mail home so I didn't try to write about it." Clark suppressed a smile. "Why don't we wait and I'll tell you and mom together."

When John turned the pickup into the driveway there was Gertie, in her yellow rain slicker, her short ponytail protruding from the baseball cap that served as her umbrella. She was walking back from the mailbox.

She heard the truck coming, turned and produced the biggest smile Clark had ever seen. John brought the truck to a stop and Clark opened the door. In her anxiousness to pile in with her returning son she slipped slightly as she came around the door. The mail flew out of her hands. They laughed as she clambered on to the seat with her second born. John went around and picked up the mail out of the mud while Gertie beamed, giving Clark a huge hug.

It was coffee and cardamom coffee bread for the next two hours around the kitchen table. Mack kept calling his grandson Doc, wanting to know all about medic training. And they all wanted to know where Clark was being sent.

"Well, I'm not being sent to Vietnam."

His parents and grandfather showed a reserved thankfulness. Inside, Gertie was ecstatic. She would have accepted the news of Clark's assignment to Vietnam with nothing more than a show of modest disappointment, but she was a mother, and the news of where her son was *not* going overjoyed her.

He then told them where he was being assigned.

"It looks like Johnny and I are going to be neighbors. I've got orders for South Korea." He let a slight grin of satisfaction show.

They were stunned for a few brief seconds. John had his chair leaning back, as usual. When he heard the news he quickly brought the chair to an upright position.

"You're going to Korea? Korea? We're going to have two sons in the same place?"

"That's it, dad. I hope the place can handle two Bergs in the same place at the same time." With a bit of self-deprecation he added, "I hope Johnny hasn't ruined the family name. I'll probably take care of that."

For a few moments John felt the pride that comes sparingly, even in the closest of families. It was a moment when they all realized what a big world it was and now the family's two young men were going to represent them in the same place; and there was a thankful feeling that they both would be away from the horror and heartache of combat.

"I'm going to write Johnny tonight," said Clark. He spoke with an interest that had always been so unlike him. "I want to let him know we'll be neighbors."

Gertie clasped her hands together. "Oh! There's a letter in the mail today from Johnny. I'll read it for all of us."

She grabbed the mud splattered letter off the kitchen counter and returned to the table, buoyed with the good news of this day.

Dear Mom, Dad, Elsie and Grandpa:

> *Big news here. Our brigade arrived in Vietnam yesterday . . .*

Gertie's voice trailed off at the end of that sentence. For ten seconds she seemed to freeze and no one said a word. Staring down at the table she pushed the letter over to John. "Why don't you read this."

It remained quiet for a few more seconds. He read cautiously.

Dear Mom, Dad, Elsie, Grandpa:

> *Big news here. Our brigade arrived in Vietnam yesterday. We are joining the rest of our division, which has been here for some time. There was no point in me trying to let you know before we left Korea because our mail was censored. We finally worked our way out of the winter weather in Korea. I was looking forward to spring. That's the disappointing part to me. Now it's straight into the hot weather. My friend Tom, from Mississippi, says he doesn't care what is going on in Vietnam, nothing could be worse than the cold. Ha! I don't know about that.*

John stopped reading and looked up for a moment. He felt a need to say something positive. The next paragraph lent itself to that.

> *The good news is that our time in Korea will count toward our time in Vietnam, so I will just carry on to complete my thirteen months.*

John looked up again and spoke with some authority. "That is good news. He'll be home in seven months."

Mack, too, could see that Gertie needed a boost. "That *is* good news. And Johnny knows how to take care of himself. Seven more months. Before you know it he'll be back home."

He looked to Clark. "Well Doc, it looks like you're going to have Korea all to yourself. Heck of a coincidence. You coming home today, telling us that you're being sent there and then not two seconds later this letter from your brother. I think it's a time that won't be soon forgotten around here."

Gertie was sitting back in her chair, arms crossed, looking straight ahead. Her eyes had taken on a glazed over look. There were some brief moments of awkward silence. The silence was not now because of the news they just received, it was because none of them had ever seen Gertie overcome as she now was. It lasted only a few moments, but they all could see her great disappointment.

Now she raised her head a little higher. She swiftly transferred her disappointment about Johnny's news to an encouragement for Clark.

"I've got two sons to be proud of, in the service of our country or not, here at home or wherever in this world our Lord intends them to be."

She quickly questioned Clark in an effort to keep her emotions in check.

"Do you think you will be going anywhere near where Johnny has been?"

"Don't know. My orders say I'm being sent to the 2nd Infantry Division. I was looking forward to the two of us getting together. Looks like we'll have to wait until we're both home for that."

21

Grandma Johnson

*but the gift of God is eternal life
through Jesus Christ our Lord.*

Romans 6:23 (KJV)

On April 25 the 2nd Brigade, 1st Cavalry Division had sailed in three Navy transport ships from Inchon Harbor, Korea for the war in Vietnam. They had traveled as a self-contained unit: men and equipment and armaments. The voyage took three days.

Johnny had never been on the ocean before. They were underway no more than twenty minutes and he was sick. He spent most of the voyage curled up in his hammock or sitting on the deck of the ship with his head hanging down between his knees. He managed to eat only dry toast and drink only water or plain tea. He either threw up or had the dry heaves a number of times. He and the few others with seasickness didn't care what awaited them in Vietnam. They just wanted off those ships.

* * *

For the second spring in a row John Berg was without the help of his sons. By the beginning of May Rollie Leach again started work at the farm. And when John requested summer help from the University of Wisconsin he was grateful to be able to get George Wistoff again.

John and Mack decided to sell eight Holsteins in order to deal with the coming loss of eighty acres to Gerald Hicks. They arranged to sell four head each to two of their neighbors. The transaction would take place at the time of the property sale.

Ann's cancer began to establish its death grip at this time. By Memorial Day weekend her inability to breath without great effort and pain had necessitated her being taken from Vanstessen's and admitted to the hospital in Madison.

Gertie's comment to her sister in February that 1966 would be a different year was proving to be true.

On a day in the middle of June Skorpie Johnson picked up Mack for the drive to Madison. Over these last few months Johnson had occasionally accompanied his friend to visit Ann. Despite Mack's heavy heart the two of them still found moments to chide each other during these trips. It was the way of two old friends who best knew how to console each other through humor.

But now Mack spoke from his heart. "I didn't think it would be this hard." He looked straight ahead while his friend drove. Johnson said nothing.

"She has never complained. But now she can't communicate and I don't have any idea how painful it must be for her."

A good minute went by before Johnson said anything. "I don't doubt that Annie is in pain, but the medicine helps a lot. I don't think she's hurting as much as we think."

He paused for a few seconds and decided to complete his thought. "You know, she's put up with you for about forty five years and she's had to do that without any medicine at all."

Mack gave back an almost inaudible chuckle. "That she has."

A couple minutes of silence passed when Skorpie ventured another thought. He spoke in the slow, measured

cadence with which he and Mack had always com-
municated.

"When I was twelve my grandmother died. I
remember my mother taking my brother and myself into
the bedroom of that old cabin of theirs. She told us that
grandma was going to die. That we needed to go in and see
her. That it was the last time we'd get to be with her. I
don't even remember what her illness was but I remember
that even though her voice trembled weakly she had a clear
mind. George and I both started to get tears running down
our cheeks and she said, 'Harold, hand me my Bible.'"

"So I gave her the Bible and I've always
remembered what she said."

"She said, 'Boys, I don't ever want you to be afraid
of death. It's getting time for your grandma to pass away
but we are only meant to be here for a while. I'm going to
heaven to be with Jesus because I've taken him as my
Savior. I want to read you these words. I want you to
remember them.'"

"Well, she had her Bible marked at a spot so she
turned right to it: *'To everything there is a season, and a
time to every purpose under heaven. A time to be born and
a time to die.'*"

He hesitated briefly, but he had not finished his
story.

"Then . . . God bless her, it took quite a bit of what
little strength she had left but she found another passage.
Can't say I can recite the exact words, but we all know it:
*'He that hears my word and believes on him that sent me
has everlasting life.'*"

The two men traveled in silence the rest of the way
to the hospital.

Two weeks later Ann Berg passed away. Two days
of visitation at the funeral home and the funeral at First
Lutheran were as heavily attended as any in Stoughton's
recent past. Ann's brother Cal Hopkins and his wife were
there as well as three of their four children, Ann's nieces
and nephews. They lived in Chicago, Cleveland and Des

Moines. The arrival of more distant relatives, four of Ann's cousins on her father's side of the family, was a real tribute to the regard with which family held her. These two men and two women were the children of George Hopkins's two brothers. Ann had last seen them at the funeral of her father in 1948. It had been the only time they had seen Ann since her parents separated in 1918. Yet here they were.

They expressed how wonderful their memories of Ann were in their youth, how good their times were together before the family became so troubled. The special bond that cousins sometimes have had been theirs.

Mack, John, Gertie and Elsie took great comfort in the expressions of all those around them. Elsie especially was comforted by the esteem with which so many held her grandmother. She wanted those in her world to know how wonderful her grandma was and she experienced just that. She missed Johnny and Clark very much at this time. In a way she felt alone because her two brothers were away in the service and it was they who knew the loss of grandma at her level.

John had called Camp McCoy to ask whether the boys were eligible to come home for the funeral. The answer was no. For overseas personnel emergency furlough for death in the family covered only immediate family. The Armed Forces defined immediate family as spouse, parent, sibling and child.

John thought it just as well. Both his sons had been well aware of the severity of their grandmother's cancer before they left. The quick trip home and the immediate return to Vietnam and Korea would probably be more of a strain than just receiving the news by mail.

John and Gertie looked forward to their permanent return.

22

Gravestone

Blessed are they that mourn:
for they shall be comforted.

Matthew 5:4 (KJV)

After Ann's passing Mack took up a renewed energy against the sale of the acreage. Even though he and John had resigned themselves to having to sell the eighty acres, he now became increasingly agitated. He tried to get through to Gerald Hicks a number of times but Hicks never responded to his calls. He then called DeVries Real Estate and demanded to talk to the owner, Robert Devries. Mack read him the riot act, unfairly chastising him for "being in cahoots with a no good swindler like Gerald Hicks."

Mack was normally not one to let anyone under his skin, but it was a backlash in response to the loss of his wife. It seemed to be a common response to grief that people make: focusing on an issue that can help deflect the sadness that one feels.

He called Charlie Stroud with no other purpose than to tell him how unhappy he was about the whole thing. Charlie was at Ann's funeral and told John and Gertie he would be calling them about a week prior to the time Hick's could make his offer. Now, with Mack calling, the lawyer went ahead and explained the strategy on how to handle the offer. He would rather have spoken to John about it but here was Mack on the phone and in no pleasant mood.

"When you receive Hicks's offer from the Devries agency let me know immediately. If you don't like the figure I will take the offer before the judge. No doubt Hicks will low ball you. Under these circumstances, with it being a mandatory sale, the judge may have to determine what a fair price is."

Mack said he wouldn't like the offer no matter what Hicks said. But he also said he understood what Charlie meant. Speaking to Stroud seemed to settle him down. The air of inevitability returned Mack to a quiet resentment.

He went in to Eastside Cemetery faithfully once a week to visit his wife's grave. These were not weepy visits for he knew full well that Ann was in heaven. Each time he recalled many treasured memories and left the place with an uplifted spirit.

The small headstone he had placed at the grave was profound in its simplicity.

Ann Berg
1898 -1966
She was loved by all

It was around the second week of October when Mack was visiting Ann's gravesite that he discovered a curious thing. He decided he would make this his last visit of the season and, in fact, visit only once or twice a year from now on. He had needed these visits, but now he decided it was time to let go a bit. On this afternoon he took a nostalgic walk among the grave markers, recalling old friends and family. He quietly spoke to some of them, smiling as he recalled so many things.

He came upon the Knudson gravesite.

"Well, Knuddy, we're in a fine fix now. I know you had only good intentions when you added that note in our property sale. I'm sure you didn't know that your son-in-law was going to come up with all this stuff thirty years later. Good acreage for sure, Knuddy. I sure don't want to give it up but, I guess, it won't be the end of the world."

"Margaret, I know that you are planted down south somewhere, but I want you to know that we're sorry to learn that your Greta passed away. I guess it's not so bad as far as you're concerned though. I mean, she's with you now. Both your girls: Greta and Maggie. Heaven is a good thing, Margaret."

As he walked out of the cemetery Mack felt as though the weight of the world had been lifted off his shoulders. Walking around recalling old friends and his decision to stop visiting Ann's grave so often left him with a mellow feeling.

As he got back to his pickup a strange feeling came over him. It was the Knudson gravesite. Something wasn't right, but he couldn't place what it was.

He walked back over to the graves. There was one modest ground level sandstone marker of rectangular form that served to recognize both graves. Mack read the inscriptions:

<table>
<tr><td>Oscar Alec Knudson</td><td>Margaret Elizabeth Meyers Knudson</td></tr>
<tr><td>Born March 12, 1875</td><td>Born Dec. 6, 1876</td></tr>
<tr><td>Died Sept. 18, 1952</td><td>Died</td></tr>
</table>

Margaret's date of death had never been inscribed.

Mack was almost back to the farm before the possibility dawned on him that the date of death might be missing because Margaret was still alive! Nonsense. He remembered reading about her passing in the obituaries years ago.

That evening Mack and Gertie enjoyed a soft autumn rain as they sat on the front porch. John was at the kitchen table updating his milk production ledger. Gertie didn't allow it to show but Mack knew her boys were on her mind. Especially Johnny. He was in harm's way. Mack thought it would do his daughter-in-law good to be able to talk about it.

"Here we are sitting in comfort on this old porch of ours and my two grandsons are trudging around on the other side of the world. It might be raining where they're at, but I don't think they're able to enjoy it like we are."

Gertie grabbed the opportunity to respond.

"I think we can be sure of that. At least it's not too cold yet for Clark in Korea; but I'm sure it is more than just warm for Johnny. Downright hot and humid, I'm sure. I'll bet that when they get back, sitting here on the porch like this, or any of a hundred other things, will be something they'll never take for granted."

She looked at Mack with a soft smile that conveyed optimism. "I think Clark might start appreciating things more."

Mack rocked in the swing and took his time responding. "I do think you could be right about that."

At no time during that evening did he think to mention about the Knudson gravestone.

* * *

At Berg Dairy Farm breakfast was always a hardy meal, but on Sundays, before heading out to church, it was always extra special. Sunday was the only time they ate breakfast as a family. Gertie and Ann had always prepared two, even sometimes three, different items. It might be oatmeal and poached eggs with toast and cardamom coffee bread, or waffles with sausage and eggs, or any number of combination of things. Fresh fruit was always a part of it: grapefruit and oranges in season, plums and peaches in August and September, their own blueberries in July and August, and their own fresh raspberries from July into early October.

Now Ann was gone and the two boys were in the Army but Gertie carried on just the same. Sunday morning was still a breakfast feast.

Mack was just finishing his poached eggs, toast and Danish when he remembered to mention the gravestone.

John was curious so after church service he, Gertie, Mack and Elsie stopped at the cemetery.

John was puzzled. "This is a little strange. I'm going to call Charlie Stroud in the morning. We'll let him know."

Mack voiced a question full of defeatism. "How is that going to help anything?"

"I don't know, dad. Charlie has always said he wants any information we can give him."

John spoke with a hint of frustration in his voice as he tried to be patient with the hopelessness suggested by his father's question.

"You did say you remember that she died?"

"Yeah, sure I remember. I've been reading those obituaries for a long time. Like I've always told you, I want to be sure my name's not in there."

The next morning John found himself much too busy to take time out to call Charlie Stroud on something that probably did not mean a thing. They were now less than three weeks away from the deadline on the property offer.

Both John and Mack worked all morning in the tool barn repairing a three point hitch bracket. They came in for dinner at eleven o'clock. Rollie Leach had just come in from the milking parlor.

"Chicken sandwiches, tomato soup, lemonade. If you behave yourself, then oatmeal cookies for dessert," announced Gertie.

"Ha! No liverwurst sandwiches?" playfully asked Mack.

Rollie chimed in. "You're just too sharp for us, oh mighty Thor. Gertie figures she has to allow a little more time before she can pull another liverwurst trick on a sharp cookie like you."

Mack grunted. "Rollie, you know, I'm your boss and you should be showing me a little more respect."

"This is true Mr. B. But what fun would that be, eh? The season's almost over for me, you know. Heck,

I'm not here for all the money you're paying me. Got to have a little fun with you. That and Gertie's cooking are the only things that keep me coming back."

John went straight to the phone. Charlie Stroud was in his office.

In a manner that was somewhat apologetic John offered the information about the incomplete gravestone. Charlie, on the other hand, was encouraged by the information.

"You did the right thing in letting me know this. I'll follow up on it." He asked John how his sons were doing overseas. They spoke briefly in that regard before hanging up.

When Charlie Stroud first viewed the deed at the Pleasant Springs Town office he, of course, read the addendum, but gave it no weight. Because he had been told by Mack that both Oscar and Margaret Knudson were deceased the addendum had become a moot point. Now, with the revelation that Margaret Knudson's gravestone had no date of death inscribed he wanted to revisit the deed on public record. The most likely thing was that Margaret was buried down south, as had been thought. Even so, it was common practice for a previously engraved headstone to be completed with the date of passing.

The lawyer was able to reschedule the two appointments he had the next day. He drove over from West Allis to the Pleasant Springs Town Hall. The receptionist and Charlie remembered each other from the lawyer's first visit. She was Tom Evans' wife.

"Yes, this is somewhat a family affair here in Pleasant Springs. A pretty low key operation." She gave out with a hardy laugh. "I remind everyone that I'm the only fulltime employee here and that my husband is just a part timer. There's just three of us, Tom, myself and our clerk, Bev Fehlsig. May I call you Charlie?"

Agnes Evans was an engaging person. By the time she retrieved the deed file in question and offered the conference room for him to read Charlie felt right at home.

When a request is made to view a deed of public record it is common practice to require the signature of that person requesting to view. The signatures are on a page that remains a permanent part of the deed file. When Charlie previously signed in he remembered that Gerald Hicks was the only other person to sign the page. This had been no surprise to him. After his wife's passing he had visited the deed file to confirm his father-in-law's note.

The rider was dated January 14, 1937, once again handwritten. This was one month and nine days after the deed had been filed:

> *If either Oscar or Margaret Knudson should determine to prevent a family member from purchasing the acreage sold to Mack Berg they may do so by signing a document stating such.*
>
> *Signed on this day of January 14, 1937*
>
> *Oscar Knudson*
> *Margaret Knudson*
>
> *Notarized on this day, January 14, 1937*
>
> Thomas L. Evans
Supervisor, Pleasant Springs Town
(notary seal) County of Dane
State of Wisconsin
Thomas L. Evans

Charlie felt a charge of intrigue go through him. This would mean nothing if Margaret Knudson was dead, as Mack had said and everyone else had presumed. But with the gravestone showing no date of death it was something to be pursued.

The lawyer then allowed himself a quick smile. He speculated that Oscar may have been less than impressed with his young son-in-law at the time. He may have felt that he needed to have a say over whether one of his family members could buy back the property, be it from the Bergs or the Piersons. Stroud was fairly convinced that this had been Knudson's thinking.

Charlie was anxious to visit the Knudson gravesite, but first he wanted to see Tom Evans.

"I'm expecting him any minute," said Agnes. "But you know these part timers. Just can't depend on them."

Just at that moment Tom Evans came through the door. Although the two had met only briefly months before when Stroud first came in to examine the deed, Evans recognized him right away.

After a hand shake and exchange of greeting Evans immediately chided his wife.

"Did this wife of mine offer you a cup of coffee, Mr. Stroud. She's Norwegian, you know. A little stiff on the hospitality."

Agnes retorted. "Ha! and ya! to you, Mr. Evans. It's a good thing you finally got here. The people of this community deserve a little service. And I think you can call him Charlie."

Back in his office the supervisor was reflective.

"Good people out here, Mr. Stroud. All of Stoughton. All of Dane County, actually. I can hardly believe I've been doing this more than thirty years. The Bergs are great people. What's happening is rotten. I know the date where this Hicks guy can buy the acreage is coming up."

"It sure is," responded Charlie. "But I'm here following up a curious lead. There is a rider to that addendum that says either Oscar or Margaret Knudson could forbid the purchase by one of their family members if they saw fit. It was a rider that you notarized."

"Yes, I'm well aware of the rider. If only old Oscar or Margaret were here now they could put a stop to our Mr. Hicks."

"Sure. But the reason I even bring it up is that the Bergs just informed me on Monday that in the cemetery here in town, at the Knudson gravesite, Margaret Knudson's name is engraved but there is no date of death.

There was either neglect in engraving her death date or . . . she's still alive. I need to follow this up."

Evans leaned back in his chair. He spoke with a tone of resignation in his voice.

"It is the law that a grave marker be completed upon the person's demise, no matter where they get planted. I don't remember her being buried up here and the funeral, no doubt, took place down south. Have you been over to the cemetery?"

"I'm going there next."

"Charlie Stroud, I'd like to go with you, if you don't mind, and then we should go to city hall to check the burial records."

"Exactly," responded Stroud.

Eastside Cemetery was within the Stoughton city limits so, after confirming for themselves the missing death date on the Knudson gravestone, the two men went immediately to city hall. Although Stoughton was considered a small town by almost any standard the impressive city hall was abuzz with activity in comparison to the little Pleasant Springs Town office. Evans was greeted warmly and quickly received permission for him and Stroud to investigate the town's burial records, located in a records room in the building's basement. Here burial records went back to 1852, five years after Luke Stoughton founded the community.

"Mack says that she died twelve to fifteen years ago," said Stroud.

"Yes. Here." Evans handed him the folders containing burial information from 1954 through 58. Evans took the folders from 50 through 53. Within thirty minutes they confirmed that Margaret was not buried in Eastside Cemetery during those years and that there was no record indicating her death and burial somewhere else.

The men expanded their search to adjacent years and still found nothing.

"I do see Oscar's burial record here in fifty-one," said Evans. "It indicates a double wide plot with a double wide ground level headstone with a pre-inscription for 'Margaret Elizabeth Meyers Knudson.' It indicates that Margaret purchased the headstone, including the future cost of her death date inscription. There is no paperwork here stating that Margaret was buried somewhere else."

"Charlie Stroud, it looks like you have yourself a real mystery here. Unless, of course, she's listed in one of the more current folders."

"And that's not likely, is it?" Charlie's words were as much a statement as they were a question. "Any chance you know where the Knudsons retired down south?"

"Yes. I do remember that. They went down to Gulf Shores, Alabama. That retirement community down there where all the Swedes and Norwegians go. Fjordland." He smiled. "I hear it's a real lively place."

23

Rider

Hope springs eternal within the human breast.

Alexander Pope

Late that afternoon Stroud called the Bergs from one of the pay phones in Stoughton City Hall. He informed Gertie that he had some new information to give them. She insisted that he come for dinner.

"Gertie, I don't know what you call this exactly, but it's one of the most flavorful meals I've ever had. With your cooking I don't how these two guys of yours keep their weight in line."

Gertie was up and about.

"They work pretty hard, Charlie. Burn it off, I guess. It's called a New England boiled dinner. Ann found it in a cookbook, years ago. You just throw everything into a covered pot: a small butt ham, whole potatoes, carrots, onion, some celery. No salt necessary. You fill the pot about a third of the way with water and you let it cook on the stove top on low heat. I like it because the cleanup is easy."

She slid a large square of her homemade gingerbread with a mountain of Berg whipped cream under the lawyer's chin.

"Oh, my! You may have to roll me away from this table."

John was emphatic. "You're going to finish that dessert before we talk business. Now, eat up."

After dessert Gertie served more hot coffee. Stroud was a satisfied man. "I may go into a stupor before I can bring you up to date."

They all laughed a little. Over the last eleven months, despite the lack of progress against Gerald Hicks, the Bergs and Charlie Stroud had grown close. This evening was just another example to the lawyer of how at peace with themselves this family was. He had important news to tell them, yet first they shared their supper with him, never asking a single probing question. He himself was a Christian, but he knew of few people who demonstrated the Holy Spirit in their lives as much as these folks. They seemed to have an assurance about things that allowed them to live above the weight of their circumstances.

"I did some digging today. Because there is no death date inscribed for Mrs. Knudson on the headstone, Tom Evans and I checked burial records at city hall. That second addendum, sometimes called a rider to the addendum, just might be important to us after all. We found no record of her passing."

He told them that Tom Evans knew right where the couple had retired to. "I'll make a phone call in the morning and see if they know anything about Margaret Knudson."

John reacted with measured enthusiasm.

"Do you mean to say that Mrs. Knudson could still be alive?"

"That undated gravestone and no paper work in Stoughton's burial records tell us there's a chance she's still alive. The rider to the addendum tells us that if she *is* alive, and wants to deny Mr. Hicks the opportunity to buy the eighty acres she can put a stop to him. Yes, John, that remains a possibility."

Mack was skeptical, emphatically skeptical. "All this is fine, except, but like I said before, Margaret is dead. It was years ago but I remember reading her obituary notice in the paper."

There were a few seconds of silence before Charlie responded. He could have given out with a cliché comment, something like, "We have no reason to doubt your claim, but." However, he knew these people deserved his forthright response. He looked Mack in the eye.

"We have an undated gravestone in Eastside Cemetery and no record of burial there or any other location. I would not be doing my job if I did not pursue this. Now, having said that, we have to realize that she's most likely planted down south somewhere. Tom Evans tells me that this sort of thing happens occasionally. One spouse is brought back for burial then, later on, for one reason or another, when the other one dies the body is not brought back. It's a sorry state that the wishes of the deceased are not granted, but it does happen."

"Heck, she could have been the one to say, 'No, I'd rather be buried down south than back in Wisconsin.' And then there's this: If she is alive she may be in no condition to understand and sign a document forbidding Hicks from purchasing your acreage. We have to realize she'd be well into her nineties by now. Alabama law is most likely similar to ours. As such, a notary is required to sign as a witness. If she is suffering from dementia, or even in a state of physical incapacity, Hicks's lawyers will just bring the notary in to testify as to her condition, making a case for an unacceptable signature."

"Besides, we're assuming a lot here. Old Margaret, if she is alive, may think that Gerald Hicks is as fine as warm bread pudding after a cold supper. She may want her son-in-law to have every opportunity. Hard to believe, but it's possible."

Stroud leaned back in his kitchen chair. He held out his hands in an apologetic gesture.

"I know I've just thrown a collection of negatives at you. I hope my phone call tomorrow has a good result. I'm just trying to be realistic."

* * *

The next morning Stroud called the Fjordland Retirement Community in Gulf Shores, Alabama. He asked if Margaret Knudson was a resident there. If necessary he was prepared to identify himself. It was not.

The bright voice of the receptionist was straight forward and emphatic.

"She certainly is. Margaret Knudson, bless her heart, has been a resident here longer than anyone else. Would you like to speak with her?"

The revelation was so immediate that Charlie came close to stumbling over his own thoughts.

"Uh. Oh. No. No. I have something I need to discuss with her. I'll stop by."

"Thank you, sir. Just a reminder that our visiting hours are from 10 a.m. until 7 p.m., with special arrangements for any earlier or later time. Thank you."

Charlie hung up the phone and tingled with excitement. Just like that he had confirmation that Margaret Knudson was alive and, apparently, well, in Alabama.

He called the Bergs immediately. Gertie was upstairs putting clean sheets on the beds. She made a mad dash down the stairs to the kitchen, picking up the phone on the fifth ring.

Stroud spoke plainly.

"Gertie, she is alive, and apparently well. She is living in the same retirement community where she and Oscar went thirty years ago!"

"Oh, Charlie! That's wonderful news. That's just wonderful. I can hardly wait to tell the men. I'm taking dinner out to them at eleven o'clock. They'll be very pleased."

The lawyer was emphatic. "Gertie, you need to tell Mack that it's vital that he go down there with me. I should have mentioned this last night. When we explain this thing to Margaret she has to be reassured about all this. If Mack is there with me we have a chance of getting her to understand what this is all about."

"I'll make sure he understands." Gertie felt another surge of excitement.

"Charlie, taking a trip like this, such an important trip, will be wonderful medicine for him."

A short while later Gertie set up dinner off the tailgate of the Ford station wagon. The location was under a line of red oaks that separated two forty acre sections at the northwest corner of the farm. She was excited that Rollie would be there to hear the good news. With the Badgers hockey season in its early schedule he was still able to work on the farm now and again.

Gertie held her tongue until John, Mack and Rollie had grabbed their sandwiches and the coffee that had replaced the ice tea and lemonade of the summer months. The Bergs were not in the habit of saying grace at these onsite meals, but today was going to be special.

"The three of you can just hold on a second before you eat. I want to say grace today."

"Our Lord, you have blessed us beyond measure. You have blessed us far more than we can begin to appreciate. We have always enjoyed a wonderful life and even when the occasional tough time comes along we have been fortified by your presence in our lives to help us through the downers. And now, on a day of great excitement like this, we pray that we will have the humility to accept hopeful news with a calm nature and a thankful heart. We bring this prayer to you in the name of our Lord and our Savior, Jesus Christ. Amen."

There was a cautious silence. John peered at his wife; then he spoke guardedly.

"Thank you, Gertie." A few more seconds of silence ensued before he asked, "You mentioned about some great excitement. Is there something that we ought to know about?"

"There just might be." It was difficult not to be a little smug. "Charlie called this morning. Margaret Knudson is alive! In Alabama!"

John, Mack and Rollie stopped chewing at the same time. John, completely on instinct, closed his eyes for a split second and quietly said, "Thank you, Lord."

For a brief moment the news was a blow to Mack's pride. "Alive? . . . How can that be? All this time and I've been wrong?"

"She is down at the Fjordland retirement home in Gulf Shores, Alabama!" Gertie looked directly at her father-in-law. "And you, Mr. Berg, need to be prepared to make a trip down there."

She let her statement sink in.

Mack quickly put aside his pride as he realized the significance of this bit of good news.

"What in the Sam Hill! Just like that? He already found out? Ha!"

"I've heard of that Fjordland place. My sister has a friend from Chicago who's down there."

A questioning look came over his face.

"But what do you mean? I need to get ready to make a trip down there? This is great news, but what do you mean, I need to make a trip?"

"Charlie Stroud says that if we want to have Margaret sign something that puts an end to Gerald Hicks you have to go down there with him. And he's right. She won't know him from Adam. Charlie says that if she's clear enough of mind at all to understand what's going on, she'll need to see you and understand that this is something important."

Mack's face went from curiosity to concern. "Well, I ... wait a minute." His eyes drifted to the ground. "The work we've got right now. I can't leave the farm right now. Look at the work we've got."

John was not surprised by his father's reaction. In a lifetime of working this land and caring for this dairy herd Mack had never been away during the spring, summer or fall for more than a few hours at any given time. He immediately dispelled his father's uncertainty.

"Dad, we just heard some of the best news we've had in some time. We're going to get along just fine while you go down there and see Margaret Knudson. Going down there is going to be the most important work you can possibly do for the farm right now. We've got no equipment problems. Ninety percent of the silage is layered and stored. The Holsteins are happy. You need to go with Charlie."

Rollie didn't mind putting in his two cents worth.

"That's for sure, Mr. B. It'll be tougher than wind sprints on the first day of training camp without you, eh, but John will get along. And I'll get over here if he needs me."

The hockey analogy may have not registered with any of them, but that didn't stop Rollie.

"It's like when you Vikings used to take those boats of yours and sail over to England and Scotland. You know; all that pillage and rape stuff, eh. Only now you're just going south to get a signature. Piece of cake."

Mack couldn't help but crack a smile at Rollie's humor. He said nothing immediately, but, in due time, he responded.

"Yeah, I guess you're right. I'm just a little stuck in my ways." He lifted his gaze to the others and his eyes lit up. He was realizing what a great opportunity was in front of them.

"Ha! We may be able to teach Mr. Hicks a lesson. Ha! This could be great stuff!"

24

Brothers

Blessed is the man who perseveres under trial . . .

James1: 12 (NIV)

The day after the revelation that Margaret Knudson was still alive, Gertie had made her occasional check of the big farm calendar that hung at the head of the basement stairs. With his time in Korea applied to Vietnam she was assured that Johnny had only six weeks remaining in that country. Clark had arrived in Korea in mid-May. He had a long way to go. In either case the news that a signature from Margaret Knudson could spare the loss of eighty acres of the Berg's farm land had buoyed her with optimism for her sons.

In a move of logistical inefficiency all four hundred men in Clark's training brigade from Fort Sam Houston, although trained to be medics, had been reassigned to the infantry. When he arrived in Korea Clark found himself assigned to a unit in the Second Infantry Division. Ironically, that unit had been moved up to the Demilitarized Zone the previous winter, filling the vacuum created when the First Cavalry brigade was sent to Vietnam.

Clark's home was Camp Johnson, named posthumously for James E. Johnson, a Korean War Medal of Honor winner. In front of them lay the DMZ and North Korea. At their backs, on the other side of the hill and down the steep embankment, was the Imjim River.

Korea was even more of a revelation to Clark than it had been to his brother. He began to see how flippant he was to the prosperity and freedom that had always been his. Johnny had given his impressions in the letters he wrote home from Korea, but Clark had been in Milwaukee, in his own world. He had seen only one letter from his brother. He had not paid much attention to it, reading it only as a courtesy to his mother. Now he was seeing for himself what he had ignored from his brother's written words.

At this austere and edgy buffer between the free world and a world enslaved to communist domination it occurred to him that he had been totally ignorant of it all.

He quickly moved to the back of his mind the possibility that he had been unconscious of it all because his world never extended beyond the reach of his small, self-serving realm.

On just his second day in camp, Clark was part of a four-man detail that traveled south to another camp to pick up some equipment for the motor pool. From the back of the two and a half ton truck that they rode in they could see a man working a rice paddy. Walking briskly, he was tipping two buckets of sludge-like material that hung from either side of a wooden yoke balanced across his shoulders.

Clark questioned the soldier next to him.

"What's going on with that guy?"

"Man, I thought you said your old man was a farmer. That's the Korean version of fertilization, man. And you can bet that it's not likely to be animal manure. A few plow oxen and some goats but not much else here. They save their own logs, man! A real John Deere operation."

Clark was also awakened to his own narrow inadequacies while on his first assignment to guard post duty.

The battalion had responsibility for four DMZ guard posts. These bare-bones installations were spaced out roughly a mile apart. They were deep within the DMZ, set back just a few hundred yards from the demarcation line with the North. Each guard post was located on a prominent hilltop that had been denuded of vegetation.

They were about twice the size of a baseball diamond and were surrounded by a twelve foot high chain link fence. Two men inside a wooden hut, manned with binoculars, an artillery scope, maps, and descriptions of Russian-made vehicles and equipment, watched and reported back to battalion HQ any suspicious behavior they observed from the North Koreans. A narrow five foot deep trench snaked its way across the hilltop, connecting the observation hut to a widened out, sand bagged sleeping and eating area for the six other men who rotated guard duty and routine maintenance of the trench.

Guard post duty consisted of a twenty-four hour cycle.

"Where ya'll from, Berg."

Clark had already determined that Ike Spencer, a kid from somewhere in Arkansas, was a backward hillbilly that he in no way planned to align himself with. He answered Spencer, but though he would spend the next twenty-four hours with him on this hilltop he made a conscious effort to distance himself from any sort of friendship.

There was a soft, warm rain during the day. That night the humid spring air was ripe for mosquito activity.

"I've never in my life seen mosquitos like this. This repellant is strong enough to take my skin off, but these things are the size of birds."

Clark's frustration had him lacing his comments with oaths. He and Spencer, having just been relieved from sentry duty, were slouched against sandbags in the sleeping area.

Spencer took his time replying. "I reckon this here is bad as I ever seen when it comes to mosquitos. But . . . I reckon we can make it through to daylight."

In the dim light that was provided by the kerosene lantern Clark could see that Spencer's face was as red and swollen with bites as his own. Yet the hillbilly kept his misery to himself while Clark realized he had been a whiner.

In the next couple of days, back at Camp Johnson, Clark came to realize that Ike Spencer had shown a great deal of maturity that night on the guard post. It was a maturity that Clark found lacking in himself.

By October the bite of the morning chill warned of the bitterness of the Korean winter that lay ahead. Clark Berg was forced to do something that had always gone against his nature. He had to suck it up. He had to gather the discipline to accept the bleak days ahead. He hoped he had gained enough grit to face the numbing temperatures of the coming Manchurian clipper.

* * *

In Vietnam, the Army's First Cavalry operated outside of Bien Hoa, a city only twenty five miles north of Saigon. Because the Division was so mobile – helicopters and armored personnel carriers – they had a large range and were often used to help other units that needed assistance. Johnny had seen fighting a few times. Twice his troop had the harrowing experience of close-in combat. He knew he would never forget it and he decided it was something that he would never want to talk about.

His gift of calm served him well on a number of occasions, but none more so than on an afternoon in August.

His platoon had engaged the enemy along a wood line when the man just ahead of Johnny was struck in the neck by a bullet. Fortunately it was a glancing strike, just missing the carotid artery, yet the initial impact was so immediate that Johnny saw blood squirt out a distance of ten feet. He made his way forward and applied one of the sterile bandage pads that every soldier carried. Within a few seconds the bandage was soaked in blood as the wounded man heaved in pain and panic. Amid shouts by others for the platoon's medic, Berg had the wherewithal to find and apply the wounded man's bandage. It, too, soon became a sopping, useless mess. By now another soldier had come forward and, at Johnny's instruction, continued to keep pressure on the wound with his bandage. Berg stripped off his equipment and fatigue shirt. He took off his undershirt and rapped it as tightly as he dare around the wounded man's neck. This slowed the blood flow enough to buy some precious seconds. As the medic approached two minutes later the shirtless Berg was so smeared with blood that the medic's initial impression was that it Berg who was wounded.

The stricken soldier survived.

* * *

The two brothers exchanged letters about once every three weeks. Johnny would say that the incessant heat and humidity were not good, but there was a certain beauty about such a tropical place. He wrote about the good things back home: how he missed the farm, the four seasons, hot water and home cooking. He wrote how rapidly things were changing: the two of them gone, grandma now passed away, how they might lose the eighty acres. He wrote about Elsie growing up. She would be out of high school and probably into college before they got home. That is, if mom and dad could come up with the money to help her go to college.

He wrote about Jenny. He told Clark about how great she was and about how they planned to get married when he finished his time in the Army, how the two of them looked forward to carrying on the work of the farm.

He encouraged Clark. He told him how there was a law that said employers had to take back service men when they returned to civilian life. Not that he would need the law to get back his job. He heard from mom that he had been doing a fine job at the radio station. And he told him that somehow, some way, their experience in the Army was going to help them. He thought the experience would help Clark in his career at WWMR. He would probably be able to stare down Uncle Frank when he got back. No more intimidation! Ha!

One afternoon, as Clark read these things, one of the others could see the amused look on his face.

"What gives, man? Good news from back home?"

"No. No, it's my brother. Can hardly get a word out of him back home. Now he's in Vietnam, writing me like there's no tomorrow. Except for our dairy farm he never says much about anything, yet he gets a pen and paper in his hand and all of a sudden he's a big time communicator."

Clark thought a moment before thinking out loud with more.

"I've been a little tough on him over the years for being square around the edges, but . . . for sure he does have some certainty about what he wants when he gets home. Gonna marry his girl, work the farm. He's always been that way. Always figured that no matter what hurdles are out there things are going to work out okay."

Clark wrote back:

These people live in such poverty and I've just taken for granted what we have back home. Freedom is big-time important to them and I've never given it a thought.

Clark was also careful to ask Johnny not to indicate to their parents that he was stationed on the DMZ:

I know it sounds kind of silly compared to all that's going on down your way, but I've not told them back home that I'm up on the border. They have enough to think about with your situation.

A turning point for Clark occurred on his first trip to the "village." After four weeks at Camp Johnson he was given his first overnight pass.

In this sparse land an overnight pass meant only one thing to anyone who wanted to get away from camp. It meant an overnight at the "village." For soldiers on the DMZ the village was Munsan. It was the first settlement south of the Imjim River. Amongst the little buildings that hugged the road in the village were bars with dimly lit back rooms of prostitution. For a trifling of money an American soldier could satisfy his urges.

Clark wanted to get away from the isolation of Camp Johnson. He was curious, and from what he heard from some of the others he could have a good time. He and two others rode the Army bus into Munsan. They entered one of the bars and they were each immediately approached by a girl. The one that latched onto Clark could have been as young as 15, though her occupation had aged her face markedly.

In her broken English she immediately asked him if he wanted to go to the back room for, as it was called, a "short time." Clark hesitated and she suggested he buy them a beer. It was the worst beer he had ever tasted. A far cry from Milwaukee's finest.

Within a few minutes he knew that this was not for him. He thought of the faithful relationship his mother and father had to each other. He thought of the two sexual experiences he had in high school. They had satisfied his curiosity and his immediate urges, but afterward they had been meaningless. He had thought he would feel a sense of bravado, but in both instances he felt a bit sheepish. Now, how much more pathetic would this be. For two dollars he could have his way with a girl he didn't know and didn't want to know. Her few English words allowing her to ply her trade.

It was embarrassing because his buddies were right there with him, but he excused himself. He walked out and caught the next Army bus back to camp.

* * *

Back home they noticed a change in Clark. His letters spoke of how he was beginning to appreciate things more. They could see that his eyes were being opened.

He apologized to them for, as he described it, "a lifetime of snotty behavior." He wrote that he wanted to live differently when he got home.

Gertie, the woman who always had such control over her emotions, suffered tears of joy when she read these things.

25

Fjordland

. . . but those that hope in the Lord
will renew their strength.

Isaiah 40:31 (NIV)

Two days after Charlie Stroud's call to the Fjordland Retirement Community he and Mack were on their way to see Margaret Knudson. It was the 18th of October. It was essential for them to obtain her signature without undue delay. The mandatory sale to Gerald Hicks was set for October 26.

They journeyed south in the Berg's sedan, a 1962 Dodge Duster. They were able to travel on the fairly new I-65 interstate highway, stopping overnight in Nashville, Tennessee. It was the first time Mack had done any long distance travel on the interstate system. It rained the last two hours before reaching the city and now it poured buckets as they secured a motel. Mack began to relax. He began to realize how little his own world extended beyond Berg Dairy Farm.

"What's so funny?" The lawyer was wondering what had Mack smiling as they brought in their bags.

"Oh, I guess I haven't been out and around much. It's just the way the clerk talked at the front desk. 'Yawl' and 'I reckon.' Just different words than we're used to up north. Anyway, it's Gulf Shores for us."

"That's it, Mack. We're half way down there. Before we get to Mobile we cut off and head straight down along the water to Gulf Shores. It's right at the bottom of the state. Right on the water."

They arrived in the late afternoon, settling on a motel four blocks up from the shore. It was about half the price of the places along the water. They would wait until the next morning to visit Margaret Knudson.

Across the street from the motel was a Waffle House restaurant. For dinner Mack enjoyed two of their large waffles, eggs and plenty of coffee. For Charlie it was a continuous battle with his waistline. He had a bowl of what the menu called Grandma's Grits, plus a fruit cup and coffee. Mack made an observation.

"I've got to give you credit, Charlie. You said you were on a diet, but Grandma's Grits and a fruit cup? For supper? I guess that's fine discipline. Or maybe it's like a friend of mine, Skorpie Johnson says, 'your taste buds are drifting through the sewers of life.'"

"Anyway, I've got to admit that I was kind of looking forward to eating out a bit on this trip, just for something different, but it gets old pretty fast. I miss that home cooking."

The lawyer may not have heard the part about home cooking because he had begun to chuckle. He lowered his head, his chin on his chest. His shoulders began shaking from a soft laughter that he did his best to muffle. After a full minute of this he raised his head. He had tears in his eyes.

He started to repeat the expression he had just heard from Mack but before he could get half way through he returned to more muted laughter. In an attempt to mask his loss of control he put his right elbow on the table and rested his forehead in his hand. Another minute passed before Charlie could take some deep breaths and regain his composure. He had gotten sufficiently watered up.

"Your taste buds are drifting through the sewers of life? That's not bad, Mack."

Mack took it with hardly more than a quick smile. "Are you up for a walk down to the water? We've been cooped up in that car for two days and my legs need a good stretching. I've never seen the ocean. It can't be as nice as Lake Michigan, but what do you say we go take a look?"

By now Charlie was under control. "Sure, Mack, but I have to ask you. Who is Skorpie Johnson? I mean, where did the name Skorpie come from? It must be a nickname."

"Oh, yeah. He's Harold Johnson. Been a friend of mine since we were kids. His mother made some of the best Swedish cardamom coffee bread you could ever want. Skorpie loved his coffee bread. He'd eat the whole loaf at one time if his mother didn't stop him."

The two men began their walk, but Charlie's question had not yet been answered.

"Okay . . . but I don't get why you call him Skorpie?"

"Oh. Yeah. You see, when a loaf of coffee bread starts to get old and dried out you put it in the toaster and let it get good and toasted—sort of burnt. Then you slap a mountain of butter on it and eat it with plenty of coffee. Sometimes you just dunk it right in the coffee. Softens it right up. It's called a skorpa. Don't know where the name came from. Anyway, we started calling him Skorpie. The name stuck."

As Mack finished his explanation a questioning look came to his face. "Now, with the Johnson's, I really don't know. The way Skorpie ate the stuff I don't think they ever had any to get old. Ha!"

The street led straight down to the water. It was lined with a blend of retail shops, restaurants, small offices and motels. There were also groupings of three or four elegant old two and three story homes, mansions in their day. They had been built by the wealthy from Mobile as ocean retreats from the heat of the city.

Just two blocks from the beach the men came upon the gated entrance to a group of well-kept buildings. A somewhat weathered looking, hand carved, wooden sign stood next to the gate. The countries that form Scandinavia were chiseled out and painted. The words, also chiseled out, said:

**WELCOME TO OUR LITTLE CORNER
OF HEAVEN ON EARTH
Fjordland Retirement Community**

"Looks like we found the place, Mack." Stroud hadn't bothered to look up the street address yet, but now they had walked up upon it. He read aloud from a small plaque next to the sign.

> *This retirement facility was built by Edgar Olmstead. Mr. Olmstead was a bank financier from St. Paul, Minnesota who, with his wife, each year enjoyed a retreat from the cold winters of the north to the sunny skies of Gulf Shores. In 1925 Mr. Olmstead brokered a financial arrangement that created this facility. Construction began in 1926. Fjordland Retirement Community officially opened in October, 1928.*
>
> *Mr. Olmstead was born in Skive, Denmark and felt an affinity with all of Scandinavia. He named this facility for the rugged coastline of Norway.*

"Looks like this is the place." In an uncertain voice Mack added, "Sure hope Margaret can help us out tomorrow."

26

Margaret

We have some salt of our youth in us.

William Shakespeare

The next morning Mack and Charlie approached the woman at the receptionist's desk of the Fjordland Retirement Community. She received them with the same bright, friendly voice that Charlie had heard when he first telephoned the place.

"Yes. Margaret is here and I'm sure she would love to see you. She is such a joy. She hasn't got any family left to visit her, yet she is one of the shining lights at Fjordland. Always in a good mood, always doing what she can to cheer up other residents. I will have her escorted into the community room where you can meet her. Oh, and yes. You should speak to her a bit loudly and distinctly. She has hearing aids, but still has a bit of trouble."

As they waited for Margaret in the community room both men were occupied with the same thought. Was Margaret Knudson really as well off mentally as they were being led to believe? Would she remember Mack? It had been thirty years. Would she be sharp enough to grasp the Berg's plight and be willing to help them?

Margaret arrived presently. She was accompanied by an aide, but was managing on her own with the help of her walker. Before acknowledging her visitors she centered herself with her back to an easy chair and eased herself down.

The aide gave a short introduction.

"Margaret, these are the men who have come to see you."

She had yet to look up, but now shifted her gaze to the aide. "Thank you, dear."

Mack and Charlie were still on their feet as Margaret looked to them. She offered not even a flicker of recognition, but she spoke with humorous self-deprecation.

"I'm a little slow, boys. I need to sit down. These bones of mine need all the help they can get."

She looked quite amazing for a woman in her nineties. She had shrunk a little from when Mack knew her, but still maintained a frame that a woman twenty years her junior could be happy with. She wore large, fairly thick glasses through which her marvelous blue eyes shown. Her pure white hair was done in curls and once she felt situated in her chair a bright smile of greeting lit up her face.

She spoke slowly, in measured rhythm, but other than a slight tremor her voice was clear and strong. "Well, this is a pleasant surprise. I have so many wonderful friends here, but it is so seldom that I receive visitors." There was mischief in the smile. "You are not from the tax man, are you?"

They all chuckled as the men sat down. It was Charlie who responded.

"No, we're not from the IRS." He paused, then continued, still smiling kindly but with a more serious tone. "Mrs. Knudson, you don't know me, but this man here is an old friend of yours."

Margaret shifted her gaze from Charlie to Mack. She stared hopefully, but without immediate recall. But as soon as she heard his gravelly voice she showed a flicker of recognition.

"Hello Margaret. We've come some way to see you. Do you remember me?"

Stroud had suggested to Mack that he give her an opportunity to recognize him before he introduced himself.

She raised her hand to her mouth as though trying hard to pull out the name of the man now seated before her.

"Oh dear. I just . . ." She reached out her left hand toward him. Mack extended his arm and she grasped the back of his weathered hand with a firm grip. "Ann. Ann. Dear, sweet Ann."

Mack almost melted. She could not quite come up with his name, but she remembered Ann. He gently squeezed her hand.

"Ann passed away a short while ago. She's gone to be with the Lord, just like Oscar."

"Oh my, yes. How wonderful for them." She held on to Mack's hand with a determined strength as her mind searched to come up with his name.

"Oh, my. Wisconsin. How young and strong we all were. I just. I just can't . . ."

"It's Mack . . . It's me, Margaret. It's Mack Berg."

"Oh, my. Oh my goodness. Mack and Ann Berg."

Tears streamed down from her eyes. She glanced at Charlie Stroud as though to say, "Do you realize who this is? This is our old neighbor. This is our old friend, Mack Berg."

For the next hour-and-a-half Margaret did an amazing job of remembering the past. She spoke of how Mack's father and mother, Gus and Ruth, had been such a help to her and Oscar after they bought their farm from Oscar's uncle.

Her thoughts came slowly, but with amazing perception. She could not quite come up with the word Depression but she spoke of how everyone struggled through "the hard times between the wars," yet how fortunate they were as farm people who never lacked for food. She even recalled details of Mack's wedding to "dear, sweet Ann." How the Steingirds were so pleased to see their granddaughter marry Mack.

As her mind continued to reach back she recalled how special Saturday nights were, taking their two girls into Stoughton where they would all enjoy just walking along Main Street, being amongst the people. How much it meant to them, after the isolation of the farm all week. And then Sunday morning. They too, were Lutheran. The four of them, being able to be there together in church. She recalled how at that time she thought those days would just go on forever.

"Tell me, does Axel still have his bakery?" As she asked this of Mack she turned to Charlie, speaking slowly, but quite distinctly. "When Oscar and I came down here we so missed Kronberg's. There is nothing here like Axel Kronberg's bakery. Just a marvelous place."

"A lot of years have passed, Margaret," said Mack. "Axel died some time ago, but John, his son, has carried on the business wonderfully. Hasn't changed any of the old favorites."

Since coming to know the Bergs, Charlie had become familiar with the bakery and could honestly report his delight with the establishment. "I agree. I've gotten to where I can't come to see the Bergs without stopping there for something. It's a wonderful place."

All of a sudden Margaret drifted off a bit, just for a second or two. Her body clock seemed to remind her that lunch time was approaching.

"Won't you both join me for lunch? It would be such a treat to show you off to my friends at the table." The thought left her fairly beaming.

At lunch Margaret went on at length about her life in Wisconsin. Although some of the others at the round table were in different stages of mental decline the elderly seem to have a special ability to communicate with each other. She spoke haltingly, and in a volume not always audible to everyone, but still, Mack, Charlie and everyone else were well entertained by her memories. A full hour passed when, again, her sense of routine kicked in. She repeated the thankful comment she had made when she first welcomed Mack and Charlie.

"I have so many wonderful friends here but it is so seldom I get visitors. I always rest after lunch. Will you come back and see me sometime?"

"That is a kind offer, Margaret," said Mack. "If you feel able right now we want to take a minute to explain something to you. Could we go back and sit for a few minutes?"

Her face took on a serious look that indicated a concern about disrupting her routine. "We should go back to my room."

Margaret did not ask what brought Mack and his friend down to Alabama to visit with her. As can happen with the elderly, even those doing as well as she, time and location can lose their context. She just saw them as visitors casually stopping by to see her. Returning to her room she struggled with her walker, obviously getting tired. Once in her room she plopped into her wheelchair. Fatigue had her staring blankly, straight ahead.

Now Mack brought up the name of Gerald Hicks.

"I want to ask you about something, Margaret. Your son-in-law, Gerald Hicks, wants to buy some of my land. Oscar and you sold some of your land to me when you retired. Do you remember that?"

Margaret's expression took on a frown. Her fatigue seemed to fade. She paused for a number of seconds between sentences, but she made her point.

"Gerry." She shook her head negatively. "He is not a nice man. How poorly he treated our Greta. He never wanted any children. Greta wanted to have children. He just made up his mind. He would just work, work, work. But not like on a farm, where you work so hard, but you are right there with your family. He left Greta alone."

She grasped Mack's hand. "Did you know my Greta died? She died some time ago. He didn't even tell me until after. He called on the telephone and told them here, after she was buried. I would have wanted to be there. Gerry never told me."

Margaret was now visibly shaken. Her fatigue came back upon her. Mack and Charlie both realized that the moment to explain the need for her signature would have to wait. They helped her out of her wheelchair and into bed. She fell off to sleep immediately.

For a few seconds Mack stood at the bedside, looking down at this woman and feeling how rapidly all the years had passed. "Life moves along quickly. Life moves along real quickly."

Charlie knew that Mack was speaking as much to himself as he was to him. He just nodded his head in agreement.

The lawyer now felt it was important to speak to Fjordland's administrator. He needed to explain the purpose of their visit and to learn if a notary were easily available if Mrs. Knudson was willing to sign a statement regarding the second addendum to the deed.

Mrs. Betty McCallum, Fjordland's administrator, made herself very accessible.

"Yes, it's a notary that you want, Mr. Stroud. We have occasion for a notary from time to time and I should have no trouble having someone here this afternoon."

"You will also need a second witness. Someone here from the home who can testify later, if the need arises, that the resident was in no way coerced into signing anything. I would be happy to witness the procedure."

Mrs. McCallum paused, as though not sure to continue.

"It should not be my place to add a personal comment, but I must say that I am not surprised to hear that Margaret's son-in-law, Mr. Hicks, is trying to take advantage of this situation. He was less than compassionate with Margaret when her daughter died. All I mean is that he never informed her until after the funeral. Even then, he refused the opportunity to speak directly with his mother-in-law. He told me on the phone that he would send a copy of the death certificate. Margaret would not have been up to the trip to Chicago but . . . can you imagine? It seemed very callous not to let her know immediately about her daughter's passing."

At this point a lesser man than Mack might have jumped all over the opportunity to smear Gerald Hicks. He simply said, "Yes, we're hoping to put a stop to him."

As the two men left the building Mack asked Charlie to hold on a second. "Could we sit on this bench for a minute?" There was something on his mind.

"Ever since you found out that Margaret Knudson was still alive I have been trying to figure out how I thought I saw her obituary all those years ago. Now I understand. It was her daughter's obituary. It was Maggie. I guess I read it and somehow thought it was Margaret. Do you know how close I was to messing up everything? Me being so sure and telling everybody that she was dead. If it hadn't been for that gravestone." He was looking down now, shaking his head.

Stroud could see that Mack was showing doubt in his own mental capacities.

"That could happen to anyone. What's it been, fifteen years since the daughter died? And the same first name. You can bet that the obit listed her as Margaret, not Maggie. The important thing is we are here and hopefully she is willing to sign our document. And I'll say this. She's none too pleased with Hicks. And . . . she remembers the Bergs fondly."

* * *

Later that afternoon they returned to Fjordland. With Betty McCallum and a notary officer in attendance Mack explained the entire situation to Margaret. She was now well rested. She listened attentively as Charlie Stroud read:

> *I, Margaret Knudson, expressly forbid Gerald Hicks from purchasing the eighty acres of land sold by Oscar and Margaret Knudson to Mack and Ann Berg on December 5, 1936, unless Mack Berg, or a member of his family to whom said land is*

187

bequeathed, is willing to sell said land to Gerald Hicks.

I acknowledge that my signature to this document is in direct knowledge of the addendum inclusive to the deed of sale of property to Mack and Ann Berg on December 5, 1936. This addendum was filed on January 14, 1937.

I, Margaret Knudson, being of sound mind, do put my signature to this document on October 18, 1966.

After reading, neither Mack nor Charlie said anything to make the document more meaningful to Margaret. They hoped she could grasp its meaning without what might come across as a condescending explanation. It was a wise decision, for Margaret Knudson had always been a woman of independent spirit. Now, even in her advanced years, she retained that spark. If she needed an explanation she would ask for it. She not only understood the document read to her, but she was amazingly insightful.

"I am glad Oscar included this in the sale of the farm. He must have known what the years allowed us to understand. Gerry Hicks is not a good person. Oscar must have realized he needed to have the last say."

She looked at Charlie Stroud and her eyes danced. "Only now it is me that gets the last say."

She reached out to receive the paper. She was given a pen, but hesitated long enough to look over to Mack. With a subtle smile she said, "We can't help but get old, Mack." She pointed to her heart. "At least we can stay young here."

Mack and Charlie stayed with Margaret for the next hour. She spoke one moment about her life in Wisconsin and the next about her life at Fjordland. In both realms she said her life had been blessed, "mightily blessed," as Pastor Keil used to say.

The two men had come down to Alabama, hoping to acquire a signature from an elderly woman from Mack and Ann Berg's past. They were about to leave with a great deal of admiration for her. Margaret Knudson was a shining example of optimism and thankfulness in the closing years of her life.

As the men began to leave Mack asked her, "Margaret, did you and Oscar ever make that visit to Norway? I remember now. It was one of the things you wanted to do when you retired."

"Oh, my goodness! Yes. That was something we wanted dearly to do." She thought for a brief moment. "We waited too long. Oscar started feeling bad and it just seemed to go on for years. Before we knew it we were unable to go."

She struggled to put another thought together. She looked at Mack with that twinkle in her eye and spoke with good humor. "We have happy hour here. I think the closest I ever got to Norway was a bottle of that Finlandia Vodka."

The three of them shared a good laugh.

27

Rollie

*The man of integrity walks securely
but he who takes crooked paths will be found out.*

Proverbs 10:9 (NIV)

Mack and Charlie were excited that evening. They had Margaret Knudson's signature in hand. They would leave for home first thing in the morning, but tonight Mack insisted that they celebrate. He wanted to buy dinner for his lawyer. He said it was going to be someplace fancier than the Waffle House. Right down on Ocean Shore Drive they found a Howard Johnson's nestled amongst the elegant high rise hotels.

"No Grandma's Grits for you tonight," he told Stroud. They both enjoyed a straight from the Gulf of Mexico shrimp dinner.

The next morning they left for Wisconsin. When they arrived in Chicago about noon the second day Mack found a pay phone and called the farm to share the good news.

"Gertie, we're in Chicago and we should be home shortly."

"Tell me, Mack Berg, did you find Margaret in good spirits? Don't you dare keep me in suspense."

Mack gave his rumble of laughter and teased a bit. "Sure have been missing your cooking. What's for supper tonight?"

"You know better than to ask. In fact, if you want any supper at all you had better not keep me in suspense. Was Margaret Knudson able to help us?"

Mack gave his daughter-in-law the good news.

"Oh, Mack! Mack that is such good news. I can't wait to tell John. You get home quickly and you come hungry. And you tell Charlie Stroud to come hungry. He's not getting away from here until he has supper with us."

Gertie took out twelve links of her homemade brats from the Kelvinator's freezer compartment. It was one of John and Mack's favorite suppers. With a small amount of water she slow cooked the sausage in a covered pot with carrot slices, green beans, diced onion, salt and pepper. Enough of the juices from the sausage leeched into the water to create a light translucent gravy full of flavorful vegetables. She served this with boiled potatoes and big slabs of her warm homemade bread and the Berg's fresh churned butter.

This was Rollie's last day at the farm until next spring. He, of course, eagerly joined the celebration dinner.

That evening, as they all gathered at the dinner table, John gave thanks.

"Our Lord, you have given us a verse in the Bible that says: *And we know that all things work for good to them that love God, to them that are called to His purpose.* We are grateful how things are working out. But each of us here needs to realize that things work out on your schedule, not ours. When things do not work out the way we think they should we ask for the wisdom to trust you; to know that you are still there for us. Amen."

It was a special time around the table. They were confident that the good land that they cared about would remain intact. Both Gertie and John thought about their boys and how much they would have liked them to be here, sharing these moments with them. They both also thought how good it was to have Charlie Stroud and Rollie Leach sharing their table.   It was good to know that family could extend beyond those who were united by blood.

Desert was simple and delicious. Vanilla ice cream with homemade chocolate sauce. The ice cream was made with the Berg's fresh cream and had bits of real vanilla bean in it. Charlie Stroud's dieting campaign once again lay in shambles.

"I need to get this Gerald Hicks business resolved. I can't lose any weight as long as I'm around you Berg people." Everyone laughed. "Gertie, that was most delicious."

"I'm glad you enjoyed it. Now . . . tell us, what do you need to do to settle things with the court?"

"I'm going to present our document and my copy of Oscar's addendum to the court clerk as soon as I can get an appointment, either tomorrow or the next day. I expect to get a phone call soon after that. The judge will convene a hearing with Mack, John, myself, Mr. Hicks, and his lawyers. At that time he will present Mr. Hicks with some bad news."

None of the Bergs gave a haughty response to Stroud's words. It was just not their way. Rollie, on the other hand, was willing to be smug for all of them.

"Oh, I'd love to be there to see the look on that chap's face when he gets the news. And what's this? You say he didn't even tell Mrs. Knudson when her daughter died?"

Rollie had more to say. It took him a second to work up his nerve, but he caught everyone by surprise. He spoke without his usual bravado.

"We boys had a Sunday School teacher back in Hespeler. He was one of the hockey referees in town, too: Mr. Fraser."

Rollie cleared his throat. "We were kids, maybe thirteen, fourteen years old. Over the years I had been mad at him a few times on the ice. For sure, every kid who ever played hockey was mad at the refs from time to time. But he taught us something in Sunday School class that I've always remembered. He had a Bible verse he wanted us to remember. In fact, he was wise enough to write it out on a three by five card for each of us. He told us to put it to memory; then find a place to keep the card so we would always have it and never forget the verse. It was Psalm 34:4: *'I sought the Lord and he answered me, and delivered me from all my fears.'* I've still got that card . . . somewhere."

It became perfectly quiet.

The Bergs knew Rollie had a good heart. They knew him to be trustworthy and unselfish. He had never demonstrated a self-serving bone in his body. But in the nine years they had known him they never heard him speak of any relationship with the Lord. He had never mentioned any church background. Although he had always shown a great spirit of optimism and seemed to enjoy just being alive, he never once said anything to them that confirmed to them that he was a Christian.

Rollie declined to look at anyone around the table. He was showing a vulnerability and a shyness that was foreign to him. Rollie Leach was anything but a shy man.

"Anyway," he paused to compose himself. "Anyway, that verse . . . I think it fits the Bergs."

He let out a deep breath. "You folks are a God fearing group. And you have a way about you. I mean, you don't seem to get excited or panicky when things go wrong, eh. It's like you have this strength that carries you through things. Anyway . . . that Bible verse makes me think of you."

They were all surprised to hear these things from Rollie, but also there was a realization that in some way, over these last nine years, maybe their behavior had served as a witness to him. Charlie Stroud heard these words and knew they conveyed the very thoughts that he felt about the Bergs. It was he who broke the silence.

"I say, Amen to that."

Elsie got up from her chair and walked around to Rollie. She was seventeen years old now and turning into quite an attractive young lady. The no nonsense feistiness she showed as a youngster was still a part of her. She put an arm around Rollie's neck and kissed him on the cheek.

"Didn't know hockey players could go that deep."

Rollie's face turned a bit red. "I'll have to go deep more often, eh!"

* * *

Five days later Charlie Stroud and Mack and John Berg were in court in front on Judge Theodore Stillwell. Gerald Hicks and his two lawyers were there.

Though Judge Stillwell had advised Gerald Hicks's lawyers by phone of the document now in hand that prevented their client from acquiring the eighty acres, Hicks insisted on the hearing.

No amount of posturing or indignation on the part of his lawyers could sway Judge Stillwell from the obvious decision. The whole farming community around Stoughton—with the exception of Midwest Agra—was gratified by the outcome of this land dispute. In his final statement on the matter the judge couldn't help but add a dig toward Hicks before slamming down his gavel.

"Based on the signed statement from Mrs. Margaret Knudson you are forbidden from purchasing the property in question, as per the second addendum to the deed in question."

The judge folded his hands together and looked directly at Hicks. "Mr. Hicks, you live by the letter of the law and you die by the letter of the law. This case is closed."

28

Family

preoccupied: absorbed in thought; engrossed

American Heritage College Dictionary

The days immediately following the court decision were a special time. The Bergs had spent the last few months thinking of all the adjustments the farm would have to make for the loss of eighty acres.

John canceled the sale of the eight cows to the two neighboring farms. In both of those cases the farmers were grateful that the Bergs had put a stop to Gerald Hicks and the inevitable sale to Midwest Agra Group.

For Mack the discovery of Margaret Knudson's undated grave marker, the trip to Gulf Shores and the eventual court decision had, indeed, been a good tonic for him. He was much better able to deal with his grief. As he had done when he last visited the cemetery his inner voice went to speaking to Ann in an uplifting way as he went about his daily work. If his mental state regarding Ann could be called daydreaming it was daydreaming in a healthy way.

This relief from so much concern allowed Mack to better grasp other thoughts. He realized, more so than at any other time, the dangerous situation his grandson Johnny was in.

This revelation hit Mack just two days after the court decision. He and John had the weigh scales set up near the milking parlor where they were logging each Holstein's weight. This ongoing record—as well as the

Babcock milk test to ascertain butterfat content—gave the dairy farmer the best indications of their stock's health.

Mack was aware his daughter-in-law was out behind the house when he told John to hold on, he would be right back.

Gertie was outside hanging laundry on the clothesline. Two years previous she and Ann had bought an automatic dryer, but she still liked to hang bed sheets, pillow covers, and towels outside. It was a chilly, but blue-sky October morning. She knew that as the sun got higher there would be plenty of warmth to dry the sheets with a freshness unmatched by the dryer.

Mack startled her from behind. As she whirled around she had two clothes pins clenched in her teeth and a look on her face that said, "Now what in the world to you want?"

Some may have seen the humor in the moment, but Mack only saw the daughter-in-law to whom he felt he owed an apology.

Gertie quickly took the clothes pins out of her mouth. "Not like you to be prowling around here at this time of the morning. Dinner won't be for another hour."

Mack stepped straight up to her. "Gertie."

He stood there for a second or two with an apologetic look on his face. Gertie responded with half sarcastic-half dramatic, "Yes, Mack."

She then put her hand to her chest, just below her throat, in a gesture of surprise. She tried hard not to laugh in her father-in-law's face, instead managing a question.

"Well, what in the world is wrong with you?"

Mack did something that was out of place for him. He gave Gertie a hug.

He backed off and Gertie looked at him with wide, wondering eyes. She still wanted to laugh, but did not dare. "Why Mack Berg, what has gotten into you?

The senior Berg retreated a step or two. He spoke in his rumbling manner. "Can you forgive a guy who's been lost in his own thoughts?"

Gertie was at a complete loss to know what he was up to.   They stood there, motionless, for a good five seconds before she responded with a frustrated sounding, "What?"

"You and John have two sons on the other side of the world. My grandsons. One of them is in the middle of a war and here I've been involved with my own concerns and you've gone right along doing your best to help an old bird like me. Ann is gone and I'll probably never get used to that, but what's important now is those two young men of yours. Of ours. I've been selfish in my own thoughts. I know you probably don't think of it that way, but it's true. I have been. The most important thing in the world to me right now is the safe return of those two boys. Those two young men."

Though Gertie had been stunned it was only for a few seconds. Her response was firm. "Now, what's this all about? Mack Berg, you've not been selfish "

She stopped for a second to gather her thoughts. "A big part of what goes into those boys comes from you. They are strong and I know we can be proud of their performance.   We may never know what they are experiencing, but I know they are well grounded, and much of that comes from their grandparents. Oh, I know Clark has been a handful at times, but I can see in his letters. I can see that he's growing up."

Mack took a deep breath. He knew his daughter-in-law would always be straight with him.

Gertie folded her arms. "Now, back you go to the scales. You've got more animals to weigh. And I need to get in the kitchen and put some dinner together for you and John." She spoke commandingly but was really doing her best to hold back her emotions.

With that Mack turned to go back to the milking parlor, but he stopped short.

"What's for dinner?" It was his way of accepting Gertie's response and putting an end to the conversation.

"Last night's ham, escalloped potatoes and tomato soup."

She hung her last item on the line and went into the house. In the kitchen she worked in slow motion for several minutes as she pondered the conversation that had just transpired.

29

The Marsh

Let your light so shine before men . . .

Matthew 5:16 (KJV)

Young John Berg continued to find himself very much in the crosshairs of war.

Coastal Binh Dinh province was the 1st Cav's designated area of responsibility, with its massive base outside of the town of Bien Hoa. The Division's mobility continued to subject them to providing help in many other places. As such, officers' map reading and communication skills were severely tested. If a comfort zone could ever be achieved in Vietnam—knowing landmarks, understanding the vagaries of streams and rivers, learning the temperament of one village compared to the next, and other essentials of warfare—such a comfort zone was most difficult to achieve for the 1st Cavalry Division.

For A Troop, 3rd Battalion, 2nd Brigade it was no exception. Johnny Berg and his fellow soldiers found themselves in unfamiliar and dangerous situations a number of times. Berg had his moments of complaints and frustration, but he continued to perform admirably.

Earlier that summer he had received a letter from his father telling him of the passing of his grandmother. John Senior left most of the writing to Gertie, but when his mother died he felt a strong need to inform both of his sons himself. Johnny had prepared himself to receive this news, but he still had some difficulty with it. His initial reaction was one common to most people. He felt that if he were home he could have made a difference. But the feeling did not last long. He had seen young men in his troop, even his own platoon, die. This proximity to death snapped him back into reality very quickly. Besides, as Tom Bradley reminded him, he had not chosen to be away from home.

Bradley and Berg's friendship only got stronger over the weeks and months. Bradley had admired his friend's demeanor in Korea and now it was the same in Vietnam. Bradley knew that when the platoon was in a tight spot Berg was scared, just like the rest of them, but he had an ability to control his fear. He had an ability to think clearly. In their time together Bradley had rarely seen his friend show any sign of panic. And he never showed a sign of a self-serving attitude. He thought that Berg was, at one and the same time, the toughest and most self-effacing person he knew.

Each in his own way Berg and Bradley were affable with, and well-liked by, their fellow soldiers, even though they refrained from some of their buddies' recreational pursuits. Having a friend of common scruples made it a bit easier to resist the vices that were so easily available to the American soldier.

While on KP duty one morning in June Berg was challenged by one of the young men who saw his quiet nature as an easy target. As was customary for those who had finished their KP assignment, the six workers sat together to eat their own breakfast.

"So Berg, what's a guy like you do for fun back on the farm? Do they have any senoritas back there, or maybe you get your kicks squeezing the teats of those cows? Hell man, all this time, in Korea or here, I haven't seen you check out the action yet."

Johnny seethed inside, but he did not have a ready response. Alberto Cruze sensed easy prey. He continued to prod.

"Hey, man. The good thing about these women here, you don't even have to sweet talk them. That should be cool for you man, since you don't ever open your mouth. Hey muchacho. Two bucks and it's all yours."

"I'm not much of a ladies' man, Cruze. I'll leave that up to you."

"Sure man. Hey, I like you Berg. I'll tell you what. You come down to Florida when we get out of this hell hole and I show you around, introduce you to a few ladies."

In deference to Johnny one of the others deflected the talk to another subject.

It was not an easy moment for Berg.

* * *

It was in mid-August, on a night of extreme anxiety, when Johnny Berg came face to face with his Christian witness.

At this time A Troop had been on a 1st Cav fire base seven miles from the Bien Hoa installation. These fire bases were manned by a troop size unit, about a hundred and twenty men in this case. Every seven to ten days this troop unit was rotated back to Bien Hoa. From these fire base locations patrols were sent out to probe the surrounding area.

John Berg and Tom Bradley's platoon, thirty- two men strong, were humping five miles back to the fire base in the late afternoon of one such patrol. As the two track dirt road they were on descended to low ground they were cut off by a force of Viet Cong or North Vietnamese regulars, they knew not which. They were forced to take a defensive posture. Because of the lateness of the hour the Americans knew they were in trouble. The enemy had learned that by forcing the Americans into a standoff at night it was difficult, almost impossible, for helicopters to aid a unit in trouble. Such was the case here, for by the time the patrol realized it was surrounded darkness had closed in. They called for assistance and were advised to hold their position. Helicopter gunships would arrive at day break.

The men hastily dug in for the night, forming a defensive circle about one hundred and fifty yards across, with the narrow dirt road intersecting the circle. As per their training the men set up in pairs.

It was a long, dark, humid, mosquito-infested night of terror. Three attempts by the enemy to breach the thin circle were made and repelled.

Johnny shared a position with the man ahead of him. It was none other than Alberto Cruze. The foxhole they scrambled to dig was nothing more than a soupy depression in the marshy ground.

They were as different from each other as the worlds from which they came. Cruze was a kid from the Puerto Rican community in Jacksonville, Florida. As he had previously shown in the mess hall two weeks earlier he was never hesitant to try and promote his image with a cynical worldly attitude. Now he was plenty scared.

As the night wore on Cruze became increasingly desperate. In his heavy accent he whispered to Johnny. "Hey, man. What the hell is with you, anyway? Mr. Cool. Yeah. Mr. Cool. Man, aren't you afraid of dying out here in the mud on the wrong side of the world. They told me you are like, the ice man. Well, Mr. Cool, you and me are maybe gonna get blown away before we see daybreak. What the hell is with you anyway?"

Cruze mumbled some oaths to himself, becoming more panicky by the minute.

Johnny said nothing for about five minutes but he was becoming acutely aware of something. He realized he had been brought to this time and place for a reason. He realized that if there ever was a time when he needed to verbally express what it meant to know the Savior that time was now. Maybe he showed his Christianity by how he lived but he had never spoken of his faith. Ha! People could hardly get two words out of him on any subject. Now, here he was, realizing that if anyone ever needed to hear from him what it meant to be a Christian it was the young man that now shared this miserable spot with him. He had asked, "What the hell is with you anyway?"

He was now almost as scared about what he should say to Cruze as he was in facing those who were trying to kill them.

"I'm no expert on things, Cruze. All I can tell you is that the difference in me is Jesus." Johnny was watching his field of fire as he spoke, then he turned to look at Cruze.

Alberto Cruze lay on his side in the low depression; his helmet off, his hands pressed to the sides of his head in confusion and fear. As soon as Berg spoke Cruze looked up and the two young men stared at each other for about ten seconds.

Cruze spoke with not only a frightened, but a confused tone in his voice.

"What the hell you mean, man?"

Johnny pulled his thoughts together as best he could.

"All I know are two things. Whenever and wherever I leave this world I'm going to Heaven cuz Christ took on my sin when he gave his life on the cross. And while I'm here in this world He's given me a peace I know I wouldn't otherwise have. He's right there with me. Every step of the way. Every day. Just like the Bible says."

Rifle fire erupted on the far side of the perimeter. Both men kept vigil on their field of fire until Cruze eventually flopped back down into the depression. After a few minutes his nerves were settled enough to speak.

"The Bible? Man, the Bible. That's for the priests to read, man."

"I'm a long ways from reading the Bible every day Cruze, but no, that's not right. It's there for everybody. You and me. Everybody."

Cruze could only respond with a long, "Maaan."

At daybreak helicopter gunships arrived. The enemy was severely punished and they soon withdrew. The men loaded their three dead and five wounded into the choppers. They then humped the remaining distance to the relative security of the fire base.

Berg and Cruze never spoke about these things again.

* * *

During this year of 1966 America's involvement in Vietnam continued to increase. Though he spoke mainly of home and of their future in his letters to his fiancée, Johnny Berg began to show his frustration:

Dear Jen:

> *We are doing the best we can to accomplish the day-to-day things they tell us to do, but I have no idea of how it all fits into the grand scheme of things. There is no front line here. We seem to gain a foothold over here while we lose it in another direction. It is hard to know if the people here like us or hate us. The best we can hope for is to get through what we are supposed to do in the day at hand, even if we don't see the progress of it . . .*

Yet in the coming days political movement in the "grand scheme of things" would have an effect on the Berg family that no one could have imagined.

30

Advice

> *we also rejoice in our sufferings*
> *because we know that*
> *suffering produces perseverance;*
> *perseverance, character;*
> *and character, hope.*
>
> *Romans 5:3, 4 (NIV)*

In Korea Clark suffered his own battles. After his mosquito-infested experience on the guard post he vowed to better handle the frustrations of whatever would confront him. His second operational assignment was stakeout patrol. From the sound of it this duty did not sound too bad. He was advised, "Hey, Berg. You better dress warm, my man. It gets cold out there at night."

Clark was not impressed by the advice he received as he geared up alongside an experienced buddy for what was sometimes called an ambush patrol.

"You've got to be joking. It must have been seventy five degrees out there today. It's nearly the middle of June."

Clark learned another lesson that night: if you're given reasonable advice, take it.

Each night, at different times to avoid establishing a predictable pattern, at least one patrol of from eight to twelve men from each company were trucked out along the barrier road that ran parallel to and just outside the edge of the Demilitarized Zone.

The men were dropped off and they walked into the DMZ. The patrol leader found a location that he thought to be adequate and the men set up in a circle; keeping a low profile, they would face outward and remain as still as possible. There they sat on the ground from four to eight hours, depending on the orders they had been given. The idea was to surprise North Korean agents as they tried to infiltrate South Korea, or as they attempted to return north.

Three hours into it Clark knew that he should have listened to the advice given him. As he sat there on the damp ground he began to feel the effects on his body of a heart at rest. He tried numerous subtle movements to create some circulation. They were of little help because his body temperature had already gone down significantly.

Throughout that night the North Korean messages of propaganda spewed out from the huge loudspeakers embedded in their mountains. Sometimes in broken English, usually in Korean, the eerie messages spoke of the "murdering American imperialist pigs that occupied our homeland. People of the South, unite with us in one mighty communal workers party."

When, after seemingly endless hours, the patrol got to their feet and walked to the road to rendezvous with the truck, Clark felt precious warmth flood through his body.

Despite the frustration of that night he never made an issue of it. He had learned his lesson from Ike Spencer.

* * *

In his letters home Gertie was uplifted to feel the change in Clark. A letter received in late September was especially encouraging.

Hi everyone,

Hope everyone is doing fine. I know I have said this before, but this is a strange, strange place. When the North Koreans broadcast their hate messages from their mountain loudspeakers it can be heard for miles down the peninsula. They sometimes speak in English. They say we are a bunch of colonial occupiers that are preventing the two Koreas from uniting. They say that we are a bunch of war mongers in Vietnam and that if we don't leave Korea we will be responsible for reigniting the war here.

Sometimes in the morning we find propaganda leaflets scattered on the ground. Some are written in Korean, some in English. Hard to believe, but they send up hot air balloons that are timed to drop these leaflets. If it wasn't so pathetic it would be funny.

Gertie paused her reading of Clark's letter, marveling at her son's description of the propaganda, wondering how anyone could think dropping such leaflets would be effective.

Staying busy is the thing that is keeping me from climbing the walls. Being right at the border, doing the surveillance things we do, helps the time move along. Special Services brings a movie and projector about once a month, so that gives us something to look forward to. I've taken up reading a little. Twice the Doughnut Dollies showed up. These are girls from the Red Cross who bring us some decent coffee and some doughnuts. We sit there and talk to and look at American women. Ha! The Army makes sure we don't have a chance to get too friendly with these girls. They are gone before nightfall.

You might not be too excited to hear this, but the thing that helps me most to pass the time is playing poker. Don't worry. I learned my lesson during my first month here when I lost my whole month's pay. Since then I've found a nickel, dime, quarter game that I can live with.

I know I have said this before, but I can't get over how different these people have to live compared to us back home. They are miserably poor and yet they consider themselves so lucky because they are free. In North Korea they have even less and their lives are dominated by the communist government. I've learned that they all work for the good of the state, that the government controls everything.

I used to snicker at how dad would just take time to stare out at the farm and say he was grateful for what he had. I get it now.

When I get frustrated here about this place I think of Johnny and how I know he's got it a whole lot worse than me. It helps me realize this is not so bad.

Home next spring.
Clark

* * *

As October gave way to November, Clark was determined to mentally fortify himself against the coming winter.

On Monday, October 31, Clark spent nine hours on a daylight patrol in the DMZ. He knew this to be good duty: cake duty or getting over, as the guys called it.

The ten man patrol humped this ghostly land that had been frozen in time when the buffer zone was first created thirteen years earlier. They passed the occasional extinct village where the forces of nature had not yet completely removed the signs of human life: collapsed thatch-roofed domiciles, iron pots and primitive plow blades, stone fences barely visible through the tangle of thorny bramble that had long ago grown up through them.

What Clark did not know was that events taking place during the previous week, events far beyond his control, were to have consequences for him and some of his fellow soldiers.

31

Hatred

Moreover, no man knows when his hour will come . . .

Ecclesiastes 9:12 (NIV)

During that summer and fall of 1966 public pressure continued to mount against the Vietnam War. In late October President Johnson traveled to Manila to meet with South Vietnamese leaders. During his visit Johnson made an unannounced fly-in to Vietnam. He inspected the troops at the American installation at Cam Rahn Bay. With Vietnam Commander General William Westmorland at his shoulder he exhorted the troops to "nail the coonskin to the wall."

After completion of the conference in Manila the president traveled to South Korea where he met with President Park.

The president's excursion into Vietnam and his trip to Korea incensed the North Korean communists. The regime in Pyongyang held little influence in the worldwide court of public opinion so their vocal objections to the "American imperialist pigs" drew scant attention. They knew only one way to make an effective statement against the Americans. That statement was through violence—and they knew just how far they could push.

It was now Tuesday morning, the first of November. Clark had some maintenance duty to perform that morning and then he would have the afternoon off. It was that evening that he was not looking forward to. He was assigned to go on stakeout patrol.

He had learned his lesson back in June. The cool fall temperatures felt refreshing during the day, but he knew the duty that coming night would be bone chilling.

That night the eight man patrol met in Company B's armory and briefing hut at 2200 hours. Clark locked a magazine in his M-14 rifle, stuffed additional magazines in his belt pouches, clipped grenades on his harness straps, and wedged a couple of flares inside his canteen belt. He wore long johns, fatigues, field jacket with liner, flak jacket, winter overcoat, and finger access mittens. The old reliable Army pile cap kept head and ears warm. He and the other men put aside their combat boots in favor of their "Mickeys." These were rubberized, insulated boots developed during the Korean War that looked like Mickey Mouse's shoes. When a soldier was moving the insulation created a great deal of heat within the boot. As they sat on the ground soldiers learned to wiggle their toes to maintain at least some warmth.

As per usual the briefing was conducted by the lieutenant who was on charge of quarters duty that night. On this night he was Lieutenant Randy Jones. Jones had been at B Company for two months. Amongst themselves the men had gotten to calling him Lieutenant Fuzz. He was a graduate of the Army's rugged Ranger School, but his idealistic attitude and his peach fuzz baby face earned him his nick name.

On the map of their sector of the DMZ Jones indicated where the drop off point would be. Tonight's patrol would set up just outside the DMZ. The lieutenant reviewed the radio identification password and radio calibration was established with battalion headquarters. Berg was relieved to see that John Benton was on the patrol that night and had been designated by the patrol leader to be RTO, or radio-telephone operator. Benton had grown up in Concord, North Carolina. He was quiet and unassuming. He took his work seriously. He reminded Clark of his brother.

Jones then went through the litany of do's and don'ts that was standard procedure during these briefings. No smoking, no talking, no standing once in position, no squelch on the radio, avoid often used locations, circle formation only, rifles on safety and no early arrival at the pick-up rendezvous.

Clark had heard it all before. This was now his twelfth stakeout patrol. But he had learned to take the instructions and warnings seriously. On just his third patrol there was an incident that taught him to take nothing for granted.

It was sometime past midnight when the men on Clark's part of the circle heard movement about fifty yards out from their positions. The moon was crescent that night, offering just enough light to make things eerily visible. For three minutes the men sat crouched or lay prone, frozen in their positions. When movement finally occurred again the two soldiers next to Clark opened fire. They rattled off six rounds each before stopping. They all immediately heard the sounds of an animal writhing in pain. Wild boars roamed this deserted land and they had just shot one. It was that three minutes of apprehension that stayed with Clark. It was enough of an experience that he never approached these patrols flippantly. Some of the others around him may be willing to compromise the patrol, but he disciplined himself not to be one of them.

It actually made him shake his head and give himself a little smile. Clark Berg, the family rebel. The one with no discipline. The good time Charlie who never thought about the consequences. Now here he was, taking his responsibilities seriously.

Lieutenant Jones told the men what they were most interested in hearing: the duration of the patrol. The length of the stakeout patrol varied to avoid creating a repetitive pattern. The operation could last from four to eight hours. "Rendezvous at 0500."

The young men groaned. They figured it would be 2300 before they would be dropped off. They would be out there for six hours.

At 2230 hours, while President Johnson slept at the Walker Hill Resort near Seoul, Clark Berg and the other seven members of the patrol were trucked out to their drop-off point. The patrol leader was in his tenth month in Korea. He had proven himself to be a good soldier, well disciplined and unwilling to join the others when the inevitable gripe sessions took place. He was only nineteen-years-old but well experienced in these patrol operations.

The patrol leader and three others had been on stakeout patrol just two nights before. It was an especially cold night for the end of October. There was a steady rain all afternoon and into the evening. A short time into the patrol the wind came up and the rain turned to snow.

Now it was just two nights later and these men were in no mood to freeze again. Fortunately the weather on this night was clear and calm. The moon was almost full and offered good visibility.

North Korean agents that were sent into the south were not average soldiers. These men were highly trained, highly motivated, politically indoctrinated career soldiers. These soldiers were the ones who had made an assassination attempt on South Korean President Park late that summer down in Seoul. The attempt failed. In the aftermath a number of the assassination squad engaged in an hour long gun battle with Park's security force and South Korean soldiers before being killed. North Korean agents possessed a hatred for South Korea's democracy and the United Nations soldiers that occupied the country, especially the Americans. They were trained to kill.

At some time after 0200, North Korean agents attacked the eight man patrol. PFC Benton got off a brief message back to battalion headquarters, saying the patrol was under attack. The radio operator at battalion later testified that weapons fire could be heard during the message. The attack was brutal and cold blooded. When troops arrived, including the battalion commander, they found some of the men shot many times, as though the North Koreans stood over the bodies and continued to fire. Some corpses had also been bayoneted. Some had fingers cut off where it appeared the North Koreans had taken the men's rings.

Miraculously, there was one survivor . . . it was not Clark Berg.

Seventeen year old PFC David Bibee was wounded in the leg and the shoulder when a grenade exploded; knocking him into semi-consciousness.

He managed to stay alive by playing dead.

The United States was engaged in a war in Vietnam. At the same time it was helping to hold together a thirteen year old truce in Korea. Now North Korea, in an effort to show its hatred for America, in an effort to show its seething resentment for the American president's visit to Vietnam and South Korea, had attacked and murdered a U.S. Army patrol performing routine nighttime surveillance in the DMZ.

Within a few hours radio bulletins announced the incident. Soon newspapers, via the international news agencies, carried the story around the world.

"Just hours before President Johnson left Seoul for home today at the end of his Asian journey, six American soldiers and one South Korean soldier of a United Nations Command patrol were ambushed and killed by North Koreans . . . This is the most brutal slaughter of American soldiers in the region since 1953.

". . . the Communists charged into the United States patrol lobbing grenades, firing submachine guns, finally engaging in a savage hand to hand combat . . ."

". . . the Communists fired a fusillade of bullets into the bodies of the dead Americans. They also bayoneted the corpses many times."

". . . The Americans fought back fiercely. One of those on the patrol, who had arrived in Korea only 17 days earlier, will be nominated posthumously for the

Congressional Medal of Honor. There was only one survivor of the ambushed patrol. He was only seventeen-years-old. Wounded by grenades he escaped death by playing dead. He said, 'The only reason I'm alive now is because I didn't move when a North Korean yanked my watch off my wrist.'"

The North Koreans had successfully ambushed an American ambush patrol. It was tragic and embarrassing for the U.S. Army. For the Johnson administration it was infuriating and frustrating. The United States could not afford a military response in Korea. For the families of the dead it was shocking. Their young men had been sent to Korea. They were safe, away from the fighting in Vietnam, or so they thought. Now six American families were going to receive the awful news. One was a family of dairy farmers in Wisconsin.

* * *

When the incident took place at 2:30 a.m. Wednesday morning in Korea it was 11:30 a.m. on Tuesday at the farm. John and Mack had been working diligently the last few days harvesting corn. The weather cooperated wonderfully. The corn was as dry as a bone and would layer well and store beautifully. Both men were confident their Holsteins would eat well this coming winter. Early that morning they worked in tandem to complete the last remaining partial section of corn. Their timing was good for a driving rainstorm began just as they put their crop and their tractors under cover.

With the hard rain pounding heavily on the barn roof the two men spent the remainder of the morning in the repair barn, doing some ongoing work replacing the brakes on their old, but still reliable, Allis-Chalmers. The tractor was in semi-retirement now, used only occasionally in place of one of the Masseys.

It was dinnertime. The wind was blowing the rain in a torrent as the two men came up the steps of the back

214

porch. They left coats and muddy boots outside, under the cover of the porch overhang.

"I'm so hungry I could eat the horns off a billy goat," said Mack as he and John went directly to the kitchen table.

Gertie did not look up from the fried egg sandwiches she was preparing. "That sounds like something Skorpie Johnson would say. That man's full of more nonsense expressions than anyone I know."

It was John who answered. "You're right on both counts. Dad stole that one from Skorpie." He looked to his dad. "What's he call it when it's raining like this?"

Mack had a bit of an annoyed look on his face as he could again see that he would get no credit for any of Skorpie Johnson's old folk sayings. "He says it's raining pitchforks and billy goats."

"Soup and egg sandwiches," announced Gertie. "Oatmeal cookies if you behave yourselves." She slid the sandwiches and the steaming bowls of her homemade cream of celery soup under their chins.

John squeezed her arm. "Wouldn't the boys like to be eating like this right now!"

Gertie quickly returned to her counter work, but looked over her shoulder at her husband.

"Well, it won't be long for Johnny. His thirteen months will be up at the end of November. That's just four weeks." She spoke with a tone of resignation in her voice that proclaimed a certainty for his safe return. She stopped her busy hands and turned to the men. "I know how Johnny will be when he gets home. Same old Johnny. But I know Clark will be different. I mean changed. He's grown up a lot. I know from his letters that it will all be for the good. You just watch and see."

At that very hour Clark was fighting for his life.

32

Bucci and Becker

Bless'em all,
the long and the short and the tall.

Vera Lynn

That evening Gertie was putting the finishing touches on supper. As was her practice she had the family's Philco radio dialed in to WWMR. The station's strong signal came in just fine from Milwaukee. At five o'clock the network newscast originating from New York came across the airwaves.

Gertie was so used to hearing the daily report on U.S. casualties and enemy body counts from Vietnam that she almost missed the broadcast's lead story.

> *Five hours ago along Korea's Demilitarized Zone North Korean soldiers attacked an American night stakeout patrol that was performing routine surveillance. Six American soldiers and one South Korean soldier attached to the American Second Infantry Division unit were brutally attacked sometime after midnight. Though wounded in the leg and shoulder from grenade fragments one soldier survived the attack. Not since the fighting was halted in 1953 by the uneasy truce, had as many as two American soldiers died in any one incident.*

As soon as Gertie heard the words Second Infantry Division uttered her hands stopped their work. The radio had her full attention.

In Tokyo, Eight Army Commander Dwight L. Beach gave a formal press conference regarding the incident.

He stated that at approximately 0230 hours last night a Second Infantry Division patrol was attacked without provocation.   The patrol was operating within the constraints of the Joint United Nations-North Korean Armistice Agreement.   The general said the attack was conducted by North Korean government agents.

Beach said that military commanders on the ground in South Korea have informed him that all indications show that the attack was premeditated. He indicated that this was not a random encounter of U.N. Forces and North Koreans but that it was a purposeful attack by specially trained North Korean agents who came across the border and attacked and murdered an American patrol performing routine surveillance just south of the Demilitarized Zone. The general said that the American patrol was well south of the demarcation line between North and South Korea and that six American soldiers and one South Korean soldier were killed in the encounter. He indicated that one American soldier, though severely wounded, survived the attack.   Beach had nothing more to report at this time.

Gertie's eyes widened as she stood perfectly still, listening. The network newscast continued.

Reporting from the president's location at the Walker Hill Resort near Seoul, South Korea, press secretary Bill Moyers said that the president will speak to the nation over the radio and on the television upon his return to Washington tomorrow regarding what he has described as a very grave development on the Korean peninsula.   The press secretary said that American, South Korean and other United Nations troops stand ready to counter efforts of aggression by North Korea.

As always the Pentagon will not release the names of those killed, pending notification of next of kin.

Gertie closed her eyes right there at her kitchen sink. She whispered a short prayer for the families of those lost in this attack and she prayed for Clark and the other American soldiers in Korea.

John and Mack would be in for supper in thirty minutes. She spent that time continuing to get supper ready and thinking about how her faith had taught her to understand and submit to God's perfect will. That was not always an easy thing to do. She felt a chill across her back. What if one of her sons was to die?

Gertie kept the radio on while she, John, Mack and Elsie ate supper. A short recorded message from President Johnson was soon played. His statement was made from the tarmac at Kimpo Air Base before he departed Korea. His speech mirrored the comments of his press secretary, adding nothing new.

"He sure sounds tired," remarked Mack.

John let thirty seconds go by before saying anything. "They all age quickly, that's for sure. Especially one leading a highly criticized war."

The president made no mention of the specific unit that suffered the attack, saying only that it was a Second Infantry Division unit. Because Clark never told them he was on the DMZ the family believed him to be safe, as long as full scale hostilities did not break out.

"Those young men, their families. What a shock this is going to be for them. I'm grateful Clark is not right on that border." Gertie looked for reassurance, while at the same time making a firm statement.

Mack immediately offered the comforting thought. "We've got fifty thousand troops there. Clark's okay."

* * *

In Vietnam Johnny heard the news at seven o'clock that morning.

Along with his partner he was on perimeter guard duty during the night in a sand bagged bunker along the fence line at the 1st Cavalry's big Bien Hoa base.

Their replacements arrived at dawn.

"Good chow, Berg. French toast, bacon. Eggs too, if you want 'em."

It was eighteen year old Andy Becker who informed Berg about breakfast. He was a skinny wisp of a kid who had volunteered for the Army right out of high school.

Johnny gave an affirmative head shake to acknowledge the scouting report on breakfast. His guard duty partner, however, had plenty to say.

"Becker, where are you from?"

Johnny gave himself a little smile as he knew Sal Bucci was going to give Becker an earful.

"Parsons, Kansas." Becker answered with an expectant look at the worldly Bucci, ready to humbly accept whatever he said.

Bucci peered directly into Becker's face. "Do they ever feed you people out there in Parsons? No matter what the mess hall shovels on your plate you seem to think it's good. Becker, where I come from we wouldn't feed army chow to a dog. And you talk like it's the best stuff you've ever eaten. Do you know where I'm from, Becker?"

By now Andy Becker was staring at the ground, doing a slow burn at the humiliation being inflicted on him. His country Kansas upbringing hadn't prepared him to joust verbally with the likes of Sal Bucci. He stood there in silence.

Bucci was tall and muscular. He had the swarthy complexion and dark flashing eyes of his Mediterranean ancestors. Always with the dark shadow of a beard, even just an hour after a fresh shave. He was good looking by any standard and, no doubt, well experienced with girls. His black hair was cropped closely now, but back in New York it was undoubtedly a thick, wavy magnet for the opposite sex. He was twenty, only two years older than Becker, but light years more worldly.

"Queens, my friend. Queens, New York City. My mother cooks like you wouldn't believe. I could stand here and give a list of her specialties that would make you drool."

"I'll tell you what, Becker. When we get back to the world you come to Queens and I'll see that you get plenty to eat. And it won't be that hayseed chow you get out in hicksville. Plenty of mama's good cooking and I'll take you out to eat, too. On me. Restaurants where you won't even understand what's on the menu."

Bucci stared at his prey while announcing his departure. "Come on, Berg. Let's get out of here. We've got to get some of that good French toast before it's all gone!"

The two soldiers began to walk back to their company area. They hadn't taken but a few steps when Bucci let out with a quick laugh and a smile. "Becker. He's a good kid."

Johnny smiled to himself. He, like Becker, was unprepared to do verbal battle with someone like Bucci. How could he run roughshod over a kid like Becker and then consider it just a bit of humor? It made Johnny realize, all the more, how different they all were.

"Hey, Berg." Johnny instinctively wheeled around. Andy Becker's partner had caught up with them. "Thought you'd want to know. Some guys got waxed up in Korea. DMZ. It was on the radio. I know you said your brother's there. Thought you'd want to know."

Johnny felt immediate anxiety. Before heading to the mess hall he made a deliberate and speedy trip to the tent that served as barracks for the platoon that he, Tom Bradley, Bucci and Becker were a part of. He needed to get to the radio that he and Bradley had bought.

The tent that the men called home had wooden slats that kept the mud at least partially at bay. The Troop's generator provided electricity. Between Berg and Bradley's cots a produce crate they had scavenged served to hold two reading lamps and the radio they shared. That radio served as a link to home. The one English speaking station they could receive was Armed Forces Radio in Saigon. The music, the news from home and the letters from home program—where girlfriends, wives and parents in the States sent song dedications to their young men—were all meaningful. Back home such simple entertainment would hold little interest. But here, half way around the world, knowing the threat of death lurked just outside the Bien Hoa compound, any time on base in the company of the radio was considered a luxury.

But now Berg was listening for the news he had just been told about. Many of the guys in his unit had arrived since the brigade left Korea. News of seven soldiers killed in Korea meant little to them. In Vietnam they were surrounded by the prospect, and sometimes the reality, of death on a daily basis. From a geo-political standpoint those who had been stationed with Johnny in Korea surely understood the gravity of such an incident but, other than the fact that they had served there, they had no emotional attachment. But Clark was there, right there. Johnny had lost his appetite for breakfast. He now found himself in a condition foreign to him—he was in a state of worry and tension.

He stuck by the radio, waiting for the hourly newscast.

In Korea, just eight hours ago, an American patrol of the Second Infantry Division, serving under the United Nations peace keeping authority, was attacked in the Demilitarized Zone. Six American soldiers and one South Korean soldier were killed in the encounter. There was one survivor. The attack took place at approximately 0230 hours Korean time, which is two hours ahead of us in Vietnam. This was the most flagrant incident involving American troops to occur on the Korean peninsula since the truce between North and South Korea was implemented thirteen years ago. We have no further details at this time but we have been told that a press conference detailing the incident in the DMZ will be forthcoming

*from either Second Division headquarters or from
KMAG headquarters in Seoul sometime this morning.*

Johnny thought of Clark one minute and his family in Wisconsin the next. He could not now relax until he knew which unit had taken the hit. He knew that it was Clark's regiment, but he needed to know that it was not Company B, 1st Battalion.

Ten minutes later Tom Bradley came into the tent. He had been on a work detail. One look and he could see the apprehension on his friend's face. "What in the Sam Hill is bothering you?"

He got no response.

"I've known you for more than a year and I've never seen you with a worried look. Am I now to believe that you are human like the rest of us, that something is actually bothering you?"

When Johnny could give him only a blank expression Bradley tried a little humor.

"Hey man, what's going on? Did one of the Holsteins die back home?"

That got a little puff of laughter out of Johnny. He went on to explain what he had heard on the news.

Bradley did an immediate mathematical analysis.

"Okay, I'm reckoning the regiment that took our place has about seven hundred line troops. So there's about a one in seven hundred chance that your brother was on that patrol. Now, I ask you, are not those pretty good odds that your brother was not involved?"

Bradley, always expressive with gestures, held out his hands, palms up, in a way of saying, "am I not right?"

But then both men immediately realized the miscalculation.

"There were eight guys on the patrol, Tom. That makes the odds less than a hundred to one." Johnny threw back his shoulders. "I need to find out what battalion and what company it was. Clark's in B Company, 1st Battalion. If it's not them, then I'll know he's okay."

33

Kringla

But thou, O Lord, art a shield for me;
my glory, and the lifter up of mine head.

Psalm 3:3 (KJV)

Berg Dairy Farm was ready for the coming winter: field harvest was in, silage for at least the next sixty days was layered with four different grains so that the cows would receive maximum nutrition. Blood samples from each animal in the herd had been taken and sent to the vet's for routine analysis.

The Bergs had come to call this day where they felt they had met the necessary time table for the winter months as kringla day. For years Ann, and now Gertie, baked a traditional Norwegian almond kringla pastry dessert for the supper meal. It was the family's own small tradition; a day of thanking God for another year of blessing on their land. The need for equipment and building maintenance would be ongoing throughout the winter as would the need for the twice daily milking sessions; but today was a day that they slept in and allowed themselves to relax for the entire day.

So on that morning, the third of November, a Thursday, Mack assumed his Sunday routine. While John and Gertie slept and Elsie caught the bus for school he walked out to the mailbox to retrieve the *Madison State Journal*. The November sun was just making its appearance on the horizon when he returned to the house and found his easy chair in the parlor. More often than not Mack would get no more than a paragraph or two read before his head tilted to one side or the other and he was softly snoring. But on this morning the headlines held his attention. The incident on the border between the two Koreas filled most of the front page. The headline story concerned the political fallout. A sidebar article addressed the nuts and bolts of the actual incident as it had been pieced together by U.S. Army authorities.

Mack Berg was not a man easily disturbed, but when he read that the Second Division soldiers killed were part of B Company, 1st Battalion, 23rd Infantry he was stunned. He had read all the letters that both the boys sent home and he had written to them a few times. He had an uneasy feeling that the unit mentioned looked familiar. He sat motionless for a good ten minutes.

Gertie kept the letters from both of the boys in an informal pile in a corner of the kitchen counter. Neither Mack nor John asked her why she didn't file them away somewhere for safe keeping, but they both rightly suspected that just seeing them sitting there in a pile was a source of comfort for her. Besides, the kitchen had always been Gertie and Ann's domain and they knew better than to question anything that went on there.

Mack knew he had to check the return address on one of Clark's letters to see if it matched the unit mentioned in the paper. He finally stood and walked into the kitchen. He hadn't felt this much weakness in his being since the day Ann died.

PFC Clark Berg
Co B, 1st Batt, 23rd Inf
APO SF 31, California

The unit designation was exactly the same.

He stood there with his hands on the counter, leaning into it. Mack was never eloquent of tongue but he closed his eyes and prayed aloud.

"Oh Lord . . . Keep our Clark safe, Lord. We are so blessed to have those two young men. Bring them both home safely to us. I know that when we leave this world we're going straight to your loving arms, but please Lord, let these young men live to know the joy of the love of a woman and children before you take them. Amen."

Mack sunk into a kitchen chair and stared again at the newspaper to be sure he had seen the unit designation correctly. He looked back and forth, from the paper to the return address on the letter. He then thought about the notification of next of kin. Could it have been accomplished yesterday? He hoped so. But what did he know of such things? He then gathered his thoughts and began to think pragmatically. He reckoned the odds that Clark was on that patrol were fairly slim. But even as that thought calmed him down he decided to put the paper out of sight. There was no point in giving his son and daughter-in-law unnecessary concern.

Later that morning Mack kept his invitation to have noontime dinner with Skorpie and Esther Johnson. As time permitted Mack's friend had been working on a project in his basement and the two of them planned to spend the afternoon doing just that. To Mack's delight Esther promised to make one of his favorites, meat pie. It was a specialty of hers that Mack and Ann had enjoyed a number of times over the years.

He did his best to ease his mind about the welfare of his grandson. He, as it is said, put it in the Lord's hands. He did not mention it to the Johnsons.

John and Gertie spent the morning in town. They strolled up and down Main Street with no particular objective in mind. This was a rare activity for Gertie and something almost unheard of for John. His visits into town consisted of church on Sunday and the occasional trip to the hardware store, the implement dealer, or the feed store. They treated themselves to lunch at the Koffee Kup restaurant. John had his eye on a chocolate milkshake to go along with his food, but Gertie swayed him.

"Go ahead and have your milk shake if you want, John Berg, but I've made something for you back at the house."

He looked at his wife knowing full well that she wasn't going to give him any more information, but he questioned her anyway. "We're having kringla tonight, aren't we?"

She gave him an expression of mock frustration. "Yes, John, we are having kringla tonight. That's no surprise. I said I have made something for you now."

John chuckled to himself but said nothing more about it. He forgot about the milkshake and settled for coffee.

They returned to the house under heavy gray clouds and high winds. Once in the kitchen Gertie revealed one of her husband's favorites. She had made him a Boston cream pie, the two layered yellow cake with vanilla pudding filling and dark, semi-sweet chocolate icing. This was indeed a decadent day for John Berg.

At about three o'clock there was a knock at the front door. John was upstairs in the bedroom in a comfortable chair which he used for the few moments of reading that he allowed himself. Like his father, it actually became a contest between reading and dozing off to sleep. Gertie was in the kitchen taking mental notes on what she needed to buy the next day at the grocery store. Even the self-sustaining Bergs bought their share of store items. She hurried to the door and when she opened it there stood two men in military uniform, an officer and an enlisted man. Gertie's heart caught in her throat, but in the split second that followed she refused to believe they could be there with bad news.

She stared at them for a good five seconds before cautiously saying, "Yes?"

The officer, a captain, responded. "Yes, ma'am. We are from the Army's R.O.T.C. program at the University of Wisconsin. Is your husband home?"

When she heard that sentence Gertie knew for certain why these men were at her doorway. They all stood there awkwardly for the next ten seconds. She then gave a slow affirmative headshake and, without further word, leaving the men on the porch with the door open, she retreated to call for John.

Gertie walked to the stairway that she had climbed a thousand times before. She ascended only three steps before sitting. She made no attempt to call her husband for more than a minute. As she did her best to pull herself together a desperate hope came to her. She knew the Army would give notification not only when a soldier died, but also when a soldier was missing. Missing in action they called it. She did not know if the Army used the same notification procedure for missing in action as they did for killed in action, but in these terrible seconds she clung to the possibility that they did. Finally, she raised her head and called John's name.

In all these years of marriage John had never heard his wife's voice sound so strange, so weak. She was the most forthright person he knew and now her frail sounding voice drew his immediate attention as he strode to the staircase.

Gertie rose to her feet as she heard her husband coming down the stairs. She always looked people straight in the eye when she spoke, but now she failed to raise her eyes.

"There are two men at the door." She then raised her head and grasped John's arms at the elbows as hard as she could. "They're from the Army."

He grabbed his wife to him. He knew immediately why the men were there. Anything less than death, be it missing in action or anything else, was handled by telegram or phone call.

John Berg was married to a very independent woman. He had always been happy to allow Gertie all the freedom her spirit required. He had always been comfortable enough in his own skin to not feel the need to be a controlling husband. He was wise enough to know that if he tried to run their lives with a dominating hand it would have been a woeful relationship. But now, with the heartache they were about to step into, he knew he needed to take charge.

"We are going to invite these men into the parlor and you and I are going to sit and hear what they have to say."

Gertie nodded, silently looking up at him.

"Come in." John closed the door and the noise of the high winds outside was cut off. "We are going to take a seat."

The house was silent except for the footsteps of four people as they walked on the hardwood floor into the parlor.

Once John and Gertie were seated the captain questioned them. "Are you Mr. and Mrs. John Berg?"

John nodded.

"Are you the parents of Clarence El Berg?"

Again an affirmative nod from John.

Though he made every effort to be respectful and empathetic the captain refrained from any emotion. As he stood there he spoke the memorized script as prepared by the Casualty Notification and Assistance Command of the United States Army.

"Mr. and Mrs. Berg, the Secretary of the Army has asked me to express his deep regret that your son, Clarence El Berg was killed in action on November 2, 1966. The secretary extends his deepest sympathy to you and your family in your tragic loss."

He paused briefly. "Mr. and Mrs. Berg, we are very sorry for your loss. The Army will be in contact with you regarding the arrival of your son's body. The Army will be contacting you to provide any assistance you would desire regarding arrangements for your son."

The captain paused briefly, then placed an official letter essentially stating what he had said on a nearby lamp table. He and the sergeant turned, then slowly left without further word.

That was it. As simply and quickly as that the Bergs were told of their son's death. It had happened countless times before in the country's history and now it was happening to them. But now mother and father of the deceased were not only stunned with grief, but they were also stunned with confusion.

The captain had said Clarence. He had said Clarence, not John. They looked at each other in a split second of utter bewilderment.

John rose to his feet and without a word to Gertie he caught up with the two soldiers, stopping them at the bottom of the porch steps.

"Wait. Wait I . . . We have two sons. One is in Vietnam. One is in Korea. You said Clarence. He's in Korea. Are you sure it's Clark? Are you sure it's Clarence?" We thought he was safe."

From his inside breast pocket the captain took out his copy of the letter he had read to the Bergs. He slowly read the name to himself.

"Yes sir. Clarence El Berg . . . Mr. Berg, your son was part of the Second Division patrol that was attacked in Korea's Demilitarized Zone."

A few seconds passed and John simply nodded his head. The two men quietly withdrew to their vehicle. John put his hands on the porch railing for support. Clark had never told them he was located at the border.

For the rest of that afternoon it was difficult for the Bergs to grasp a sense of their own emotions. They felt confusion as well as grief. They had each steeled themselves for the possibility of losing Johnny in Vietnam. But Clark was in a country where the fighting had stopped thirteen years before. It was a fragile truce, yes, but he was reasonably removed from the border. Or so they thought.

John called the Johnsons. When Esther called down the basement to tell Mack that John was on the line his shoulders slumped. John would not be calling except with important news. Skorpie Johnson recognized the body language immediately.

"What's wrong?"

Mack said nothing, but went upstairs to take a phone call that he dreaded.

When she arrived home from school Elsie burst into tears with the news. In her youthful optimism she had not allowed the thought of losing either of her brothers to enter her mind.

That evening John gathered his thoughts well enough to deal with the need to let their son in Vietnam know what had happened. Without some prodding by him the Army might not research the fact that Clark had a brother in Vietnam.

He wanted to speak to Johnny on the telephone. He didn't know if that was even possible. With letter in hand he called the Randolph Casualty Notification and Assistance Center at Fort Knox. He received no answer for the office was closed for the evening. A second number put him in contact with Fort Knox headquarters. He left his phone number. He was told the center would open at 8:00 a.m. and that someone would phone him first thing in the morning.

John slowly sank into a kitchen chair next to Gertie, Elsie, and his father. Certainly, he wanted his son to hear the news from him before the names of those killed were released to the public. But this was also an unconscious form of therapy for John. It was as old as the grieving process itself. The attempt to accomplish something, in this case the notifying of his son, helped take the spotlight off his own grief.

By eight o'clock that evening the Bergs had yet to notify any of their extended family. They sat at the kitchen table, sometimes going ten minutes at a time without a word being said. Gertie pulled herself together in her usual deliberate way, only to lose composure when she began to speak of her son. When she attempted to talk about how she could see in his letters how Clark was changing, how he was growing up and appreciating things he had always ignored, her voice was a rollercoaster between blessed assurance and trembling emotion.

She took out one of Clark's letters, the only one that she had placed safely in a kitchen counter drawer. The others had all read it before, but she wanted to read part of it to them. She composed herself, showing a brief smile of a proud mother.

> *I want to ask your forgiveness for the way I have acted for so long. When I look around me here at the poverty in this place and have become aware of the importance of the prosperity and freedom that I have always taken for granted I know what a jerk I have been. Yet you have always stood by me. All of you. Grandma and grandpa; being so patient with me. Poor Elsie, putting up with the selfish behavior of her brother. And Johnny, just being Johnny. He's never tried to show me up. He's never talked down to me. Yet there I was, jealous of him because of my own crummy behavior; resenting him because he was not the self-serving person that I have always been.*

Gertie was not finished reading, but she put her hands over her face, just briefly, before continuing. Tears streamed from her eyes and, for a couple seconds, her voice trembled at a high pitch.

> *And you, mom and dad. You have always worked so hard to give Johnny, Elsie and me such a great home. You gave us great security and love. But there I was, manipulating and calculating and thinking only of myself. Some of the guys I am here with come from homes where the father mistreated them or where the parents divorced and yet I see a lot better behavior in them than I see in me. I want to come home and be a different person. I want to be the kind of son you can be proud of.*

Tears streamed from Elsie's eyes. She sat leaning against her mother. The two of them buried their faces in each other's shoulders. They sobbed very quietly.

In due course Gertie raised her head and through her grief she stated that she needed to contact her family.

"No Gertie . . . No . . . I'll make the phone call." John's voice was adamant. "I've let you carry more of the emotional burden of this family than I should have because you just . . . you just don't need me to lean on."

Gertie squared her shoulders. "I can let my parents know." She gave her husband a weak smile. "I know you're trying to help me out, but the best thing I can do right now is to let my family know."

* * *

The next morning John paced around, first outside in the darkness, then inside the house, waiting for the eight o'clock hour and the call from Fort Knox. He could not recall a time when he felt so anxious. When he had not heard from the Casualty Center by 8:30 he called. He spent the next few minutes either waiting or being shuffled between three different people.

Finally, a woman came on the line who introduced herself as Florence McIntyre. Her sincere voice carried a soft mountain drawl. John recognized her as being, as they say, very down home. He felt that he had reached someone who could help him.

"Yes, I see you did call last evening. I'm sorry you had to wait until this morning to speak with us. How can I help you, Mr. Berg?"

"We have a son in Vietnam and I urgently need to speak with him. Is there any way you folks can arrange for that to happen?"

"We occasionally arrange for folks to speak to loved ones but it must involve an emergency, that is to say, the passing away of a family member or a situation where death is imminent. I hope you'll forgive me, Mr. Berg, I don't mean to sound callous, but I am required to ask you what the need is?"

After a few seconds of silence Mrs. McIntyre spoke again. "Mr. Berg?

John gathered himself. "Yes, I'm here. You see, we have two sons in the Army at the same time. One is in Vietnam. That's the one I need to speak to. Our other son is . . . our other son was Clark. He was just killed in Korea and I need to let our son in Vietnam know. He has to know his brother is gone. I want him to hear it from me."

As an employee at the Randolph Casualty and Assistance Center Florence McIntyre knew immediately that Clark Berg must have been on the DMZ patrol that was attacked. From the folders of casualty information on her desk she quickly retrieved the information that listed the American soldiers killed in Korea less than forty eight hours before. There was the Berg name.

She resisted the common human response to express her sympathy at this moment. Instead, she explained to John the procedure that would take place in order to get hold of his son.

"Mr. Berg, in a situation like this it may be the Red Cross that takes care of notification to a soldier. If you will be so kind as to give me your son's unit in Vietnam I will forward the information to the Red Cross. They will use their infrastructure on the ground there to arrange a phone call. When we are told the status of that arrangement we will surely get back to you."

After getting the information the woman retained a professional composure. "Mr. Berg, from the time we pass this information on to the Red Cross it can be anywhere from two hours to possibly a full day before a phone call can be set up. With your son being in Vietnam he may be in the field, which would require the longer time."

She paused only a brief second before asking John if he had any questions.

"No. No, I think I understand." The sincerity John felt in the woman's voice prompted him to add a comment that he would otherwise not have shared. "I'm just hopeful that I can speak to him before he hears his brother's name over the radio. We do appreciate your help. God bless you."

"Yes, I understand." At this point the woman paused. John's comment of "God bless you" prompted her to speak from her heart.

"Mr. Berg, this is such a tragic and unexpected event for your family. I am sure you have been so shocked to have lost a son who you thought was safe. If there . . .

In the woman's hesitation John sensed that she wanted to say more. He knew, however, that in her position she must be careful in what she said.

"Mrs. McIntyre, I want you to know that our son was a Christian and we know that he is now in heaven."

There was a moment of silence before she responded. "Mr. Berg, I do believe that at a time like this for your family that is the only thing that can sustain you."

Up to this moment John had yet to shed a tear, despite the heartache and shock he was feeling. He was trying to be as strong as he could be for his wife and his daughter. Now his eyes welled with tears. He turned away as he hung up the phone so Gertie, Elsie and his father could not see his face.

34

Phone Call

He that loveth his brother
abideth in the light . . .

1 John 2:10 (KJV)

The special day of November 30 was drawing closer for young John Berg. It was the day he had been pointing toward since he first arrived in Korea and then Vietnam. His rotation day. The day his tour was finished. It was the day, as some of them liked to say, that he would "return to the world." In his troop he and Tom Bradley and the four others that had been assigned to A Troop that first day back in Korea were still in one piece and they were "getting short."

Twenty-seven hours had now passed since Johnny heard the news about the incident in Korea. He, Tom Bradley, and a number of others had been on a work detail filling sandbags at the Bien Hoa base.

"What do you think, Tom? Do you think that I would have heard by now if my brother was hurt?" Johnny used the word hurt. He couldn't force himself to use the word killed.

As his friend opened sandbag after sandbag, Tom Bradley shoveled in the sand. "Man, what's happened to the guy who always handles trouble like it was a walk-in-the-park? You're tied up in knots when the odds are that right now your brother is up there counting the days he's got left, just like us."

Sal Bucci was sandbagging nearby and overheard the talk. In his New York way he offered a way for Johnny to stop worrying.

"That's right, Berg. If he's not up there counting the days, he's wondering what kind of slop the mess hall is going to throw at them tonight. Now stop dragging around here and start pulling your weight with these sandbags."

* * *

It was after midnight when the Red Cross made contact with A Troop. The runner from the orderly tent quickly entered fourth platoon's tent.

"Berg. Where's Berg?" The runner was none too delicate as he ran his flashlight up and down the two rows of cots that flanked the walls of the tent. Men groaned and cursed at the awakening.

He spotted Johnny, beaming the flashlight into his eyes.

"Yeah? What is it?"

"How should I know, man. They told me to come get you. I think maybe you got a call on the land line. On the double."

As he left, the runner responded to the grumbling, cursing men by flashing his light into the faces of as many of them as he could.

"Get back to sleep, gentlemen. This platoon has perimeter patrol in the morning. I'll be back to wake you low-lifers at 0500."

Johnny sat on the edge of his cot in the dark, slowly pulling on his fatigues and boots. Tom Bradley lay in his cot staring at his friend in the darkness. He knew what was going through his mind. He felt it best to say nothing.

35

Home

But as it is written,
Eye hath not seen, nor ear heard,
Neither have entered into the heart of man,
the things which God hath prepared
for them that love him.

1 Corinthians 2:9 (KJV)

Three days later Berg was back home in Wisconsin. He was met at the Dane County Regional Airport by his mother, father, Elsie and Mack, and his fiancée Jenny Watson. The emotional stability that all parties had gained in the time since they learned of Clark's death came unraveled briefly but quietly as the six of them gathered in one large hug. Not a word was spoken. Johnny's body trembled as he fought tears. He felt that if he separated from their collective embrace too soon he would just sink to the floor. After these few moments they exited the gate area, Johnny with one arm around Jenny and the other arm around his mother. Still, no words were exchanged.

Once back at the farm Jenny excused herself, insisting that Johnny have time alone with his family.

It wasn't until Johnny, his parents, Elsie, and Mack were all seated around the kitchen table that any real conversation took place. It was Johnny. He looked down at the kitchen table and spoke in a measured cadence in order to get his words out.

"It must have been . . . such a shock. When they told you it was Clark."

Gertie responded weakly, but still in her pragmatic way.

"We were shocked, yes."

She paused, then said matter of factly, "Heartache's the same."

She had more to say, but it took a moment before she could let her human grief give way to her Christian reassurance.

"Your brother's life has been cut short, but he's with his Savior now. For that we can be forever grateful. It is the only consolation I can know."

A short while later Johnny phoned Jenny. When he heard her voice he lost his composure. He had been away from them all for more than a year, all the people who were dearest to him. In that time his most earnest thought was how great it would be when he returned to them, never thinking it would be like this. By now it was seven o'clock in the evening and Jenny could hear the exhaustion in his voice. She said he should get some sleep and come over in the morning. He would have none of that. He was soon over at the Watson house. They sat there alone on the couch in the parlor, mourning quietly together, until Johnny fell into a deep sleep.

* * *

Since America's involvement in Vietnam first began no one from the Stoughton area had yet to lose his life. Now Clark Berg, stationed in Korea, had been killed in what most everyone thought was a safe place. The community was stunned.

The day after Johnny got home Clark's body arrived at the airport. A crowd of about ninety people, family and friends, were there. A military escort took his body to the Gunderson Funeral Home in Stoughton. The Army officer that escorted the body from California advised the officials at the home to recommend to the family that the casket remain closed.

What happened in the next three days was a testament to a family's, and a community's, faith. John and Gertie insisted that the funeral be one of hope. Despite their heartache they made sure that everyone who came to share in their sorrow knew that they believed that the Lord had fulfilled His promise and taken their son into Heaven.

The Bergs asked Glen Masterson to take up his guitar and sing his rendition of *There Will Be Peace in the Valley*. Red Foley himself could not have done a more sincere arrangement than Clark's uncle. Carl and Flo Feskreig sang *It Is Well with My Soul* in a soothing *a cappella*. Both of these offerings could not have been more perfect.

Pastor Mantlund's words were clear and strong.

"The Bible tells us that once a person has truly received the Lord Jesus as his Savior He will not let that person go. We all stumble, we all sin. He has left the Holy Spirit with us, yet none of us, even the most determined Christian, can live a life totally pleasing to Him. Some of us drift farther away from Him in our behavior than others. Yet He loves us and He will not let go of us."

"The Bergs are not a family to readily share their family concerns with others, even with their pastor. But John and Gertie have made it clear to me to let all of you here know how, for so long, Clark struggled to find the contentment that the Lord wants for his followers. How he, in trying to find a replacement for that contentment, sometimes was irresponsible. John and Gertie also wanted you to know that our Lord would not let Clark go; that the Lord is true to us, even when we fail to be true to Him. And be assured, all of us, to one degree or another, are guilty of being untrue to Him. And so our Lord would not let Clark go."

"I was here at First Lutheran only about a year or so when Clark, in confirmation class, confessed his faith in Jesus Christ as his Savior. He received the gift of salvation, salvation from eternal death, by confessing that he was a sinner and confessing his belief that Christ came as the Son of God to die on a cross, taking upon himself the sin of all of mankind.

"Our Lord, on His own timetable and in the way He chooses, brings each of us back to Him if we have confessed our belief in Christ. And so He sent Clark away from us. He sent him away from his wonderful family, away from this bountiful land that He has so wonderfully blessed to an austere and struggling place. John and Gertie have told me that Clark's time in Korea had shown him that he had been unappreciative of the life he had here. They showed me a letter from Clark in which he talked about wanting to be a better person."

"And so we are here and we grieve. We grieve because God has given us the capacity to love and along with that love we can't help but grieve, especially when we lose someone so young and in such a violent way. But as Christians, He has given us expectation of the great reward."

"We can leave here today with two verses from the Bible. One is a verse of great comfort and one is a verse of great excitement. In the Gospel of John these words of comfort and assurance come to us from Jesus: *'I am the resurrection, and the life: he that believeth in Me, though he were dead, yet shall he live.'* We can take comfort that Clark Berg is alive today in Heaven."

"And the verse of great excitement is this. I Corinthians 2:9: *'But as it is written, Eye hath not seen, nor ear heard, neither have entered into the heart of man, the things which God hath prepared for them that love Him.'*"

* * *

Clark was buried close to his grandmother in Eastside Cemetery. They were the first of the Bergs buried there. The old Skaalen Cemetery, a gentle slope near the northwest corner of County Road N and Skaalen Road was the burial site for the generations past of the Bergs. Elmer and Muriel Berg were laid to rest there. So were Gus and

Ruth Berg. Other family members as well. That old cemetery, with sandstone markers losing more of their inscriptions with each passing year, had been closed to further burials in 1939. It was on property donated by Oscar and Sonia Skaalen, the very couple that Elmer had become friends with on his journey from Norway.

Epilogue

Life went on for the Bergs. Though they had lost Clark in a faraway land they never showed bitterness toward America's occupation in Korea or its war in Vietnam. As the protests against the war increased through the rest of the 1960s and into the 70s they refused to accept the attitude of those who held America's leaders in contempt.

Johnny had twenty seven days left in his tour of duty in Vietnam when he came home for the funeral. The Army's policy was that if an overseas stationed soldier came home for an immediate family member funeral he would return to that duty station, Vietnam or otherwise, if he had two or more weeks remaining at that station. But because it was his brother who had been killed in action they made an exception. Johnny was sent to Fort Benning, Georgia, where he completed his military obligation.

Johnny Berg and Jenny Watson were married upon his return to civilian life. They built a small home on Spring Road, at the northeast corner of the farm. Johnny never wavered from his commitment to carry on the legacy of Berg Dairy Farm.

Mack lived another fifteen years. They were productive years. He continued to work the farm with his son and grandson until he was eighty two. He was able to spend his final days at home. In those days he grew fond of using the old expression that he was about to be "called home." When his life-long friend Skorpie Johnson, hail and hardy at age eighty three, visited him in those final days Mack would always chide him, saying that he, Mack, would be called home first. "I always did lead the way for you, Johnson."

Harold Johnson gave his gruff and hardy chuckle. "If He lets in an old Norseman like you I know I've got it made."

Elsie, married and the mother of two, visited her grandfather's bedside one Sunday afternoon. She was sitting there with Gertie and John when Mack asked her to read the passage from the Bible that Fred Mantlund had read at Clark's funeral years before.

"But as it is written, Eye hath not seen, nor ear heard, neither have entered into the heart of man, the things which God hath prepared for them that love Him."

A very contented look came upon his face.

"I know you're going to put me in the ground next to Ann. That's a good thing. But I want you to know that I'll not be staying there. Like the Word says, we hardly know how great it's going to be in Heaven. I'm hoping she and I will be part of it together."

Two days later Mack Berg passed from this world into the next.

* * *

John and Gertie remained the same shining example of the unchanging, down to earth couple that they had always been. As youngsters they had grown up in the Great Depression and then been part of the great effort of World War II. Since then they had raised a family and met their responsibilities as diligent contributors to the American way of life. Like all of God's children they were imperfect; but they stood on their own two feet: meeting life's challenges, overcoming its disappointments and accepting its rewards with thankful humility. When they were given praise for their accomplishments they were able to deflect that praise to their God.

The loss of their son was something they never were to forget, but it was something they kept to themselves, accepting it as one of the many heartaches that a family experiences. When acquaintances brought up the loss of Clark they never turned their eyes away. They looked optimistically at the person and said how grateful they were to know that he was in Heaven. They never spoke of the great confusion of that day when they braced themselves for the death of one son, but were told of the death of the other.

John and Johnny continued to partner in the farm. John and Gertie invited Johnny and Jenny, with their three children, to buy the homestead; provided, of course, that they could continue to live there. It was a cycle familiar to this family. Five generations on the land.

* * *

Tom Bradley had kept in touch with Johnny. Twenty years after their Army days Tom made good his promise to visit. As he pledged while in Korea, he came in the summer. The closest he wanted to get to a Wisconsin winter was to look at the family's photos of the farm in its snowy landscape.

One afternoon Tom sat privately with Jenny on the Berg porch, saying that her husband was the best friend and the best soldier he ever knew. He told her how he could never understand it. How his friend could be the most unassuming, self-effacing, reliable person he ever knew when all about them seemed so out of control.

Then he told her that he now knew the answer.

"In these last twenty years my faith has come a long way. Johnny was so quiet he never expressed it, but he had a great inner peace that he could only get from his faith."

Jenny nodded. "Yes, I see it in him all the time."

She reflected for a moment.

"But you know, Tom, he must have spoken up at least once when you guys were over there. He got a letter a few years ago from Florida. A man named Cruze. He wrote to thank Johnny for what he told him that night in the marsh. That's how he said it. 'That night in the marsh.'

He said it led to changing his whole life. He said it led to the most important decision of his life."

The end.

246

A Note from the Author

Although most of the characters in this story are fictional, the events leading up to and including the night of November 2, 1966, are historically accurate.

The news wire reports about the events of that night are accurate. Though Clark Berg is a fictional character the soldiers mentioned who lost their lives that night and the one survivor are real.

In the ensuing years the free Republic of South Korea has become an economic powerhouse. North Korea, still communist, remains a land where its people live in fear and abject poverty. Although strides have been made to ease tensions, the Demilitarized Zone between the two Koreas continues to this day.

In 1965 I, like many young Americans, entered the military service during the turbulent Vietnam era. I have not forgotten the encounter of freedom and communist enslavement on the border of the two Koreas. Neither have I forgotten the morning of November 2, 1966, when seven young men from our battalion were attacked while on routine stationary night patrol.

It was important to me to write this story for two reasons. The first reason was to show, through the fictional Berg family, God's faithfulness to us and our need to be faithful to Him. It has been my hope to show how the Berg family lived out their Christian inheritance in order to deal with their sometimes difficult experiences.

Jesus said it to us in the Gospel of John, Chapter 16, Verse 33: *These things I have spoken unto you, that in Me ye might have peace. In this world ye shall have tribulation: but be of good cheer; I have overcome the world.*

The second reason was to honor those who lost their lives in the darkness of the morning of November 2, 1966. The picture I have tried to describe of what Johnny Berg and then his brother Clark saw and experienced in Korea was not a product of my imagination. As a young twenty-year-old these were things I saw and experienced myself. I can be grateful to God that I was not on that patrol that suffered the hatred of the North Korean communist regime. We continue to live in a dangerous world.

In memory of those American soldiers who tragically lost their lives the morning of November 2, 1966.

Sergeant James Hensley/Horn
Private First Class John Benton
Private First Class Robert Burrell
Private Morris Fisher
Private Leslie Hasty
Private Ernest Reynolds

Survivor:
Private First Class David Bibee

A Special Note from the Author

God's Providence and Getting History Right

I have learned how important it is to do diligent research while in the process of writing a novel, this novel, which will soon be released.

On the morning of November 2, 1966, seven American soldiers of the Second Infantry Division and one South Korean soldier attached to the American unit were ambushed and murdered while on stakeout surveillance along Korea's Demilitarized Zone. There was one survivor. This was an unprovoked attack of aggression by North Korean agents. It occurred thirteen years after an uneasy truce was declared between North Korea and the Democratic Republic of South Korea in alliance with United Nations forces.

The November 2, 1966, incident was a memorable event for me because I was in a Second Infantry Division unit stationed a short distance down the road. We performed the same surveillance activities as those in the ill-fated patrol. A short time later, after next of kin had been notified, I heard via Armed Forces Radio Korea the names of those slain. The one name that stayed with me was the patrol leader. He was the same rank as myself, he was from Michigan, as am I, and I remember his name being remarkably similar to mine: James Horn.

Many years later in my life I set about writing a novel. One of the events central to the story was the tragic event of November 2, 1966. In trying to get information about that night, especially the names of those slain, I spoke with the then reference librarian at the Cromaine Library here in Hartland, Michigan. This was in the early years of the internet, something that I knew almost nothing about. Via the internet she was able to retrieve an account of that incident which included the names of those slain and the one survivor. According to this account the patrol leader was Sgt. James Hensley.

I accepted that over the years I had mistakenly thought the name was Horn when it actually was Hensley.

Fast forward to the present time—the winter of 2021. I was determined to clean and reorganize our basement this winter. I eventually arrived at four boxes tucked away in a corner. I have often saved written material and mementos in these boxes, everything thrown into these boxes in a casual, disorganized manner. I eventually got to the last and oldest box. This included material from the time my wife and I were first married, more than fifty years ago.

To my surprise, near the bottom of the box, I found five newspaper clippings about the incident in Korea. Among these yellowed old clippings was a *Stars and Stripes* newspaper story listing those killed that night— including James Hensley of Stockbridge, Michigan. I remember this being a clipping I brought home from Korea. Another clipping was from *The Detroit News* that included a picture of, and a few words about, Sgt. James Horn, age 19, of Stockbridge, Michigan. Since I was in Korea at this time I do not recall how I knew about, or saved, this article.

I now googled the internet and came up with an accounting of U.S. Army deaths from 1966 through 1969 in Korea. It included Sgt. James Hensley of Stockbridge, Michigan.

I was now no closer to the correct name than when I first discovered two sir names for this young soldier who had lost his life.

As part of the dedication page on this soon to be printed and released novel the names of those slain and the one survivor is to be included. For the sake of accuracy and with respect for either Sgt. James Hensley or Sgt. James Horn and his family I needed to have the correct name—and the novel's publication was looming.

Stockbridge is a quiet farming community in south/central Michigan, about an hour's drive from my home. I decided to contact the local funeral home in hopes that records might show arrangements for a James Hensley or James Horn, most likely sometime in November of 1966. As it turned out I wisely decided to go to Stockbridge in lieu of making a phone call.

The funeral home was closed when I arrived.

In Michigan burial records and cemetery records are maintained at the township level. I soon found that the township of Stockbridge office is in the village square of Stockbridge. To my good fortune the deputy clerk, Mandy Urquhart, kindly listened to my story. Although she did not personally know anyone named Horn she had heard the name. She called a local resident who she described as the genealogy guru in Stockbridge. Vickie Osborne answered her cell phone in Arizona, where she was spending the winter. She either had her genealogy information right in front of her or she had a great memory. I explained my concern and she responded immediately.

"James Hensley and James Horn are the same person."

I was a bit stunned. Before I could say anything she continued with a short and guarded statement.

"There was an illegitimate birth. That's why you see two different names. I did know him from high school and I do remember when he was killed."

I had my answer!

She went on to give me the location of the grave in the nearby cemetery. I went grave hunting, but after kicking snow off of tombstones for twenty minutes without success I decided I would come back in the spring.

Some would say that it was by sheer luck that I stumbled on those fifty-five-year-old pieces of paper that had been buried in a box in our basement. After all, I wasn't even looking for them. I prefer to think that it was by the grace of God that I found that information and that I was able to understand that both names were meaningful.

A few days later I received a phone call from a Mrs. Linda Winnie. Word of my inquiry had reached her. She told me she was the younger sister of Jim Horn. She was a teenager when her brother was killed in a place that everyone thought was out of harm's way.

It would be presumptuous of me to think that our conversation offered her closure on the loss of her brother, but I do believe it was meaningful for her to speak to someone who could remember that night long ago when her brother lost his life.

I later spoke to Linda again by phone. I asked her what Jim's legal name is. His legal name is Hensley. Apparently neither Jim, nor any of his Horn siblings, were aware of this until it was revealed upon his entrance into the army.

I asked Linda if she recalled if Horn or Hensley was posted on his gravestone. She did not remember. A Michigan listing of American military deaths in Korea from 1966 through 1969 that listed James Hensley had a post from a cousin of Jim who seemed upset that the name Horn was not recognized.

I explained to Linda that the names of those slain the night of the incident are listed on the dedication page of the novel and near the end of the novel. I asked her if listing "Hensley/Horn" was appropriate. She gave me a definite "yes."

And so, I am humbled to provide a small contribution to history and to the memory of this fine young man, and perhaps some helpful recognition to his family.

Acknowledgments

Thank yous go out to Sally Brodie, now retired librarian at the Cromaine Library in Hartland, Michigan. Many years ago you impressed upon me the power of the internet when you found the news wire reports referenced in this story. I wish to thank Major Vardon Jenerette whose article *The Forgotten DMZ* and Richard Kolb whose article *Fighting Brush Fires on Korea's DMZ* were helpful to me. I also thank the Lyndon Baines Johnson Library and Museum in Austin, Texas, for supplying the hour-by-hour activity of President Johnson for the time period I requested. To Bill Carmichael and staff at Deep River Books in Sisters, Oregon. You encouraged me and were the first to expose my writing to the public. Most of all to my new publisher and editor Donna Nakagiri at Red Recliner Books of DMS Onge Publishing. You saw something in my writing that made you take a chance on me. You have patiently dealt with my mediocre computer skills. Of course to my wife, Sue, whose quiet determination at whatever she attempts has always impressed me. She is reserved on platitudes and long on "get 'er done." To Stockbridge Michigan residents Mandy Urquhart and Vickie Osborne whose township connections and genealogy information offered needed clarity to me. To Linda Winnie for telling me about her brother. And a huge thank you to my immediate and extended family and to friends whose care and whose example have helped me so much in this life. Finally to our Lord, who has blessed my life so much and made all things possible.

Jim Hodge

254

About the Author

Jim Hodge is a veteran who served in the Demilitarized Zone on the Korean peninsula in 1966 as a Sergeant in the U.S. Army. He served in Company A, 3rd Battalion, 23rd Infantry, 2nd Infantry Division. He later served as an assistant instructor at the Army's Officer Candidate School at Fort Benning, Georgia.

He graduated from Wayne State University in Detroit where he met his beautiful wife Sue. Her family's good-natured and sincere character provided him with inspiration for this story.

The home front scenes of this novel are set in the environs of Stoughton, Wisconsin, a place he visited during its annual Syttende Mai festival (he stayed away from the lutefisk). It was there that Jim found a joyful Mid-West American community with great pride in its Norwegian heritage.

The military scenes are set in the austere Korean peninsula where Jim learned to appreciate a people's yearning for freedom. The struggle to preserve the precious gift of freedom by a then desperately poor people has never been lost on Jim.

The Hodges live in the semi-rural countryside northwest of Detroit. Jim and Sue have two adult children and three amazing grandchildren. They are members of an Evangelical Presbyterian Church. Jim is also a member of the Military Writers Society of America.

256

About the Publisher

We hope you enjoyed this wonderful book, *When Troubles Rain: A Novel*, by Jim Hodge. It is the first book under our new imprint, Red Recliner Books.

We will publish a nonfiction work by Jim Hodge in the near future. We also hope he continues to write and that we may continue to publish his works, as well as works by other equally wonderful American authors.

Our books are available through your favorite bookseller, online at *Amazon.com*, *BarnesAndNoble.com*, and our own website, *DMSOngePublishing.com*.

If you would like us to consider publishing your manuscript, please visit our website for current manuscript submission guidelines, *www.DMSOngePublishing.com*. We are a traditional publisher and accept a limited number of manuscripts each year.

*DMS Onge Publishing, LLC, publishes
fiction and nonfiction works under a number of imprints,
including this imprint, Red Recliner Books,
as well as greeting cards and other printed products.*

258